"SHALL I CARRY YOU ACROSS IN MY ARMS?"

Sloane led Diana toward the bridge, laughing when she gasped in alarm. It was nothing but a collection of swaying vines and rotting pieces of wood. The walls of the gorge were so steep that Diana's head spun when she looked down at the distant ribbon of water at the bottom.

"I'll carry my own weight," she said with a shaky voice. Sloane moved up close, his body behind her guiding her across.

When they reached safety, he pulled her pliant softness even tighter against the unyielding hardness of his strong and powerful body.

Diana wanted to cry for help—fighting her own desire to give in to his passion.

But there would be no one to hear—and the jungle sounds would drown the feeble cries of her protest....

INTRODUCING A NEW SERIES OF CONTEMPORARY LOVE STORIES...

HARLEQUIN SUPERROMANCE

Harlequin has been publishing romance novels for more than thirty years. Now we are proud to offer a new type of love story to our millions of readers—a longer, exciting and dramatic story...in keeping with today's life-styles.

Love's Emerald Flame is the second great HARLEQUIN SUPERROMANCE. Written by Willa Lambert, it is a passionately beautiful love story, as intriguing as it is thrilling.

So...sit back and enjoy the kind of read you've been waiting for!

LOVE'S EMERALD FLAME

WILLA LAMBERT

Harlequin Books

TORONTO • LONDON • LOS ANGELES • AMSTERDAM
SYDNEY • HAMBURG • PARIS • STOCKHOLM • ATHENS • TOKYO

Harlequin first edition, September 1980

ISBN 0-373-70002-4

CHAPTER ONE

DIANA GREEN didn't know the man. If her expression didn't sufficiently denote that fact, she quickly reinforced it verbally.

"I beg your pardon?" she said, her forkful of *cebiche de corvina* interrupted halfway to her attractively pouted mouth.

"I'm sorry I'm late, darling," he said casually, as if he had known her for her full twenty-five years.

Diana felt suddenly as if she were a character in a low-budget film. The locale was certainly exotic enough.

"I see you've gone ahead and ordered the salmon trout," he observed, flashing her a wide smile. He had sensuously full lips that now revealed a wide expanse of large white teeth. Not only did the locale suggest some B-grade movie, but the man seemed to fit the bill, too. He had the rugged good looks that one would possibly attribute to an actor still quite handsome, but past the attractiveness of youth.

Diana looked curiously around the room, wondering if she was unknowingly appearing on that popular old show called "Candid

Camera," but doubting that its crew would have been sent all the way to Lima, Peru.

"I think maybe I'll have the *conchitas* made with tiny scallops and *anticuchos* of chicken livers, shish-kebab style," he decided. "What do you think?"

"Is this some kind of a joke?" That was what she thought!

"Lovely place, isn't it?" the man commented, smoothly getting the waiter's attention at the same time. "Tambo de Oro, from Spanish and Quechua, the native language of Peru. A Rest House of Gold."

"You've seen the brochures, too, I see," Diana said, hoping her sarcasm showed.

It had been the brochure in the lobby of her hotel, complete with its enticing phrases, that brought her there in the first place. Diana had immediately been entranced by those mental images conjured by "twenty-foot-high double doors beyond which many claim to have seen the ghost of Belén." Nowhere, however, had the pamphlet prepared her for the man who had unexpectedly joined her.

It wasn't his joining her that so much disturbed her. Mistakes, after all, were made by everyone. What disturbed her was that he showed no indication of moving on after it was obvious the mistake had been made.

Diana was on the point of muttering something more pithy regarding the violation of her privacy, but with the arrival of the waiter she decided there was little sense in causing a scene over a matter that might be cleared up very shortly.

Her companion ordered just what he had said he would, and when finished he flashed another of his wide smiles in Diana's direction.

He had two dimples, one in each cheek. He had dark, brooding eyes, gleaming black pupils surrounded by brown starbursts within otherwise ebony irises; thick eyebrows and long sooty lashes. He had a cleft in his chin. His tousled jet black hair added to those dangerously dark, well-tanned masculine looks and physique that, despite all of his small talk and expert commandeering of the waiter, would have seemed more appropriate in some outdoor setting.

He seemed a bit too physical for this elegant restored house, built, according to the tourist leaflet, by the Pazos Verela family and once owned by Gustavo Berckemeyer, father of Fernando Berckemeyer, Peru's one-time ambassador to the United States. The man's rugged presence made a sharp and somehow challenging contrast to the refined atmosphere, the quiet hum of the diners enjoying their meals.

Diana gave him her best sardonic smile, able to enjoy a good joke as well as the next person. But every joke had to have its punch line....

"Excuse me for just a moment, won't you, darling?" he interrupted her thoughts, scooting back his chair and standing. He looked far larger when he was on his feet than when sitting, his bulk appearing to be all solid muscle, too.

His turning to disappear suddenly down a back hallway left Diana flabbergasted. Had he finally realized his mistake? Was that why he had left? He must have been pretty confused if it had taken him as long as it had to find that he didn't know her. Funny. . .he hadn't looked rattled, but you could never tell by looks alone.

Clarie Johns, a sorority sister of Diana's at the University of Washington, had seemed perfectly normal, too, but she had ended up talking to the statues along the mall. What's more, Clarie had confessed to Diana that she had got A's in physics only because of her discussions with the bronze bust of Albert Einstein in the courtyard of the science building!

Diana picked up her fork, her piece of fish—direct from the waters of Lake Titicaca, or so said the menu—finally making it to her mouth. She chewed it slowly, only absently aware of its moist flakiness permeated with the tang of lemons, the bite of onions and red peppers.

"Strange," she said aloud, hearing her own voice and glancing self-consciously at the surrounding tables, feeling very much like Clarie Johns. She took another mechanical bite of her fish, washing it down with a swallow of the house white wine, having actually reached the point of wondering if she hadn't imagined everything. Had some mystery man sat down and called her "darling," or had it been wishful thinking, a harmless little daydream? No, hard-

ly the latter, because had she conjured anyone out of her thoughts, it certainly wouldn't
have been that strangely disturbing hulk of a
man.

She decided to chalk it up as one of those intriguing little anecdotes that would make conversation interesting once she got back from
vacation: "And in Lima, at the Tambo de
Oro—that's Spanish and ancient Incan for Rest
House of Gold—this ruggedly attractive man
sat down at my table and . . . ." The only problem was, no one would believe it; Diana wasn't
even sure if she did herself.

Her mind was wandering, but she was
brought quickly back to reality by the arrival of
the waiter.

"¿Qué es?" Diana asked.

"Conchitas," the waiter answered grandly,
describing the dish of food he had just placed
ceremoniously on the table across from her.

Diana glanced around the room. This was
carrying the joke a bit too far. Was that man
who had ordered this meal waiting in the wings
now, getting ready to jump out and yell, "Surprise!"

No, he wasn't, and the piquant scallops, followed immediately by a generous serving of
chicken-liver shish kebab, got cold while Diana
sat there watching.

From all sides she imagined people staring at
her and wondering, *where is her companion
who ordered his meal? Why hasn't he come*

back? Have the young lovers quarreled? A perfectly good meal had been spoiled by his joke.

The waiter came to ask if her fiancé had been called away.

"My what?"

The waiter, thinking he had confused his English, gave a Spanish equivalent: *"novio."*

"I've never seen that man before in my life!" Diana said, sensing she was going red with anger and blushing all the more. People at the adjoining tables were looking her way and smiling. Mockingly? Sympathetically?

"He will be coming back?"

"I should hope not!" Diana replied tartly, causing a few more curious glances in her direction.

When the waiter began clearing away the untouched food, Diana ordered a pisco sour, thinking she could use the extra lift the famous Peruvian drink of potent local grape brandy would give her. She hoped it would lift her right out of her chair and float her across the room to the front door.

The brandy did help. When she got the bill for *two* meals, she even managed to keep her indignant gasp down to a hardly audible hiss. To add insult to insult, the mystery man had stuck her with his bill! Diana simply couldn't believe it, especially since there wasn't much to be done about it. She gave the waiter her American Express card, not having brought enough of the local *soles* with her.

She left the place with as much dignity as she could muster under the circumstances, telling herself she was only imagining that she was the center of attention.

Every time she thought of all that wasted food, and all the starving people in the world, she got absolutely furious. She was forced to think about it, however, when her cab arrived at the Gran Hotel Bolívar, where even at that hour there were a few young children hanging around begging for coins. What Diana had been forced to put out for the extra meal would probably have fed the lot of these youngsters for a week.

Feeling guilty, she was more generous with her centavos than she probably should have been, and as a result she was met by a frowning desk clerk when she entered through the revolving doors. The children were already somewhat of an embarrassment to the management, and giving them doles only encouraged them to stick around. Diana's attempt to melt the clerk's disapproving grimace with a friendly smile as she picked up her key was met with abysmal failure.

A posted Circle-SA tour bulletin listed her schedule for the next day. Wake-up calls (optional). Breakfast from 9:30 to 10:30. Lunch from 11:30 to 12:30. Baggage out at 1:00. Bus for airport at 2:00. Flight to Cuzco at 3:00.

Carol wasn't back yet when Diana let herself into their room, and for once she was glad. Sharing a bathroom, even with someone you had grown to like, was often an inconvenience if you wanted a long relaxing bath.

Diana's teaming with Carol Wiley had been the result of one of those mix-ups that occasionally find a tour group with one too many people for the available rooms. Such foul-ups were never discovered until later, this one popping up when the group was seated in the lobby of the Hotel Crillón in Caracas.

Diana and Carol had graciously volunteered to share, since actually there was very little else they could do. The only other single on the tour was George Culhaney, who, even though somewhere in his seventies, could hardly have been expected to share with one of the young women.

Besides, neither Diana nor Carol had any real reason for complaint; Diana less so than Carol in that most of her tab was being picked up by Circle-SA as part of a press promotion. Carol, on the other hand, was on her yearly gem-buying trip for a custom-jewelry house in Portland, Oregon.

Diana, in fact, had spent most of that morning with Carol, going through the seemingly inexhaustible selection of gemstones at the branch of I. Bern located in their hotel. In Caracas Carol had taken Diana to the I. Bern at the Tamanaco and the Hilton hotels. In Rio they had disappeared into I. Bern, Amsterdam-Sauer, Maximino, O. Lange's, until Diana had had gems coming out of her ears. In Buenos

Aires it had been the I. Bern shops in the Hotel Plaza and the Hotel Sheraton.

"I. Bern," Carol had said knowledgeably, "gives you the largest choice for the most reasonable prices. In more than thirty years they've built up an international network and reputation."

She obviously bought enough to make an impression, since there was almost always some I. Bern representative waiting at the stops to take her out to supper. It was usually someone who was quite willing to let Diana tag along as part of the bargain.

"Don't be silly!" Carol had insisted on the occasions Diana voiced doubts about the ethics of so often taking advantage of the largesse of a company that had got nothing from her but seventy-five dollars for a pair of small—very small—topaz earrings. "These people have bigger expense accounts than you and I put together. How much does that newspaper of yours have you budgeted for meals, anyway?"

At present, though, Diana had no interest in seeing one more diamond, tourmaline, amethyst, cat's-eye, opal, morganite or garnet that she didn't have the money to buy. Free meal or no free meal, she was not so much of a masochist that she enjoyed the temptations offered by all of that exquisite jewelry.

She could actually get butterflies even thinking about how she had almost succumbed to temptation that morning and gone into hock for an emerald ring.

She had always been extremely partial to emeralds, probably because they were her birthstones, and could remember being particularly captivated as a child by hearing somewhere that emeralds, like people, were seldom perfect, and that "emerald without a flaw" had passed into proverb as signifying unattainable perfection. She had also heard that the verdant color of the stone suggested to many a new spring or eternal hope.

Then, of course, there were the five emeralds Cortes had been bringing to his bride when his ship was wrecked in the sixteenth century, one made into a bell with a pearl for a clapper, one a rose, one a horn, another a fish with gold eyes. The last, rumored to have been the most exquisite of the quintet, was an emerald in the form of a cup with a base of gold.

Anyway, the ring Diana had wanted hadn't been anything nearly as exotic as Cortes had managed. It had been merely a small stone, but still worth a king's ransom as far as Diana's budget was concerned.

Carol had had a special appointment that evening at the Lima-Sheraton branch of I. Bern, followed by supper with a representative of the store.

Diana drew water for a bath, testing it with her elbow. She gratefully peeled off her clothes, feeling sticky, the restaurant having seemed exceptionally hot after her mysterious supper guest had made his exit. Still, she procrastinated momentarily to check herself in a full-length mirror on the bathroom door, neither overly pleased nor overly disappointed with what she saw.

Her hair was a corn-colored blond that she wished were a lighter shade. Her eyes were large and green, which was okay. She considered her nose too snub, her mouth somehow not ripe enough. Her breasts weren't too bad, but Carol's were better. She chided herself for making the comparison. And when she viewed her own waist and good legs, she thought she wasn't in bad shape, even if she wasn't going to set the world on fire.

She slipped down slowly into the tub and stayed there luxuriating for a good half hour, buried to her neck in hot water and dissolving suds.

By the time Carol got back, Diana was in bed trying to read a book. Her attention, despite all her efforts to keep it focused on the printed page, kept returning to that man at the restaurant who had so swiftly come and gone, leaving her with very little except an uneasy memory— and, of course, the bill for his meal.

"I think there's still a little hot water," Diana said by way of greeting her roommate.

"You're a lifesaver!" Carol responded, heaving her overstuffed purse onto the twin bed parallel to Diana's. "Now, how could you have guessed that I would at this moment give anything for one tub of hot water?''

"Because I know the feeling,'' Diana said simply.

"And how was your evening?'' Carol asked, sitting on the edge of the bed and kicking off her shoes. A petite shapely brunette with large hazel eyes, upturned nose and a Cupid's-bow mouth, Carol was an expert gemologist and a skilled lapidary. She had a reputation, at thirty-two, of being a knowledgeable buyer who knew a good bargain when she saw one. You didn't easily put one over on Carol Wiley where gemstones were concerned, as any of her business peers would tell you.

"I met a man,'' Diana said. "He was tall and muscular. He was tanned and handsome.'' She was determined to milk this story for all it was worth—considering what she had been forced to pay for it!

"Well?'' Carol prompted, her curiosity obviously piqued, since there wasn't a man in their tour group under fifty.

"He asked if he could join me for dinner. He kept calling me 'darling,' and—''

Carol's sudden laugh was spontaneous. "Oh, Diana! Do you know, I actually believed you for a moment? Must be the altitude making me giddy. Either that or—''

There was an interrupting knock on the door.

"Who do you suppose it is at this hour?'' Diana asked, checking her travel clock by the bed and noting that it was almost ten o'clock.

"Maybe your mystery man, huh?" Carol said with a shrug. "More likely, though, it's Al dropping by to make sure we both got back." Al Scalipas was the guide who had been assigned the group by Circle-SA Tours.

Carol went to the door, leaning her ear against it. "Al?"

"Señorita Green, *por favor.*"

Carol glanced curiously toward Diana on the bed. "You didn't really meet anyone tonight, did you, Diana?" she asked.

"Police, Miss Green," the voice said in heavily accented English. "If we could possibly have a moment of your time, please?"

"What do you think?" Carol asked, frowning. "Do you think it's really the police, or some Peruvian hotel mugger?"

"Who would want to mug a Peruvian hotel?" Diana responded, too curious about what the police wanted with her to smile at her own attempt at humor. Getting out of bed, she reached for her robe and wrapped it securely around her nightdress, nodding for Carol to open the door.

Two of the men on the other side didn't wait for more than a crack before placing all of their weight against the door and shoving.

"My God!" Carol exclaimed, that being all she could manage as she was caught by the door and thrown back into the room. If it hadn't been for her bed, she would have landed on the floor.

Diana watched in shocked surprise as a third man entered, gun drawn. She dropped reflexively to the floor, scooting quickly behind a chair and waiting for the sound of bullets, knowing full well how they sounded at close range.

Wouldn't her mother be surprised to find Diana had been shot in South America! Would Jessica appreciate that irony? It was, after all, because of other guns once aimed in Diana's direction that Jessica had arranged for her daughter to be sent off on this little junket.

After the plaster-splattering crash of the door against the wall, all three men moved quickly, one continuing to fan the room with his weapon while another went to Carol's bed, aiming his gun at her and commanding her not to scream. The third man moved to a position over Diana.

"What is this?" Diana spoke up when she realized they weren't immediately going to kill her. Her voice wasn't any too stable and her heart was beating five times its normal speed.

"Up!" the man ordered.

The man in the middle of the floor moved to the bathroom. Once assured that the room was empty, he came back and shut the door to the hallway, replacing his automatic in the shoulder holster beneath his suit coat. His companions didn't follow suit.

"What do you want?" Diana asked, now on her feet and being motioned over toward the bed next to Carol. Her initial fear was fast changing into indignation. "Just what do you think you're doing here?"

"Miss Green?" the man with the now concealed gun asked, shifting his gaze between Diana and Carol.

"I'm Miss Green," Diana said, so angry she was trembling. She would have sat, but she doubted the weakness in her legs would have allowed her ever to get up again.

"So sorry to disturb you ladies at this hour of the night," he began. "I'm Captain Sipas. Lima Police." He was tall with thin brown hair, his long angular face looking as if it had been chiseled from cold stone, his eyes a sickeningly pale gray. "We would just like a few words with you, Miss Green. About your fiancé."

"Fiancé?" None of this made sense to Diana. "What fiancé?"

"Mr. Sloane Hendriks," Captain Sipas said obligingly.

"I don't have a fiancé," Diana insisted, using her right hand to hold her robe together at her throat. "I certainly don't know anyone called Sloane—"

"Hendriks," Captain Sipas finished for her.

"Hendriks," Diana echoed.

"We have found people at the Tambo de Oro restaurant who have sworn that you were there with Mr. Hendriks this very evening," Captain Sipas explained in oozing politeness.

"I ate alone," Diana said.

Carol still hadn't recovered. She had pulled her body up tightly against the headboard of the bed and was now clutching a pillow in front of her as if somehow to deflect any bullets fired from the gun still aimed in her direction.

"Your waiter said Mr. Hendriks joined you, ordered his meal and then quarreled with you," Captain Sipas said, pulling out a small notebook but reciting from memory as he thumbed through its pages. "Mr. Hendricks left, but you remained. You had one after-dinner drink, a... a pisco sour, then paid the bill and left the premises."

"This all has something to do with *him*?" she asked, having felt uneasy about her encounter with *that* man from the very start.

Captain Sipas marked a spot in his notebook with his thumb, concentrating for a moment on a maze of small scribbles that were obviously his own special shorthand.

"He was heard to call you by endearing terms on more than one occasion," he said.

"That man was a complete stranger!" Diana blurted, getting angrier by the minute at these strong-arm tactics being used by the Lima Police; angrier still at Sloane Hendriks, who apparently was responsible. "He came into the restaurant and sat down at my table completely uninvited, obviously having made a mistake."

"He called you 'darling,'" Captain Sipas reminded her. "He then proceeded to order a

meal of. . .of *conchitas* made with scallops, and beef—"

"Chicken," Diana corrected absently.

"Chicken?" Captain Sipas echoed. He seemed confused.

"He ordered *conchitas* made with scallops and *anticuchos* of chicken livers," Diana said, able to remember every little detail of that meeting, down to the dark black hair that grew on the back of Sloane Hendriks's large and powerful hands.

"The waiter said beef," Captain Sipas muttered, taking a pen from his pocket and adding something to the hen tracks already in his notebook. Diana wondered why she had even brought it up. It could hardly make a difference, since Sloane Hendriks hadn't eaten any of it anyway.

"Look, are these guns really necessary?" she asked. She herself didn't like the threatening presence of the weapons, but she was thinking even more about Carol, who really looked as if she had been unnerved by Sipas's unorthodox entry. Diana had been shaken, too, but. . . .

"You're right, of course," Captain Sipas agreed. Although even after he had given orders for the guns to be put away, his men continued to look menacing. "Better?" His voice held just a trace of amusement. "If so, maybe you might now explain why, if you don't know Sloane Hendriks, you paid for his meal with your American Express card. I have the restaurant copy of the signed credit charges, if you would care to see it.''

"That won't be necessary," Diana responded. "I have my own copy."

Carol's wide-eyed gaze kept going from Diana to Sipas and then back again.

"And are you accustomed to paying for the meals ordered by complete strangers who call you 'darling' and tell the maître d' they're your fiancé?" Captain Sipas asked, his momentary veneer of politeness having slipped slightly as a bit of definite sarcasm crept in along the edges.

"I didn't want to cause a scene," Diana explained.

"Of course," Captain Sipas said. "Being in a foreign country, you were naturally afraid you might be penalized for the truth. You have heard tales of how we are...shall we say, unsympathetic to tourists' complaints, *sí*."

"It had nothing at all to do with that," Diana said, knowing it probably had, since it was easier to get into trouble in countries with unfamiliar customs, languages, rules and regulations. "I would probably have done the same thing if it had happened in Seattle."

"But, then, I forgot Americans are so rich they think nothing of throwing away their money," Captain Sipas commented. "You are rich, Miss Green?"

"I am not rich. I work hard for a living."

"Work?" he echoed, eyes widening in exaggerated amazement. His tone oozed sarcasm.

"Yes."

"Ah!" Captain Sipas exclaimed. "A working girl on vacation. Now you will rush home and tell everyone you were cheated by a Lima restaurant, not bothering to mention that you never tried explaining how you happened to be charged for a meal you never ordered."

"I have found nothing bad to report about your country—*until now,*" Diana said, firmly. The man was really being impossible! "I can assure you, it would be enough to scare off many tourists to hear of armed police breaking into Lima hotel rooms with so little provocation."

Captain Sipas shrugged. "Be sure to mention that not every tourist is likely to be seen dining with a wanted man," he said.

"Just what exactly has Sloane Hendriks done?" Diana questioned, having forgotten even to ask in all of the excitement.

"I suggest that if you *really* don't know anything about Sloane Hendriks, you would be far better off maintaining your present blissful state of ignorance."

"I do not know Sloane Hendriks!" Diana insisted, wondering how many times she had to keep repeating herself.

"Then, as soon as we complete our search of your room we will leave you to rest for your departure tomorrow. I believe you are scheduled out for Cuzco, are you not?"

"Search our room?" Diana asked, genuinely indignant.

"Only to assure ourselves that Mr. Hendriks didn't drop off certain items."

"I think, before you begin any searches, I had better call our embassy," Diana said, wanting to kick herself for not having thought of that before.

Carol noticeably blanched. She had been to Peru on and off for the past five years and was well acquainted with Peru's history as a military state and with the political tensions always bubbling beneath its surface calm. If Sloane Hendriks were indeed involved with any such politics—and Carol couldn't help thinking he must be—then Diana would be far better off cooperating than making waves. This wasn't the United States, and it would be very easy for two American women to just up and disappear, especially if that disappearance was engineered by the powers that be. At least that was how it seemed to Carol.

"By all means call your embassy," Captain Sipas said, nodding indulgently toward the phone sitting on the night table between the twin beds. Diana surprised herself by moving in the indicated direction. "However, I had high hopes we could get this taken care of without your embassy's involvement."

"Yes, I can very well see how you might have had such hopes," Diana said. "On the other hand, you certainly must understand my position."

"It will undoubtedly mean staying in Lima

far longer than you had anticipated," Captain Sipas pointed out, his tone insinuating far more warning than his actual words. "You certainly won't be making any flight to Cuzco tomorrow."

"Diana, forget the embassy," Carol broke in.

"Forget it?" Diana echoed, turning to Carol with the definite feeling she had just been stabbed in the back by a friend. "How can you *not* want me to do something?"

"I think you would be wise to listen to the lady's excellent advice, Miss Green," Captain Sipas said. "Unless, of course, you have plenty of time—and money—to spare. There will be questions, reports, red tape. There will be language problems, communication difficulties. There will be letters written and answered, phone calls made and returned. In the end your own people will not thank you for having caused so much trouble over so small an incident."

"So small an incident?" Diana said in echo. "Small? You have pushed your way into our hotel room. You have pointed guns at us. You have made completely unfounded accusations. You now want to search our room. I do not call *that* a small incident."

"Possibly because you aren't as innocent as you pretend, *sí*?" Captain Sipas suggested, raising a hand to keep Diana from interrupting. "You're not hiding anything, are you, Miss Green?"

"Diana, let them make their search," Carol pleaded, her voice almost breaking with barely restrained tears. "We've got nothing to hide. I just want them out of here!"

Diana knew she should have stuck to her guns, picked up the phone and made that call to the embassy. She should have raised all holy hell, prepared to spend the extra days, weeks, months, whatever time it would take, to show these toughs that American citizens couldn't be harassed. That's what she *should* have done.

"So, search the room!" she said.

Because, despite what she should have done, she really wasn't prepared to go through the inconvenience of major schedule interruption, just to prove some point that—as Captain Sipas had so smugly indicated—would probably have none of the embassy people thanking her. She had been looking forward too much to seeing Cuzco and Machu Picchu to miss her flight the next day, especially with so little compensation being offered by the present alternative.

In the final analysis, she reasoned, Captain Sipas was probably just a policeman doing his job in a country that didn't have as many laws to protect its citizens as the U.S. did. How could he understand why Diana was so upset when he might be used to violating human rights every day of the year? He was just a dedicated officer of the law, albeit not a very personable one, who wanted Sloane Hendriks off the streets and thought Diana might be out somehow to thwart that honest objective. If by searching Diana's and Carol's room he could be convinced that they were merely innocent bystanders, then let him get on with it and get on his way.

At the same time Diana knew she was compromising certain of her principles, even if compromises weren't new to her. It had been one, after all, that put her on this trip to write fluff travel pieces, when she should have been off somewhere doing in-depth investigative reporting!

However, remembering that man Sloane Hendriks, who was responsible for all of the hassle she'd just gone through, didn't make this particular compromise any easier. She had intuitively known, from the very first glance, that he was going to upset her life far more than his brief stop at her table in the restaurant would have suggested.

CHAPTER TWO

NEITHER DIANA NOR CAROL got much sleep after Captain Sipas left. Every time either thought she was finally drifting off, she would imagine hearing something out in the hallway. Both eventually dozed from pure exhaustion, Diana not managing to do so until long after daybreak. They looked anything but refreshed when they boarded the Faucett flight for Cuzco.

Diana had never heard of Faucett Airlines. But, then, before this trip she hadn't heard of Avianca or Varig airlines, either.

She found a small tag in the pocket of the seat ahead of her. It had a picture of a parrot with a yellow string tied in its beak, and it said, "Would you like to rest without being disturbed? Just hook this sign on the back of the seat in front of you, or hook it to yourself." Diana pinned it to her sweater and went to sleep.

An hour later she awoke to the sound of Carol gasping.

"What's happening?" Diana asked, her eyes wide open even if she wasn't yet awake.

"Better go back to sleep," Carol warned, her

voice rising a good octave by the time she had reached the end of her sentence.

Diana stretched across Carol, who was by the window, and looked just in time to see a large hunk of the Andes rushing by seemingly within feet of her face.

"Are we crashing?"

"The pilot assures us we're merely landing," Carol said.

"In the middle of a mountain?" Diana asked as the plane dropped. Then, feeling her stomach rise suddenly to her throat, she leaned back into her seat.

"I see it, I see it!" Carol announced.

"See what? The Pearly Gates?" Diana asked. Her seat was shaking beneath her, making her extremely nervous.

"Cuzco," Carol said. "Look. There's the main plaza. There's the city hall and the church."

"Where's the airport?" Diana asked.

"I don't see it," Carol answered.

"And that's what I was afraid you'd say," Diana mumbled as the plane dropped again. There was the loud grating of metal against metal as some mechanical marvel lowered a wing flap even farther. She shut her eyes.

Still alive, Diana found herself outside the small terminal a few minutes later, waiting for Al to load her into one of the small cabs taking everyone, a couple at a time, to the Hotel Savoy. While she was waiting she was confronted by a dirty-faced child who came up and stuck out his hand. Diana automatically reached into her purse for a couple of stray centavos. It seemed she would forever be obligated to put out for anyone who begged for money, just because she had watched a huge dinner of scallops and chicken go to waste.

She thought of Sloane Hendriks; then, reminding herself that she had resolved to wipe all details of that unsettling experience from her memory, she gave the boy a couple of coins. She was surprised when he put up his free hand, spread fingered, indicating he wanted five centavos more. Lucky for him, he had caught her when she was feeling guilty, or she wouldn't have reached into her purse for the requested money and handed it to him. Immediately he yelled something to a boy on the sidelines, pointing to Diana.

Thinking he was broadcasting to the world that he had found an easy mark, Diana was surprised when the boy on the sidelines came forward and thrust a book into her hands. She had apparently just conducted her first business transaction in Cuzco, without even knowing it. She had bought a copy of *The Photographic Guide to Cuzco and Its Environs.*

"Diane, over here!" Carol screamed, standing half in and half out of one of the small taxis. Diana hurried over and climbed in after her, finding the back seat so cramped that for once she found herself wishing she could have exchanged her long legs for a stubbier pair.

"Oh, you bought one of those books," Carol said, taking it from Diana and beginning to leaf through it. The taxi shot out into the traffic as if the driver were a kamikaze pilot bent on his and their suicide, and Diana was pushed back into her seat by the resulting force.

"I was going to buy one of these," Carol said. "But Al said we could probably get them cheaper at the hotel."

"Just my luck," Diana sighed. Then, realizing she had thought she was giving the money away, she acknowledged that she hadn't come out too badly in the deal.

"'Cuzco,'" Carol began reading, "'was once the capital of the mightiest South American empire that has ever existed. Today it is the capital of thirteen provinces that form the department of Cuzco, one of the twenty-four departments into which Peru is divided.'"

Before they had reached their destination Diana had also been informed that the town had roughly one hundred and forty thousand inhabitants; it was a Spanish city built on Incan foundations; its most famous yearly event was the Procession of the Señor de los Temblores, or Lord of Earthquakes, during Catholic Passion Week; and its *ayuntamiento* had served as police and army headquarters since the Colonial Period. She would undoubtedly have heard more, but just then the cab pulled up in front of the hotel.

They were greeted at the head of the stairs by a young Indian boy who was wearing a colorful woolen poncho and *chucu* cap. He smiled, showing crooked teeth, as he pointed Diana and Carol into the lobby, where they took seats with the rest of their group gathered there.

"Did you believe the size of that cab?" Diana commented leaning back into the chair. "I felt like a pretzel."

"It was pretty bad, wasn't it?" Carol admitted, leafing through the guide book as Diana prepared herself for an onslaught of new information on Cuzco and its surrounding territory.

Al, fat, balding and with a thick accent, arrived and raised his hands for silence. Quite typically, he didn't manage to get it until five minutes later. "Let me remind all of you that you are at an elevation of approximately eleven thousand four hundred feet. It may not seem high, but it is. You must be extremely careful not to overdo. As a matter of fact, I suggest you all spend the next couple of hours in bed, because we have a full itinerary this afternoon. I don't want any of you coming down with *soroche.*"

"*Soroche?*" came the chorus.

"Altitude sickness," Al explained. "Now, before I give you your keys, tea will be served, compliments of the management." There were

grunts of approval. "The tea is an Indian pre-
ventive for *soroche* called coca that...."

"Don't they make cocaine out of coca
leaves?" someone whispered, causing Diana to
miss much of what Al was saying.

"...so take one or two cups, but not three,"
Al finished, and then began passing out room
keys.

The boy from the door, now joined by a little
girl, shyly handed around trays of teacups.

Diana found the brew weak but palatable. It
had a slightly greenish tint. After finishing one
cup of it, though, she went to her room, finding
no difficulty in falling asleep while Carol read
aloud something about the railroad to Machu
Picchu following the course of the Sacred River
of the Incans, first known as Vilcanota.

When Diana woke up she had a slight headache. As that was one of the symptoms of
soroche, she decided to pass up the evening's
festivities in favor of the comparative quiet of
the hotel. Carol, on the other hand, was prepared to play tourist, saying she hadn't been to
Cuzco before. Which was possible, since there
didn't seem to be a branch of I. Bern in sight,
but Diana suspected Carol suddenly felt safer
with the group than with her roommate, having
weathered Captain Sipas's visit in even less good
form than had Diana.

Sight-seeing was going to include a pagan fortress, ritual Incan baths, the Kenco Amphi-
theater. Dinner was to take place in a restaurant

made up to look like an underground Incan sacrificial chamber. And entertainment was to be the reenactment of an Incan human sacrifice.

Diana lay in bed until all the slamming doors, loud voices and trampling feet faded, then dozed for a few more minutes before getting up to take a couple of aspirins.

After a deliciously wicked tub bath, she dressed in a plain white wool dress, because at an altitude in excess of eleven thousand feet the air was a bit nippy.

Down in the lobby she bought another guidebook of Cuzco and Machu Picchu from the desk clerk, since Carol had run off with the first copy, and found a thoroughly comfortable chair in the hotel lounge in which to thumb through it. She sank down into accepting cushions, raising her feet onto a conveniently placed footstool.

"You are very smart, my dear," someone said in a disturbingly familiar male voice, making her jump with surprise—and something else? Diana had thought she was alone. She wasn't; she saw him now sitting in a large wing chair opposite her: Sloane Hendriks, just as calm as you please!

"You must be sure not to overdo at these altitudes," he went on casually. "Most tourists foolishly think they can run around like ants. On the train ride to Machu Picchu tomorrow they'll be dropping like flies. I presume you are scheduled for Machu Picchu tomorrow. Right?"

"You!" Diana exclaimed finally. Actually, she couldn't immediately think of anything else to say.

"I am sorry about the other evening," he said, flashing a wide smile that was too attractive to be safe. "I am, of course, prepared to make financial restitution." He fished into the pocket of his slim-fitting jeans, pulled out a wad of bills that would have choked a horse and began peeling them off one by one.

"You tell me when to stop," he said. He looked far more handsome than she had remembered. His arrogance, however, hadn't changed.

"I really can't even remember how much that meal cost me," Diana said coolly, coming to her feet. Of course that was a lie, since she remembered every last detail—including the sizable bill.

"Well, I think this should certainly be sufficient," he said, extending several folded notes. "If you should find it's not you must be sure to let me know, won't you?"

Diana, though, didn't reach out to take the money, almost fearful she might become contaminated by mere contact with it. She was afraid that, through some accident of chance, she might actually touch him, this man who was for some reason wanted by the police. His hand, securing one edge of the folded bills, had black hair running along the backs of fingers that seemed strong enough to hold so tightly to whatever they captured that there would be no question of escape.

"At least, you must allow me to pay you back with supper tonight," he said, putting the money back into his pocket.

"You think buying me supper is going to pay me back for what you put me through?" she asked, surprised that her anger seemed to make her feel almost hysterical.

"You have a more enjoyable suggestion in mind, do you?" he asked, raising his left eyebrow inquisitively. Diana read the sexual innuendos, becoming more angry.

He saw her tensing for flight and came to his feet to block her. He was bigger than she had remembered. Bigger, but not nearly as old. Diana, who had mistakenly equated age with size, now decided he couldn't be much over thirty. Poured into his jeans and chamois shirt, the latter open at its collar, his muscled legs, arms and chest all emphasized to good advantage, he might have been considered overpoweringly attractive by anyone whose standards of handsomeness were based on the wild and macho image featured in some cigarette ads.

Diana was only thankful she preferred her handsomeness in smaller doses, telling herself that Sloane Hendriks's jaw was too square, the cleft in his chin too deep, his eyelashes too long, his dimples too pronounced, his chest too hairy and his arms definitely too muscular.

"I'm sorry if you took that the wrong way," he said. "Actually, my intentions are quite admirable."

"Just what is it you're doing here, Mr. Hendriks?" Diana asked, immediately afraid of the answer he might give her. She felt a sudden pain in her right hand, and realized her fingers were clenched, her nails digging into her palm.

"You know my name?" he asked, seeming genuinely surprised.

"Hendriks. Sloane Hendriks. Wanted for who knows what by the Lima Police and probably by every police force in South America, for all I know."

"Just one damned minute!" he said. Diana thought he managed feigned indignation very well.

"Oh, drop the great innocent act, Mr. Hendriks! I've been thoroughly briefed by Captain Sipas—"

"Sipas!" Sloane interrupted. "You've seen Sipas? Damn, I *am* sorry!"

He did seem sorry, too, but Diana refused to be taken in; the man was obviously some kind of con artist who, for all she knew, made a practice of preying on women tourists. Well, he had another think coming if he thought he had found an easy mark in Diana Green! She didn't need to be burned more than once to recognize the danger of fire, and there was fire here, all right.

"Your sympathy is really quite commendable," she said icily, feeling the heat of her nervousness. "So I do thank you for it. Now, if you will excuse me, I'll just go up to my room and wait patiently for the next policeman to break down the door to find out what you happened to say to me this time."

She had every intention of shoving past him, but he reached out his hand to stop her, wrapping those feared strong fingers around her right wrist. Diana's whole forearm was instantly lost within his grip.

"Please, I'm afraid. . ." he began.

"Don't touch me!" Diana said in a low whisper, at the same time wondering why she didn't scream it to the rooftops and bring everybody—possibly even Captain Sipas—running in from the wings. Suddenly a quick jerk left her wrist free, Sloane having obviously released her of his own volition, since there was no physical way Diana could have pulled away herself.

"Look, I really am sorry," he told her. Diana was trembling, her arm still feeling the sensuous burn his fingers had left on her skin.

She wished he didn't sound so genuinely sincere. It was, after all, highly doubtful he *was* sorry. He was probably amused by the additional complications his little prank in the restaurant had caused her. He would have been delighted to know how unnerved the mere touch of him had left her just now.

"Couldn't the two of us sit down for a few minutes and discuss this sensibly?" he asked.

"Look, Mr. Hendriks," Diana said. "Why don't you just leave me alone?"

She didn't know what repercussions this little meeting was going to have, but she couldn't imagine they'd be anything to relish. Captain Sipas would hardly believe this second encounter was an accident, since even Diana had trouble doing so. Then again, Captain Sipas was in Lima. This was Cuzco, several hundred miles away.

"Don't you think it's only fair to hear *my* side of the story?" Sloane asked.

Diana was surprised to realize she hadn't the vaguest notion of what Sloane's side might be, which wasn't saying too much for a woman who had aspirations of becoming a good investigative reporter. On the other hand, the purpose of her trip to South America was not to investigate its criminal element but to write innocuous travel pieces.

Even if she did smell a potential news story with underworld aspects, it would simply be too hard to follow up. She didn't speak the language and she didn't have the contacts required for the type of in-depth article that might interest the readers back home. Just *might* interest them, because there was too much crime in the States, taking up the limited newspaper space, to warrant substituting something about everyday crime on the streets of faraway Peru.

Besides, Captain Sipas had warned in no uncertain terms that Diana was far better off not knowing anything at all about Sloane Hendriks; and these strange feelings he was causing inside her must be intuitive affirmation that Sipas was right.

"Come on, please sit down," Sloane cajoled, not touching her but motioning toward one of the nearby chairs.

"I'll just pretend that somewhere, somehow, there are logical explanations for all that you did," Diana said. "I'll even give you the benefit of the doubt in regard to your criminal guilt or innocence, okay? But since I'm just passing through, I don't think I want to get involved in something that might bring Captain Sipas back for more interrogations at gunpoint."

"And if there really isn't a Captain Sipas?"

"I saw the man, remember?"

"You say Raphael Sipas," Sloane said. "He's never been a captain of any organization that I know of, except maybe his own. Not the military and certainly not the Lima Police. The police, in fact, would probably be most interested in hearing what Raphael is up to these days."

"But he said—"

"And he showed you identification?"

"Three guns were all the identification I needed," Diana responded, knowing she should have been experienced enough as a reporter not to accept anything at face value. The whole problem was, of course, that she had been thrown a little off kilter by being in a strange country where she wasn't even vaguely familiar with the rules of the game. In the States she wouldn't have been caught off guard. She certainly hadn't been caught napping during the investigation leading to the biggest drug raid in the history of Seattle.

"Do you really think that's the way the Peruvian police act with foreigners?" Sloane asked. "Breaking into their rooms? Threatening them with guns? Actually, the authorities are usually willing to bend over backward for people like you. Tourism brings in big money, and Peru isn't so rich that it can lightly risk alienating any source of income. Even during times of intense political upheaval you'll find opposing sides taking great care to see that tourists are kept ignorant of the real, and often bloody, internal struggles."

Diana remembered how unconcerned Sipas had been when she had suggested she might complain about police harassment. "So who is Raphael Sipas?" she asked, and sat down, her natural curiosity having finally got the best of her despite silent alarm bells warning her to beware.

Raphael Sipas, according to Sloane Hendriks, was the modern equivalent of a grave robber.

"The country is riddled with Incan graves,

many filled with artifacts," Sloane explained. "There are still whole cities overgrown with jungle, none of which have been scientifically excavated. Artifacts bring good prices to collectors who can get their hands on them, especially as a hedge against spiraling worldwide inflation. People like Sipas have made a big business of exporting Peru's past without going through official channels."

"The government can't stop him?"

"The government tries, but how can it, since it doesn't have the manpower or the resources necessary to patrol close to five hundred thousand square miles of deserts, mountains and jungles? Areas, I might add, that usually don't have roads or even donkey trails leading into them. It's physically impossible just trying to guard known archaeological sites, without keeping track of unrecorded finds made by local Indians. It's the latter, of course, that offer Sipas his best clandestine source: he and a few others like him have communication networks that give them immediate notification of any important finds. More than one poor Indian, thinking he has struck it rich, has been killed in the rush of Sipas and his competitors to get the booty first."

"It seems fantastic that the government can't do *something*. Couldn't it set up a network, too? I mean, the Indians would surely be anxious to get government help in keeping their ancestors' treasures out of unscrupulous hands.''

"Yes, you would think so, wouldn't you?" Sloane said, with just a trace of mockery at Diana's obvious naiveté. "However, keep in mind that more than a quarter of Peru's sixteen million people are suffering from malnutrition. If you were one of those starving people—the majority Indians, I might add—where would you go with a trinket you happened to dig up out of the ground? To a government agent, who'll confiscate it as a national treasure and tie up your finder's stipend, if any, in time-consuming red tape? Or to Raphael Sipas, who'll give you enough ready cash to buy food for your hungry family for a day or two? With more than one half of the working force of this country lacking adequate employment, there are Peruvians today who must live literally on chicken feed.''

Diana might have thought Sloane prone to exaggeration had she not seen the legions of beggars all through Peru. Aside from that visible evidence, she had once worked on a UNICEF news story in which a regional director at the U.N. had told her that more than forty percent of Latin America's sixty million children lived in homes with incomes below the poverty level.

"All of which hints at Sipas's rather unscrupulous character, but doesn't explain his interest in you," Diana reminded him.

Sloane settled back in his chair. There was such a long pause, Diana wondered if he was going to continue.

"Twenty years ago, a plane supposed to be piloted by my brother and flying from Manaus, Brazil, to Lima, Peru, turned up missing," Sloane said finally. "My brother, on the other hand, turned up safe, sound and drunk in the company of a prostitute. There were nearly ten years between us, and Jack had always been one for the wild life," he added wryly.

"Your brother hijacked the plane?" Diana asked, that certainly being one obvious conclusion.

"Jack landed the plane in Leticia, Colombia, a fueling stop near the Colombia-Peru border. While there, at least according to his story, he turned the plane over to a friend called Gary Holsteen, a procedure my brother and Holsteen had apparently followed on the quiet before, in order to give Jack some time with certain ladies of that town."

"Holsteen hijacked the plane, then?" Diana ventured.

"Since, according to Jack, it wasn't the first time he had entrusted his friend with a plane-load of valuable cargo, he kept insisting the only possibly thing that could have kept Holsteen from arriving in Lima on schedule was for the plane to have gone down. Most everyone else figured Holsteen had simply hijacked the plane, given the perfect opportunity by my irresponsible brother. All of which, I'm sorry to say, put a black spot on our family name and honor that remains to this day."

"The cargo wasn't insured?"

"Insurance, had it been available for such a high-risk undertaking—and it probably wasn't—would have required a detailed manifest of all cargo. The men my father dealt with in those days were fortune hunters and others of similar ilk: a secretive lot, hardly prepared to reveal any aspects of their business to strangers."

So the father, too, had moved in shadowy worlds, Diana noted. Like father, like son.

"And all of this presumably has something to do with Sipas?" Diana pressed on, nervous again while not knowing why.

"Among the cargo were several Indian artifacts, two of which were recently put up for sale through an outlet in Lima. I discovered that a man called Dan Jacos had brought the items in question to the dealer—Jacos, it seems, often acts as middleman between buyers and certain big suppliers in the field."

"And the suppliers include Raphael Sipas?"

"In this case I persuaded Jacos to admit that the supplier in question was Sipas's chief competitor, a man called Dennis Carlyle."

"You *persuaded*?" For some reason, that conjured up all kinds of macabre visions of medieval dungeons, complete with the appropriate accoutrements of torture. As far as Diana was concerned, Sloane's air of mystery very easily lent itself to suggestions of that sinister scenario.

"I didn't have to break Jacos's legs to get the information out of him, if that's what you're thinking," Slaone said, obviously having read her thoughts. "I think you have me confused with our friend Sipas. Who, by the way, is involved in all of this because he knows I've been making arrangements to get to Carlyle. Carlyle is the man who can get me to the downed aircraft, since his men have located and sacked it."

"Why do you want to get to the plane after all these years?" Diana asked, playing reporter, not able to remember when she had ever been so nervous during an interview. For some inexplicable reason, the air around them seemed charged with high-voltage tension.

"Can any woman ever really understand a man's need to experience real adventure at least once in his lifetime?" Sloane asked, and just the way he said it indicated he thought he knew the answer already. But he was wrong. Not that Diana could answer for every woman, but she personally could understand. Despite what Sloane might think, such needs weren't always the domain of the male gender: Diana herself had felt the call of adventure when she had submerged herself in the world of illegal narcotics to get the one big news story of her career. She felt it again now.

"I see this undertaking as my last chance to

do something adventurous before being forced into the routine of day-to-day existence, controlled more by external forces than by my own desires," Sloane explained.

Diana could certainly understand that. While Sloane evidently had come to Peru to indulge one brief flicker of adventurous freedom, Diana's being there to write innocuous travel pieces was for her a mere return to her confining box. The fact that she was talking to Sloane here and now could be considered one final protest against the areas of dull reporting into which certain people back home were determined to put her. Well, as feeble an effort as her token rebellion might be, it was good to feel once again the exhilaration of approaching the brink of danger. Sloane was for Diana a powerful fire, drawing her dangerously nearer and nearer its hypnotic flame. But she must remember not to get burned; the key to her success—and safety—was in knowing when to retreat, in surviving to tell the tale.

"And then there's the old-fashioned bit about family honor," Sloane said. "I know that might sound trite to you in this modern day and age. I guess I'm more old-fashioned than most, probably because I was so impressed during my formative years by the value my father put on such things as family honor. He considered that we'd lost it when suspicion arose that Jack had inadvertently lent himself to a hijacking. My father literally worked himself to death in an at-

tempt to pay off those debts he figured he had
incurred to every man who had shipped cargo
on that lost plane.''

Diana felt herself being hopelessly drawn
to Sloane during the course of his story. Surely he didn't really imagine she would find
it old-fashioned of him to want to restore
what his father had so sorely suffered in
losing!

''So, my finding that plane is important to
me, because it's going to prove that the Hendriks family name was never really tarnished,
that it wasn't an act of my brother and Gary
Holsteen, but an act of God that kept that plane
from setting down on schedule in Lima,''
Sloane concluded. ''Even though there is no one
left who gives a damn but me.''

''What about your brother?'' Diana asked,
figuring that if anybody should have been there
with Sloane at that moment, it was Jack Hendriks.

''Dead at twenty-five from the big H.''

''The big H?''

''Hepatitis, complicated by a general loss of a
will to live. Dad didn't even want to see the
body before burial. I remember. . . .''

He paused and flashed a guilty look that really had no bearing on the present explanations.

''Why would Sipas want to get to Carlyle?''

''Quite aside from a continuing desire to
eliminate the competition permanently, you
mean?''

"To kill him?" Diana asked, frankly shocked.

"Oh, our friend Sipas wouldn't think twice about killing Carlyle, and vice versa," Sloane answered her. "The death of either one would leave a nice share of the market up for grabs. Remember, we're talking about big money here."

Diana shivered slightly, brought back once more to the potential danger of any relationship with Sloane Hendriks.

"However, this time around I suspect Sipas wants him for another reason. It's been rumored that Carlyle has come across a major find—a whole temple complete with artifacts, or some other such thing. Sipas would do just about anything to get his greedy hands on that. Carlyle, though, seems to have kept pretty quiet on this one, which is why he's suspicious of everything that moves in his direction—including me."

"He thinks you might be working for Sipas?"

"The going price for artifacts on the open market has tripled in the last two years. Buyers are paying out fabulous sums just for slabs hacked indiscriminately from ancient buildings. Wars have been fought in these jungles for a few ruined heaps of stone that the majority of the world will never know existed. If Carlyle is a little paranoid at the moment, he has every right to be, especially since his spies undoubtedly will have told him Sipas has been paying a good deal of attention to me lately. I was, in fact, in the process of shaking one of Sipas's men the night I ran into you. I might add that if I had thought for a moment that Sipas could have so thoroughly sniffed out my escape route, I wouldn't have sat down to say hello.''

''Why did you sit down?''

''You were too pretty to resist.''

Diana gave him a look that told him that story, while flattering, wasn't really going to hold water.

''Actually, I was just looking for someplace off the street to alight for a while,'' he said. ''You were alone, and I figured a woman alone might not resent male companionship for an evening.'' Diana found she was suddenly sorry she had pressed for the less complimentary explanation.

''I really had all intentions of coming back,'' Sloane continued.

Diana gave him one of her best dubious looks.

''Really,'' he insisted, as if it were actually important that she believe him. ''I merely left the table to make sure I wasn't being followed. Unfortunately, I spotted a couple of suspicious characters and decided not to risk going back into the restaurant and possibly implicating you. Though my good intentions do seem to have been to little avail, for which I have already tendered heartfelt apologies.''

''You are now going to tell me you flew all the

way to Cuzco to offer those apologies personally?'' Diana said, wishing that were true and wondering why she suddenly found herself liking Sloane, when but a little while before she had been quite prepared to think the worst of him. Possibly, she assured herself, because compared to Sipas he certainly came off the more personable and sympathetic. And honest, if she was any judge. If there was a further reason, she was prevented from seeing it by some protective reflex inside her, admitting only that Sloane's ability to change her attitude toward him so drastically made him seem far more dangerous to her, in a different way, than Sipas could ever be.

"All tourists visiting Peru can be expected to stop at Cuzco," he said, once again disappointing her. "The Savoy usually sees more than its share of the tourist traffic."

"Which tells me why *I'm* here, but what about you?" Diana asked, determined to pin him down. She found something decidedly unnerving about the idea of his turning up at every leg of her journey—whatever logical explanations he might come up with.

"I'm here on instruction."

"From Carlyle?"

"Right you are."

"And where is Sipas all of this time?"

"Back in Lima, I hope. I certainly went to enough bother to shake the tails he had put on me."

"And you don't think he might have had me followed?" Diana asked. "After all, he did seem quite convinced there for a while that I knew you."

"I know Sipas. If he had really been convinced you knew anything about me, I doubt very much whether you would be here talking to me now."

Diana felt a shiver run the whole length of her spine.

CHAPTER THREE

DIANA AGREED TO MEET SLOANE for supper. Why not? She had to eat—if not with Sloane, then alone. Besides, he *did* owe her a meal, and it seemed a little unsporting of her to continue refusing his offer of repayment.

"Just give me a couple of minutes to freshen up in my room," she said. Then, wanting him to know she was ready to believe him, she added, "And I promise not to make any phone calls, in case you think our friend Sipas might have left me his number."

"I'll meet you in half an hour back here in the lobby, then," he told her. If he had any reservations about her being convinced of his story, he didn't show it.

Once in her room, Diana opened her suitcase. Realizing she was looking for another dress, something a little more...yes, more *sexy* than the one she presently wore, she stopped. The dress she had on would be perfectly fine with some freshening up; the situation certainly didn't call for something more seductive. Sloane Hendriks was hardly a typical dinner date. Maybe he was attractive, but he wasn't someone

Diana had to impress. In fact, she still couldn't be one hundred percent sure he wasn't some shifty underworld character—except that she found she really did want to believe he had been telling her the truth.

All she really had to do to check out the truth of his story was call the Lima Police and ask for Captain Sipas. But if Captain Sipas was in fact there, wouldn't Diana be morally obligated to tell him she had run into Sloane in Cuzco?

If she did tell him, things were bound to get more complicated. There would be questions. Specifically, how was it that Sloane just happened to run into Diana at the Hotel Savoy? Diana found the coincidence a little difficult to accept herself, even with Sloane's explanation that every tourist in Peru eventually ended up in Cuzco.

Aside from the fact she had promised to make no phone calls, it simply remained easier to take Sloane's story at face value. If Diana hadn't just been passing through, the situation might have been different. But she *was* just passing through. She had only this evening in Cuzco, another week in Machu Picchu (where she was leaving the group), and then she would fly back to Seattle, her job, her friends and her mother. So she would go to dinner accepting that Sloane was who he said he was, and Sipas—who certainly fit the bill—was the villain of the piece.

She shut the suitcase. Sloane would undoubtedly notice any change of her dress, maybe even read something into it that he shouldn't. It was best to keep their dinner on a purely "repayment" basis.

She went into the bathroom and splashed her face with cold water. After reapplying some light powder and a bit of lipstick and running a comb through her soft blond hair, she looked plenty good, she decided, for a tourist going to dinner in Cuzco, Peru. She couldn't be expected to come downstairs looking like a fashion plate fresh from the pages of *Vogue*.

She dabbed a bit of perfume on the pulse spot on her neck, then on her wrists. She told herself her opening of the small and expensive bottle of Joy that she had bought as a special treat at the airport duty-free shop had nothing whatsoever to do with the man downstairs.

Back in the bedroom, she checked her watch: still twenty minutes to go. She sat down and reached for her guidebook of the city, at the same time hearing a noise in the hallway that gave her a start. It was only when she realized that she had been expecting an ominous knock on her door, accompanied by an all-too-familiar voice asking, "Señorita Green, *por favor*?"

She told herself she was being silly; the noise had to be either a tourist or a maid going into one of the rooms down the corridor. This was Cuzco, not Lima, and Raphael Sipas—or *Captain* Sipas, depending upon whose story she believed—was miles away. Anyway, Sloane seemed pretty convinced of that.

On the other hand, Sloane had thought himself incognito at the Tambo de Oro, and Sipas had tracked him there, indicating that Sloane's judgment—like everyone else's—wasn't infallible.

Diana got up and went to the small writing desk by the window, opening a drawer to find the typical one postcard, one envelope and one sheet of stationery all emblazoned with the hotel logo. She sat down and began writing a letter to her mother.

As had happened during all such previous efforts on the trip, she developed writer's block when it came to writing to Jessica. The logical subject to have written about was the incident in the Lima hotel room; in fact, it would probably have been easiest to write about that, if only because Diana could then gloat over Jessica's ironic assumption that a tour around South America would keep her daughter safe and sound. But no, she decided, she wouldn't write her mother about either Raphael Sipas or Sloane Hendriks. She would tone the story down and deliver it personally—gently, if at all. Jessica was very likely to conclude that this new exposure to violence was directly connected to an assignment for the paper, which could only make things worse for Diana.

Diana loved her mother, could even understand how Jessica came to be so concerned about her welfare, but whether she accepted her mother's rationale or not, the fact remained that Diana was of age and had every right to a life of her own. She should never have attempted to avoid the inevitable mother-daughter Armageddon by agreeing to this trip in the first place.

Glancing at her watch, she couldn't believe only eight minutes had passed. Did time have a tendency to stand still at high altitudes, or did it just suddenly seem that way?

Briefly, she contemplated going down to the lobby and waiting for Sloane there, but decided against it. Not because she was one of those women who believe it's de rigueur always to keep a man waiting: if nothing else, her career in journalism had taught her the virtue of punctuality. However, there was no point in letting Sloane think she was overly anxious, either.

Not that it really made any difference what Sloane thought. They were, after all, ships passing in the night. Although that particular metaphor was somewhat overworked in this particular instance, in that these two ships had passed before, just yesterday.

She checked her watch again, then went back to the mirror in the bathroom, asking herself why she was so nervous. She *was* nervous.... Maybe it was because she had had a few minutes alone to remember just how frightened she had been when Raphael Sipas and his men came barging into her hotel room; or maybe she was only now beginning to realize fully that her reunion with Sloane here in Cuzco was apt to bring on a repeat performance of those horrors.

Then, too, perhaps she was so nervous because Sloane suddenly appeared far more attractive than she had believed, or wanted to believe even now.

Picking up her purse, she headed for the door. If her hand paused momentarily on the night chain before unlatching it, it was only for a moment.

She confronted her paranoia and quickly opened the door, stepping out into a hallway empty except for the young boy who had greeted the tourists upon their arrival at the hotel and later served tea. Leaning against the wall where the corridor made a right angle toward the elevators, the boy smiled at her, showing his crooked teeth. He was hardly the enemy Diana had been expecting, which left her feeling a little ridiculous for her preceding fears—some of them, at least.

Sloane was waiting downstairs. He had changed into a blue blazer, dark pants, a white shirt, even a tie, and Diana thought her cocktail dress of light blue silk would have been the perfect complement to what he was wearing. On the other hand, that particular dress was probably too formal for the occasion. Its neckline was so revealing that Diana hadn't even worn it to a special press party in Rio, which was what she had bought it for in the first place.

"You really are quite lovely," Sloane said, standing back with an appraising look that could have had Diana suspecting he was really seeing her for the first time. He smiled, his cheeks dimpling and his eyes crinkling attractively at their corners. "And even a bit early, too."

He stepped in close, so close that his faint lime-scented cologne mingled with her perfume, enveloping them both in a cocoon of exotic fragrance. Diana was acutely aware that his sheer physical presence, so casually dwarfing her one-hundred-fifteen-pound, five-foot-five frame, left her exceptionally uneasy.

He lightly took her left elbow and guided her skillfully across the lobby.

"It would seem the tourists have decided to dine elsewhere," he said as they were greeted by a dining area deserted except for two other couples, neither belonging to Diana's party.

Diana was about to point out that she was a tourist, too, albeit a working one, and would have probably been off with her group if she hadn't found herself with a headache earlier. She was distracted, however, by realizing her headache was gone, and trying to remember when it had faded.

Sloane directed her to a table in a corner, and they were both seated by the time their waiter appeared. He declined menus, having already decided what they would be having.

"We'd like *chicha morada*," he said, "and *chupe a la limeña*." He added a bit of further instruction in Spanish, which Diana couldn't catch, then turned his full attention to her.

"And now you must tell me all there is to know about Miss Diana Green," he said, somehow managing to let her name linger almost affectionately on his tongue. "You do realize I had to resort to asking the desk clerk your name, don't you?"

As unbelievable as it seemed, Diana hadn't told him herself. "Diana Green was born and raised in Seattle, Washington," she said, noticing his cuff links, small gold sunbursts. "She went to grade school, junior high school, high school...." She stopped, feeling suddenly a little foolish, smiling the question, *you don't really want to hear any of this, do you?*

"Now you've finished studying but are taking some time off to see South America. Right?"

"I haven't been a schoolgirl for some time," Diana corrected him, frowning. "I work for a newspaper. This is not a vacation, or if it is one it's a working vacation. World Travel Unlimited recently expanded its operation into South America, opening a subsidiary, Circle-SA. In the hopes of some free publicity, they offered to pick up part of the tab for certified members of the press who decided to join segments of the Circle-SA tours."

The waiter arrived with their drinks and momentarily interrupted the conversation.

"So your official title is what? Travel editor?" Sloane asked when they were alone again.

"Hardly an editor," Diana said. "Just a

reporter. Actually, these are the first travel pieces I've ever done." Then, not wanting him to think she was a complete novice, she continued, "My last assignment was an exposé on the drug traffic over the western U.S.-Canadian border. The piece was even picked up by the wire services."

"From drugs to travel? Or are you down here researching the famed South American connection? Colombian marijuana? Andean cocaine?"

"During the course of my on-the-spot coverage for the drugs article, there was some gunfire that had my mother figuring it was about time I was packed up and sent somewhere safe and sound. She has a tendency to worry. So I'm afraid it's purely travel pieces I'm doing here." She wondered if her disappointment showed.

"Your mother decided this, or your editor decided it?" Sloane asked, obviously confused.

"My mother is a very old friend of my editor," Diana said. "She quite frankly pulled his strings." Then, wondering if that hadn't painted Jessica in an entirely unfair light, she decided to give a more sympathetic picture of her mother.

"My father was a foreign correspondent for a major U.S. wire service. He was killed while covering the North Vietnamese offensive in March of 1972. His death was something my mother had been expecting for years. I mean, everywhere there was gunfire, or the possibility of gunfire, my father managed to be: Korea in the 1950s, Bay of Pigs in 1961, Panama Canal riots in 1964, Dominican Republic Civil War in 1965, and on...and on...and on."

"Your mother isn't too keen on your following in your father's footsteps?"

"Don't get me wrong," Diana said. "I do realize why she feels the way she does. But I sometimes get a little tired of her continual behind-the-scenes manipulations. When she found out I had landed the job with the paper on my own, she made some calls to make sure I was assigned only the fluff stuff. You know: the fashion scene, the cute cuddly animals at the pound—"

"Major drug raids don't impress me as being in the category of fluff," Sloane said.

"I wasn't exactly assigned that story," Diana admitted. "Actually, I just spent all of my free time hanging around the police stations, and a few of the guys finally decided to take pity on me at the right time."

"Are you good?" he asked. Then added, "As an investigative reporter, I mean?" He smiled, his eyes saying he really *was* trying hard to be a gentleman.

"I'm a damned good investigative reporter!"

"Then, I'd say your editor isn't tapping good potential if he doesn't better utilize the talents of someone who hit the wire services with a story she went out and drummed up on her own."

"My editor says I should give my mother a little time to cool down."

"This trip, you mean?"

"He thinks if we take it slow and easy, eventually we can talk her over to our way of thinking."

"And if you can't?"

Diana only wished she had the answer. However, she didn't, hinting to Sloane none too subtly that she would prefer a change of subject.

Sloane diplomatically took the hint, saying, "You now see before you what is known in these parts as a *chicha morada*. Nonalcoholic, I might add, since I wouldn't recommend touching cocktails on your first night in Cuzco. One drink at this altitude, you see, is the equivalent of three or four in Lima." He smiled, eyes twinkling darkly. "You see how careful I'm being so as not to be accused later of plying you with liquor for immoral purposes, even though the perfect opportunity did present itself."

"So nice to find a gentleman these days," Diana remarked lightly, wondering if she could really be beginning to wish he were bit less of one. She took a small sip of the sweet drink.

"It's made from purple maize," Sloane said. "I thought you might find it more interesting than the usual tourist standards of bottled water and Inca Kola."

"And our main course? *Chupe a...?*"

"...*la limeña*," he finished for her. "In deference to your digestion, not to my pocketbook, by the way, I figured we'd have a light meal this evening."

As if on cue, the waiter returned with a fish-shaped tureen filled to the brim with soup Diana had to admit did smell inviting.

"It's made from prawns, fish, cheese and potatoes," Sloane told her. "I'd also recommend the *chilcano*, a type of soup that's equally delicious, but it contains lemon, tomatoes and *ají*, a hot Peruvian pepper, and those ingredients can raise havoc with the digestive system at these high altitudes. You must try it sometime, but tonight we'll play it safe."

"You certainly *sound* as if you know what you're talking about," Diana said, humming her appreciation of the soup, which was indeed delicious.

They talked of other things, safe things, things that touched on neither of them personally: of Rio, which Diana had loved; of Sao Paulo, which Diana had hated; of Iguassu Falls, where Diana had braved the boat ride across the rapids to the small island vibrating on the edge of the drop; of Bogota's Gold Museum, which had overwhelmed Diana not only with its gold collection worth millions on today's market, but also with its display of Colombia's most valuable collection of emeralds.

When Sloane finally glanced at his watch and said it was getting late, Diana was amazed at how quickly—and enjoyably—the time had passed in his company.

"You'll find yourself in better shape in the morning than most of your group who are still our partying, I guarantee it," he said in the elevator.

The Indian boy was still in the upstairs corridor, and Sloane playfully tousled the youngster's thick black hair as he and Diana walked past.

At the door to her room, Diana opened her purse and took out the key. When Sloane reached for the key, her hand reflexively jerked it away.

"I just wanted to unlock the door for you," he said. It was a kind of little-boy hurt, not anger, that came through. "I forgot, I guess, that you were a liberated woman who could open her own hotel-room door."

Diana hesitated momentarily and then offered him the key as a peace symbol. For a breathless moment she thought he wasn't going to take it. Relief washed over her as he did... followed by a pang of disappointment when he gave it back so quickly once the door was open.

"Thank you for an enjoyable evening," she said, unable to think of anything less trite.

"You're most welcome," he responded.

She wondered if he expected her to invite him in for a nightcap.

"I'm sharing the room," Diana said. Then, realizing how that sounded, she hurried on, "I mean, I'd invite you in for a drink, but...."

"Too bad," he said. "A drink would have made the perfect ending."

Diana tried to detect sarcasm but couldn't. "Anyway, thanks again," she said, moving to enter the room. After all, she couldn't keep him standing in the hallway all night. Then she felt his hand on her arm, firm but not demanding. She turned back to face him.

"May I kiss you good-night, Miss Diana Green?" he asked. "I usually wait until at least the second date." Somehow Diana doubted that. "But it's highly unlikely the two of us will ever meet again, isn't it?" Which was true. Diana would be heading for a week at the Hotel de Turistas at Machu Picchu. And Sloane...?

He pulled her in closer to him, his hand slipping from her arm to her waist.

When I was in Cuzco, at the Hotel Savoy, this man—remember my telling you about him sticking me with his meal at the Tambo de Oro in Lima—well, he took me in his arms and....

He kissed her, and Diana found herself almost eager in letting him do so. As his mouth lingered on her own, increasing its pressure, Diana felt more and more of her inner resistance giving way as easily as her lips parted. Her reserve was steadily crumbling, protective walls, so carefully erected, tumbling down to leave her more and more vulnerable to the dangers waiting in any breach. Yet there was pleasure to be had in her apprehension, enjoyment to be realized in testing just how much she could afford to give way before the animal was let loose inside her.

She told herself that what she was feeling had really nothing whatsoever to do with Sloane Hendriks. It could have been any man kissing her. Then again, Diana couldn't remember ever having been kissed quite like this before. There was exceptional excitement in the way his mouth made almost imperceptible movements against her own, the way the tip of his tongue seemed sensuously to trace the outline of her lips, the way his kissing drew heat upward through her body as if he were fanning some mysterious inner flame.

If Diana had been concentrating on letting her defenses drop only to a point that would still keep in check the animal inside her, she hadn't counted on any unexpected flaring of passion to quickly burn down the barriers. But when his arms pulled her in tightly against him, the feel of his virile body somehow adding fuel to the flames already well kindled, Diana made one more effort to remember there was no safety to be had in any kind of surrender to this man.

She pushed him away, frankly surprised that she had allowed herself to let things come this far, especially with someone who, knowing their time together was limited, could very well think himself safe to play Don Juan on her doorstep. Diana—unlike Sloane, apparently—had never been one to relish the idea of love caught on the run. If such quick encounters could even be called "love" at all. For Diana, intimacy was to be shared only with a man she truly loved, someone who was willing to make a genuine commitment in return for her own; certainly not someone like Sloane, who for all intents and purposes was a virtual stranger and undoubtedly always would be one.

Granted, Diana could hardly consider mere kissing as important as the ultimate surrender. But she had experienced enough melting of her reserve during that one kiss of Sloane's to know she hadn't even begun—before now—to know how potentially threatening this man could be, not only to her person but to all of the moral principles she held dear.

"I see your holding to old-fashioned ways goes only as far as your own family honor, not extending to mine," she said, hearing her voice come out disturbingly breathless.

She wished she knew what was to be read in his dark, flashing eyes.

"You felt it, too, did you, Diana?" Sloane said hoarsely, his hair attractively tousled. Diana felt tempted to run her fingers through that thatch of black hair, simultaneously despising such feelings for coming so quickly on the heels of what had just happened.

"Now, don't get any wrong ideas from one little kiss," Diana warned, frightened by the idea that he was strong enough to make her quickly helpless in his strong arms, more frightened by a shameful suspicion that she would be too weak in the end to resist him. There were, after all, still embers glowing inside her, waiting only for another kiss to arouse them to flash-fire intensity.

"I've had many 'little' kisses in my time," he said, "and believe me, that wasn't one of them."

Diana immediately was set to wondering how many kisses he had sampled before this one, how many times he'd bragged to other women that his kisses were never just small ones.

She would fight him if he tried to kiss her again. She would scream and bring out everyone in the hotel to save her from—what?

"Goodbye, then, Diana Green," he said. "And thank you for believing I wasn't the villain Sipas made me out to be." He turned abruptly, leaving Diana momentarily confused by his retreat.

"How do you know for sure I didn't call Sipas from my room when I went upstairs before dinner?" she called after him in challenge, telling herself she hadn't asked the question just to keep him there for a few seconds...a few minutes...longer.

However, as soon as the question was asked, Diana knew she shouldn't have asked it. As a newspaperwoman she had heard such questions, many just as seemingly innocuous as this one, spoil a whole interview that had been going excellently at the time. Her suspicions were only verified when Sloane stopped suddenly and turned back to face her, anger flashing on his handsome face because she had ruined a certain delicate something that had been building between them all evening.

"I *could* have called Sipas, you know," Diana reminded him, figuring she might as well eat the devil as drink his broth. "'If you ever see Sloane Hendriks again, Miss Green, you can reach me at this number.' That's what he said. I had plenty of time to place the call."

"You didn't make any calls," Sloane said, and his eyes asked her to leave well enough alone.

Diana, though, had a reporter's instinct for knowing when she had, unintentionally or not, backed someone into a corner. It was almost second nature for her to move in for the kill. "How can you know for certain?" she asked.

"Because I've paid someone a good deal of money to monitor all of your outgoing and incoming calls."

"You *what*?"

"And you couldn't have called from anywhere else without my knowing it, either, because I've paid someone to keep a close eye on all of your movements. And I know your roommate didn't call Sipas, because I'm having her watched, too. Does that answer just about everything?"

"Yes," she said faintly, no longer wanting him to stay. "It does."

He hadn't trusted her word, had paid people to bug her telephone and watch her every move. Diana couldn't possibly feel anything for a man like that but pure, unadulterated abhorrence.

Sloane turned and headed down the hallway, and Diana watched as he disappeared around the corner. She stood there alone, except for the boy with his crooked teeth, who was leaning against the far wall down the corridor, watching...watching...watching.

Momentarily the remembrance flashed through her mind of how it had been with Sloane's body pressed so tightly against hers. She told herself the embers inside her had flared unexpectedly but were now safely cold, dead ash. That's what she told herself, despite the fact that her cheeks immediately blushed warm when she reflected, even briefly, on how lucky it was she had stopped that one kiss from going dangerously further.

CHAPTER FOUR

THE BOY WAS STILL THERE at 6:00 A.M. when Diana left her room for breakfast. *"Buenos días, señorita,"* he said, and smiled. Diana smiled and wished him a good morning, too; it was hardly the boy's fault he had been made an offer he couldn't resist, making sure the American woman didn't go sneaking off to a telephone in the middle of the night.

Actually, after a good deal of thought Diana had decided she had probably been wrong to get so upset with Sloane. The kiss had been as much her fault as his, and in having her watched he had merely been taking precautions he thought necessary. He couldn't have known definitely that Diana believed his story. He couldn't have known she wasn't going to call Sipas. She could have been a person who made empty promises with all intentions of breaking them at the first opportunity.

When Diana reached the dining room she found it more crowded than it had been the evening before, although she could pick out very few of her Circle-SA tour group. She told herself she wasn't really looking for Sloane. He had, after all, tendered his farewells the previous night and was probably already off to keep his rendezvous with the mysterious Dennis Carlyle. Which was probably for the best.

Diana had found Sloane affecting her in ways she couldn't quite explain. She, for more reasons than one, was probably far better off with him completely gone from her life.

Across the room George Culhaney was sitting by himself, and Diana went to join him. George was one of the most remarkable men she had ever met. In spite of his advanced years he was forever in good humor and full of seemingly inexhaustible energy. His head of thick white hair was always combed neatly; he had bright blue eyes, and if his teeth weren't his own, they certainly looked it. As now, he usually wore a suit complete with vest and tie, though he never looked uncomfortable or out of place in such formal attire.

"Miss Green...Miss Green...Miss Green." George came immediately to his feet when Diana stopped at his table. "I must say, you are looking chipper this morning." His voice dropped to a conspiratorial whisper. "Not like the majority of our traveling companions, I should imagine."

"Would you mind some company?" Diana asked, thinking she might enjoy, for a change, a man who was in no way threatening.

"Please, do sit down," George insisted as he pulled out one of the chairs for her, and Diana seated herself opposite him. "Will Miss Wiley be joining us?" he asked, signaling for the waiter at the same time.

"Carol isn't feeling much like eating this morning," Diana explained.

"Yes, yes," George said with a wry nod, as if to indicate that further details were unnecessary. "Why these tour groups insist upon crowding so much into such a short time, I will never understand. Especially here at Cuzco. *Soroche* is nothing to play around with, my dear. No indeed. I have seen people die of it. The only thing that saves many of these silly tourists is the fact that they're whisked off to lower elevations before they know how much danger they are really in."

As hungry as Diana was, she decided to wait until later before eating anything too heavy, taking George's example in ordering tea and toast.

"Very smart. Very smart, my dear," George commended her. "Let your system adapt slowly. Acclimatization is the key word. Your intestines have enough trouble adjusting to these heights without trying to dissolve a bellyful of heavy food. Try to tell that to some people, though, and they think you're stark raving mad. I gave up trying to tell them after my third trip—I discovered it did no good anyway. They have to learn by their own gross errors."

"You've been here three times?" Diana

asked, making a place for the small metal teapot and saucer of cold toast.

"Oh, more than three times," George said. "Much more than three. More like forty-three."

"Forty-three!" Diana exclaimed. She would have laughed, except she got the feeling George wasn't kidding.

"I think I missed 1964," George said. "I had a gallbladder operation that laid me up for quite some time."

"That's fantastic!"

"Not really. A lot of people my age have gall-bladder problems." George gave a sly wink to let her know he had really caught her meaning.

"You must be pretty fond of this place to keep coming back," Diana persisted, smearing butter onto a thin piece of hard toast that seemed bent on crumbling beneath her efforts.

"Fond?" George seemed to think that over for a moment. "No, not fond. Certainly not fond. It's merely memories that keep bringing me back, Miss Green. And not too many pleasant memories, either, my dear. I often think I'll welcome death just to be rid of them."

Diana looked up, genuinely surprised. George hadn't appeared to be the kind of man who tolerated the morbid in himself or in others.

"You'll have to excuse an old man his ramblings," he apologized, flashing a cheerful smile that didn't quite cancel the absence of gaiety beneath it. "I should have warned you before you sat down that I become less and less good company as I get nearer and nearer the jungles around Machu Picchu."

"I hope I haven't intruded," Diana said, wondering how she could manage a gracious retreat.

"Actually, it's probably healthier for me not to sit by myself, brooding over the past," George said. Although she was naturally curious, Diana was considerate enough not to pry for specifics. "And I must apologize for insinuating that I don't appreciate your company when the truth is I certainly do," he went on.

Diana took a bite of her cold toast.

"So how was your evening last night?" George asked lightly, channeling the discussion into another direction. "Enjoy that ceremony, did you?"

Diana was momentarily uncertain what he was talking about, then remembered their group had been scheduled to watch the reenactment of an Incan sacrifice of a virgin. "I'm afraid I missed it," she admitted. "I stayed here at the hotel and went to bed." She didn't bother to tell him she had got very little sleep. In fact, she had been wide awake when Carol returned, although she had pretended otherwise. Diana had been in no mood to go over with Carol the pros and cons of Sipas versus Hendriks.

"You'll excuse me if I seem too much awed by such common sense in one so young as yourself," was George's comment. "It's just...

well, you heard about Mrs. Similian, didn't you? And she's certainly old enough to know, far better than you, not to overdo.''

Diana hadn't heard anything about Mrs. Similian. She knew the woman and her husband, a retired tailor, only vaguely as members of the tour group.

"Now, that dear lady would have benefited by your example of taking it easy last night," George said. He lowered his voice. "She had to have oxygen given her at three o'clock this morning."

"Oh, my goodness!"

"She'll undoubtedly survive," George said, adding hot tea to the cool liquid in his cup. "She won't, however, be fit enough for our little train ride this morning. Just look around. Not too good a turnout, wouldn't you agree? If things run according to form, you can expect very few of our party to be up to Machu Picchu this morning. As often as I've seen it happen, it makes me wonder if the tour guides don't purposely plan it this way, just so they won't have to herd too many people on and off the train, up and down the ruins. No skin off my teeth, you understand, but I could have told these people, and they wouldn't have paid the least mind."

He took a few swallows of tea, eyeing Diana over the rim of his cup. "You'll be leaving us in Machu Picchu, if I recall correctly," he said, replacing his cup on its saucer.

Diana couldn't remember telling him, but she

wasn't surprised he knew. Several people in the group knew—it was certainly no secret.

"Yes," she admitted. "I'm staying on there for a few days to write an in-depth travel piece on the ruins, complete with pictures. It's hard to really see a place and get a good selection of pictures in just one short afternoon."

"Sometimes you never get the one picture you need," George replied cryptically. He didn't elucidate. "You're with a magazine, aren't you?" he asked.

"Newspaper," Diana corrected him.

"Ah, yes," George said absently, as if his mind were suddenly a thousand miles away. Diana became a little concerned by his glassy stare. He was, after all, getting along in years, and this was more than eleven thousand feet up. For a moment she thought she might have to call Al, who had come in and taken a table by the window, but George's eyes came back into focus.

"If you're ever in Los Angeles, Miss Green— Los Angeles is where I live, you know—you must make it a point to stop by for a visit. I'll pull out all the old articles and newspaper clippings and let you read them."

"You were a writer?" Diana asked, realizing quite suddenly that she didn't actually know what George had done before his retirement. And she only knew he was retired because someone in the group had commented on it in passing.

"Oh, no!" he said. "Got horrible grades in composition and spelling in my day. I would have given any editor apoplexy had he tried to make head or tail out of my literary efforts!"

He sat back in his chair, looked at her and smiled. If he had seemed a bit out of sorts a moment earlier, he was now in full possession of his faculties. "Are you a *good* newspaperwoman, Miss Green?" he asked.

Diana couldn't help remembering that Sloane had asked her the same question. She wondered briefly where he was at that moment, and whether he had found his mysterious Carlyle, but she pulled herself back to the present as the thought of him brought a disturbing warmth to her body.

"Yes," George was saying, proceeding to give his own answer, "I would imagine you are. There are newspaper people, you know, who really aren't very professional. But anyone who knows how to take care of herself at high altitudes must certainly be good at taking care of anything else she puts her mind to."

"Thank you," Diana said, unable to think of anything else.

George finished his tea, wiping his mouth on a linen napkin starched to the point of being quite able to stand on its own. "I do envy a person who is good at what he or she does," George said. "Although I must admit to thinking, at one time in my life, that no newspaper person could do a purely unbiased piece of reporting. Since then I've mellowed—probably because I've discovered I've never been all that good at anything myself.''

Diana was going to accuse him of obvious exaggeration, but he raised a hand to stop what he suspected was coming. "No, please, don't try to be kind to an old man and say it's otherwise, Miss Green. For, while I do appreciate the thought, you really know nothing at all about me, do you? We've just bumped into each other on occasion over these past few days. I, on the other hand, have lived with George Culhaney for seventy-seven years now. I know him better than anyone, and he is indeed a failure, my dear. Oh, he might have been something once. He had his chance, but he lost it. He. . . .''

He paused, smiled apologetically like an old man suddenly caught talking to himself, and reached into the pocket of his suit coat to pull out a small spiral notebook and pen. He opened the notebook to a blank page and filled the space with his name, address and telephone number, ripping out the page and sliding it across the table to Diana.

"Do be sure to stop if you ever get to my neighborhood, Miss Green," he said. "I really would enjoy talking to you. Now, if you'll excuse me. . .?" He stood, hesitating momentarily to survey the room around him, then inclined his head in Diana's direction.

"I make a head count of only six out of the fourteen in our group," he said. "I'll give you odds that that isn't far from the number of our party who will be making this little jaunt to the ruins this morning. You can usually spot the survivors as those who come down for breakfast.''

Out of the Circle-SA group, seven decided to stay at the hotel, and by the looks of Carol, she should have made it eight. "Are you all right?" Diana asked as their cab was nearing the train station. It wasn't yet seven, and cocks were already crowing from every direction.

"Not really," Carol admitted, "but I'm determined to survive. I can almost hear everybody back home now: 'Did you get up to Machu Picchu this time?'''

"*Down* to Machu Picchu," Diana corrected her. "Cuzco is more than eleven thousand feet, Machu Picchu closer to eight thousand.''

"Whatever," Carol said, opening her purse and taking out a small bottle of aspirin. She popped off the lid of the bottle and dumped out a pill, which she swallowed, giving thanks when it didn't stick on the way down.

"You'll feel better when we get there," Diana assured her, trying to give comfort while at the same time remembering Al's warning that altitude sickness could happen at eight thousand feet just as easily as at eleven thousand.

At the station Al was waiting to give directions and pass out the tickets. "All of your seats are in the sixth car," he said. "The sixth car. Got it?"

"Got it," Diana said. She and George Culhaney were the only really chipper ones in the bunch, most of the others looking as if they had come down with hangovers or something much worse.

"This is first class?" Carol moaned when she eyed the thinly padded seats.

Diana took the window position, since she doubted Carol much cared. No sooner were they seated than there was a mad rush of children back and forth along the aisle. They kept frantically checking tourists' faces and comparing them to those in the stacks of photographs clutched in their small hands. One of the young photographers shoved a picture in front of Diana's nose.

Diana gazed at a shot of herself trying desperately to get into the taxi at the Cuzco airport, her dress hiked so far up her legs that the photo bordered on indecency. She bought it immediately and put it in her purse for later destruction.

Few of the other children paid much attention to her, because most of their work had been done during the previous afternoon and evening when Diana had been absent from the group. When she had been at the hotel with Sloane. . . .

Once again that pervasive warmth crept into her as she dwelled on the image of the man who had somehow drawn her into his net of intrigue. Then she started, aware suddenly that a wide-eyed youth, possibly eight years old, was standing before her seat, looking first at her and then at Carol. He shuffled through his photos and ended up sticking a neat pile underneath Carol's nose.

Carol, revived by the strong smell of chemicals still clinging to the hastily developed pictures, opened her eyes, took one look at the top photo of herself and a llama, and frowned.

"Forget it, kid," she said, and shut her eyes again.

The boy looked absolutely crestfallen. Clearly he had used a good deal of time and film on Carol and was now shocked that his efforts had been wasted.

"Here, let me see those," Diana intervened, reaching out and taking the rejected photographs. She was sure Carol would have been more interested if she hadn't been so under the weather, since things like these made the best souvenirs. Diana began going over the shots one at a time, deciding which would be the best to give Carol as a farewell gift.

The boy, though, shrewd businessman that he was, didn't remain inactive while Diana viewed and pondered. He turned across the aisle, registering Mr. and Mrs. Powell's fat, cherubic features. Quickly separating their pictures from the rest of his stack, and dropping the excess pile on the empty seat across from Diana and Carol, he began bargaining with the interested couple.

Diana, meanwhile, selected five pictures of

Carol, some amusing, some attractive. As she waited for the boy to turn back in her direction, she decided there might be one or two more pictures of Carol the boy had missed, actually hoping for one of herself that didn't have her looking like a contortionist. She began a haphazard shuffling of the photo collection now on the seat opposite her.

There was Mrs. Kelly with a llama. There was Mr. David wiping something from the sole of his shoe. There was Mrs. Denver bargaining with a little old lady for an alpaca shawl.

There was a picture of Sloane Hendriks, talking to some unkempt character on a Cuzco street corner.

Yes, it was Sloane! Diana would have recognized his rugged face and body anywhere. Just by the way the two men were postured in the photo, it was apparent they were in deep discussion.

Diana took the photo from the pile and added it to the ones she had of Carol, then began hurriedly riffling through the boy's selections once more. Her search was interrupted by a whistle from the engine and the simultaneous removal of the photo stack from the bench. The boy began yelling something as the train started to move.

Carol's eyes were mere slits. The whistle had scrambled her poor aching brains, and now every Peruvian kid in the world seemed to be screaming bloody murder in her ear.

"I want these," Diana said, shaking the handful of pictures. "How much?" She hadn't the faintest notion what was being answered, having enough trouble figuring out Spanish when someone was speaking it at a slower than normal pace. This combination of Spanish and Quechua, the language of many people of South America, screeched to her at breakneck speed, was completely beyond her.

Opening her purse, she pulled out the first medium-denomination note she could find and gave it to the boy, who looked panic-stricken. She took a stroke in the dark and motioned for him to keep the change. The boy took the money and ran as the train picked up speed.

Diana stuck her head out of the window, expecting to see the boy's body sprawled by the side of the tracks amid a flutter of scattering photographs. Instead she was greeted by the sight of a group of young entrepreneurs engrossed in comparing daily cost-profit margins. She brought her head in, gratefully settling back into her seat.

"Am I saved?" Carol asked dramatically, apparently not believing the comparative calm that had settled over her. When the engine whistled in reply, she groaned softly.

Diana heard someone ask if there was oxygen on board, just in case, followed by Al's assurance that there was. She looked once again at the photo of Sloane Hendriks, wondering if thoughts of him would ever come without an accompanying blush to her cheeks.

"That's really not a very good likeness," the low male voice said. It was a voice Diana knew very well by now. It made her actually afraid as she glanced up to see Sloane standing there in the aisle beside her, smiling down at her.

"Surprise!" was his greeting.

Diana thought her mind must be playing tricks on her; no doubt her reflections on what had happened the night before had brought the image in the photograph vividly to life beside her. She found her conjurer's trick unsettling, fearing first that it wasn't an illusion and then that it was.

It took several seconds for her to recover her senses before she could come up with a logical explanation that would satisfy her obviously curious roommate. She could hardly admit to Carol that she had revived any kind of relationship with the man responsible for the frightening incident in their Lima hotel room. Any detailed explanations also might have forced Diana into a too thorough analysis of the fearful fascination this man held for her. Such an analysis was the last thing she wanted to further complicate her life.

She introduced Sloane as Mr. Black, because his eyes, such hypnotic pools of jet speckled with brown, seemed all she could think of at the crucial moment; the length of her pause had already become suspect. "I met Mr. Black at the hotel last night," she explained, in as casual a tone as she could muster, noticing the dreaded suspicion already sparked in Carol's eyes. "He was kind enough to keep me company while you were out having a good time."

Sloane, taking Diana's hint, nodded as if her words were gospel.

"I thought you wouldn't be going to Machu Picchu today, Mr. Black," Diana said with an inquiring look at Sloane, hiding her real feelings. She was experiencing that special electric fear and exhilaration that charged their every meeting, especially evident now because, if their meeting at the Hotel Savoy in Cuzco could, by some wide stretch of the imagination, have been chalked up as coincidence, this latest appearance of Sloane was definitely one coincidence too many.

"Rowdy," Sloane said. Diana looked confused. "That's my name," he explained, and smiled; it was obvious to him, and most likely even to Carol, that Diana wasn't a very good liar. "Rowdy Black. But you can call me Rowdy...ma'am."

"Oh," Diana replied, finally understanding.

"That friend I was telling you about last night?" Sloane said. "Well, it seems he's decided to meet me at Machu Picchu. So...."

"So here you are," Carol finished for him. It looked as if she was prevented from saying more only because the ache in her head diverted her thoughts.

"Your condition, little lady, is bound to improve as we drop in altitude," Sloane encouraged her.

"I'll try to take heart from that...Mr. Black," Carol replied, continuing to eye him nervously.

George Culhaney, one seat forward, glanced back curiously. When Diana caught his eye he smiled a little guiltily. "We've both picked the best side of the train for seeing the sights," he told her, obviously making an excuse for turning around in the first place. "The left side is always the best on the way in. I meant to tell you that this morning."

He quickly turned back to the scenery passing slowly outside the train window, not really very exciting scenery at the moment because the train was moving through the dilapidated outskirts of Cuzco. Most of the visible houses had no doors and only dirt floors, chickens scratching in many of the unkempt yards.

"Do you mind if I make use of this space?" Sloane asked, indicating the vacant seat opposite Diana and Carol. Without waiting for permission, he sat down. He was wearing western boots and tight jeans. His shirt was open at the neck revealing a V of tanned muscled chest.

As the train suddenly began slowing down, Carol said loudly, "We're stopping!" Her paranoia concerning the possible true identity of Mr. Rowdy Black was more than evident in the hysterical pitch of her voice. Diana glanced nervously at Sloane.

"Cuzco sits in a bowl formed by a circle of mountains," Sloane explained calmly. "In order for the train to make the descent to Machu Picchu, it must first climb *out* of that natural depression in which Cuzco sits. It does so by proceeding upward in a zigzag pattern, going forward and then backward a total of three times."

At that moment the train came to a complete stop. A short while later, just as Sloane had predicted, they began backing uphill. After reaching the rim of the natural bowl that contained Cuzco, the train began to descend on the other side to a large plain that had been a lake during the Quaternary geological period. At one end of the plain the train dipped into the narrow canyon of the Anta River, then followed the Anta to its merging with the Urubamba and crossed to the right bank of the river via the Concevides bridge.

Diana sat by the window, fascinated by the way the vegetation was changing before her eyes. The plant growth became thicker, greener, lusher, as the train entered more tropical climes.

From January through March there would have been flowers everwhere: orchids, begonias, lantanas, even lilacs. Now there was mostly green, punctuated here and there by a splash of yellow or orange blossoms. While Sloane couldn't identify the plant life in such hasty passing, he made up for it by sharing with the others a plethora of interesting bits of information.

Even Carol—her headache, as Sloane had predicted having become less painful—began to show a genuine interest in spite of her fears concerning the sudden appearance of the mysterious Mr. Black.

"Ollantaytambo," Sloane said, pointing out the giant fortress on the hilltop where remains of defense towers still guarded the lower slopes. "It supposedly sheltered the Inca Manco when he fled the advancing Spaniards."

He indicated a distant wall formed by six large polished stones. "Those polished slabs are red porphyry," he said. "Each weighs fifty tons and is believed to have been brought from a quarry all the way on the other side of the mountain. The builders had no derricks, no pulleys, no wheels. They used only man power and dirt ramps, and their tools consisted of simple stone implements and bronze crowbars. Yet when that wall and many like it were completed, the seams were so closely knit that it was impossible to insert even the point of a knife between them."

"I take it you've been here before, then, Mr. Black," Carol said.

"Yes, several times," Sloane admitted. "At one point in my life I rather fancied becoming an archaeologist. I've since tried to keep up on the subject as a hobby, having done extensive research on this particular area...."

"Just what exactly is it that you..." Carol began, but didn't finish.

Diana knew Carol had been about to ask just what exactly it was that Sloane *did* for a living, but had caught herself in time. *The less you know about Sloane Hendriks, the better,* she thought.

"I must look a sight," Carol sighed, veering from the direction in which she had recklessly been headed, and opened her purse to take out a tiny folding mirror. She busied herself with rearranging her hair and applying rosy lip gloss in an effort to amend the lingering effects of *soroche*.

"If we were coming to Machu Picchu by car, we'd find the road stops here," Sloane said. "It's about a sixty-five-mile hike."

"Thank God we're not going by foot!" was Carol's vehement response showing she had continued to listen.

Diana noticed, by the peculiar tilt of George Culhaney's head, that Carol wasn't the only one keeping track of the conversation. She casually stood and leaned forward over the back of Sloane's seat, coming so close that she could feel the male warmth of him through the thin fabric of his open-necked shirt. If she felt any giddiness—and she told herself she didn't—she attributed it to the altitude.

She tapped George on the shoulder and he gave a guilty little jump, very much like someone caught with an eye pressed to a keyhole.

"Oh, it's you, Miss Green," he said, as if Diana were the last person he had been expecting.

"I thought you might like to join us, Mr. Culhaney," she suggested. "Mr. Black has just been telling us he's been this route several times before. Who knows, maybe you two have even more than that in common."

George hesitated. "I wouldn't want to intrude...."

"If I thought you would be intruding I wouldn't have asked," Diana said. "Please. As a favor to me." She didn't know why she hadn't thought of bringing George into the discussion before now. Between herself, Sloane and George, Diana figured they could keep Carol occupied with other things besides whether or not Rowdy Black might be Sloane Hendriks. Diana, after all, still wouldn't have felt right in letting Carol in on the secret. Not only had Carol been more upset than Diana by the incident with Sipas, but she could hardly be expected to understand her friend's sudden compulsion to court danger, since not even Diana herself completely understood it.

Sloane, upon whom the burden of conversation had fallen during the past miles, turned now in George's direction. "Do join us—Mr. Culhaney, is it?" He obviously approved of Diana's idea.

"Yes," George said, coming to his feet and moving around to shake Sloane's offered hand. "George Culhaney. Just George, if you will."

"Rowdy Black, George," Sloane said, committed to his new identity. "Rowdy, if you will."

"Mr. Culhaney has been over this route forty-seven times," Diana said.

"Closer to forty-three, my dear," George corrected her with a forgiving smile.

"Forty-three?" Carol echoed in a combination of marvel and disbelief. "*Forty*-three?" Before her headache had dropped to its now bearable drumbeat, Carol had decided that *once* to Machu Picchu was probably one time too many.

"That is an impressive figure," Sloane admitted. "Are your trips purely for pleasure, George?"

"Pleasure?" George responded vaguely. Diana saw that same faint glaze cloud the blueness of his eyes as in the dining room at breakfast. Carol, too, noticed George's faraway expression, and glanced nervously at Diana, her eyes saying, *all I need is for this old man of yours to keel over dead in front of me!*

"George?" Sloane tentatively reached out a strong brown hand to touch the other man's arm. He, at least, was prepared to try to do something. "Are you feeling all right?"

"I'm certainly feeling no pleasure at the moment," George said, his eyes slowly coming back into focus. "It was you, was it not, who asked me about pleasure?"

"Is it your heart?" Diana questioned, genuinely concerned.

"It really is nothing physical, my dear,"
George assured her, a faint smile playing across
his lips. "You are looking at an old geezer who
is in surprisingly good physical condition—considering. The doctors have assured me that I
shall go on to live to a ripe old age if I but take
the time to pace myself properly."

Diana, Carol and Sloane all looked a little
dubious.

George's smile grew wider. "You really
mustn't concern yourselves," he said. "None
of you. Honestly." He turned to Sloane. "And
you were once interested in archaeology, were
you not?" No one commented that George
would have had to overhear that bit of information prior to his officially being asked to join the
party.

"Most boys dream of being firemen or police-
men," Sloane said. "I guess my fantasies were a
little more esoteric."

"You were well to have eventually separated
your fantasies from reality," George said.
"Some of us have not been nearly so lucky."

"I'm afraid I don't quite understand, sir,"
Sloane said.

George turned his head and watched the green
jungle sliding by outside. Diana was quite sure
the old man was again withdrawing into himself. She wondered if it had been such a good
idea after all to ask him to join them.

"I once had aspirations, too, of being an archaeologist," George said finally. "And what better place, I thought, for discovering something than Peru. I mean, where else could a whole city like Machu Picchu be accidentally stumbled upon in the undergrowth?"

"You were an archaeologist?" Diana asked, only a little luckier with that assumption than she had been with her earlier one that he had been a writer.

"I was a very spoiled, very rich, very young man," George responded, still looking out the window, where a blurring profusion of trees, liana creepers, bushes and ferns all merged into a backdrop of variegated green. "I was a deluded nobody, thinking that to become an archaeologist I needn't bother spending years studying dusty old books. Oh, no, I needed simply to come out into the field and begin finding lost cities. Lost cities just waiting...just waiting...for George Culhaney to discover them."

He turned back to the group and focused his attention on Diana. "And do you know what I did find when I went traipsing through these jungles with a few of my equally spoiled, rich, horribly ill-equipped young friends?"

"Nothing?" Diana ventured. Considering the lead-in, that did seem the most logical answer.

"And *that,* my dear Miss Green, is the exact biased conclusion to which most of your journalist counterparts seemed to jump at the time!'' George declared loudly with ill-concealed anger. His outburst brought stares from most of the other passengers, many of whom were from other groups besides Circle-SA. "I'm sorry," he said, reaching into his suit coat for a square handkerchief with which to wipe the sweat from his forehead. "Truly, I am."

"You did find something, then?" Sloane asked.

George didn't answer immediately; he seemed to be deciding whether Sloane was really a sympathetic listener. "We eventually could distinguish a total of three larger buildings," he then went on. "Three very large buildings. Temples, I think. Then, of course, there was The Keep. It looked as if there might have been even more, but it was difficult to tell. The jungle had completely swallowed most traces."

"The Keep?" Sloane echoed. There was no disguising his interest, and Diana was fascinated, too. Although by this time she wasn't sure George was all that well—no matter what he might have said to the contrary.

"I didn't, of course, know what it really was," the old man admitted. "I called it The Keep merely because it looked so very much like one. It was round and tall, constructed of stone tightly fitted together without mortar, in the Incan style. With no indications of windows or doors. At one time it had probably jutted well above the surrounding vegetation, but when we reached it it was shrouded by all manner of creeper.''

"Where exactly did you make the find?'' Sloane asked.

"Isn't that what *I* would like to know!'' George shot back. Carol looked to Diana for confirmation that Mr. Culhaney had just dropped off the deep end. "We were attacked by natives. I was the only one who got back. The rest...dead. Anyway, there was never a trace of them found. No trace of the ruins, either. We'd had no time for pictures or plottings, you see. So in the end everyone thought I had merely fantasized my Incan Keep.'' He was sounding genuinely distraught.

The train slowed again, and Diana thought they were arriving at Machu Picchu. George and Sloane, however, knew better.

"We shouldn't be stopping here,'' George said to no one in particular, his face turning back to the window.

"No,'' said Sloane, "we shouldn't.''

Carol went white.

"What is it?'' Diana asked breathlessly. There was certainly no denying her nervousness. Being with Sloane was reason enough for her to feel apprehensive, without having the train stop unexpectedly out in the middle of nowhere.

As soon as the train came to a complete stop, Sloane rose from his seat to find out what the trouble was.

George was quick to point out that he would

gladly have gone, too, but he wasn't as spry as he had once been. "Many years have been spent scampering through this underbrush, looking...looking...always looking...for what I lost," he said. "Now I'm relegated to tour groups that can offer the amenities required by my old age." He moved back to his own seat, for a better view, seeing as Carol and Diana had pretty much monopolized all immediate window space at theirs.

"He's Sloane Hendriks, isn't he?" Carol asked in a low whisper that didn't in the least conceal her anxiety.

"Mr. Culhaney? Don't be absurd!"

"How could you get involved with him again after what happened to us in Lima?" Carol asked, not even smiling at Diana's attempted levity. "I shudder to think what's going to happen to us now."

"Rowdy Black could hardly be held responsible for this stalled train," Diana said, wishing she could be more convinced of that herself.

A man who had been up the tracks now headed back, passing beneath their window, and Diana asked what the trouble was. "Someone said there was an animal on the tracks," the man told her. "They're moving it off now."

"An animal..." echoed Carol. Hanging out the window had made her faintly dizzy, so she pulled her head inside and sat down.

"What, I'm wondering, were you expecting it to be?" Diana asked sternly.

"How do I know?" replied Carol, shutting her eyes and not looking at all well.

Diana certainly hadn't been expecting an animal on the tracks. She had chided Carol for expecting the worst when she herself had been equally guilty.

Several men began clambering aboard a few of the cars up the line. The engine whistle sounded, to Carol's dismay; the train gave a jerk, a pause, another jerk.

Diana spotted Sloane, who had stopped walking the minute he realized the train was on the move. He quickly grabbed hold when his car came past, swinging lithely aboard.

"It was a goat," he announced in response to the simultaneous questioning of several passengers. "We're on our way once again, as you see."

George had more questions, but he waited until Sloane was seated before turning to ask them. "A *dead* goat?" he probed. If Sloane wasn't willing to volunteer the information, the old man wasn't above digging for it.

"Yes," Sloane admitted. Diana noticed how his voice had suddenly dropped to the same level as George's.

"Killed by what?" George asked.

"Looked like a big cat," Sloane said, figuring George wasn't a typical tourist who would be put off for long by attempts to skirt the issue.

"Jaguar," George said. It wasn't a question. "I read there was one giving the villages trouble in this area. There's a small settlement just off through there.''

Diana didn't see anything but green jungle in the direction George was pointing; however, she didn't doubt there was a village where he had said there was, since the goat had to have come from somewhere.

"Did the train scare the cat off?'' George asked.

"The goat was still and dead cold,'' Sloane replied.

"It's apparently realized domestic livestock are easy to come by,'' George said. "It can afford to leave its leftovers lying around for those that are less fortunate. Let's hope it sticks to animals.''

Sloane frowned, inclining his head slightly first at Diana and then in Carol's direction. The two women however, had already read George's insinuations.

"There won't be anybody to take care of a man-eater,'' George continued, not seeing, or not heeding, Sloane's silent request to leave the subject alone. "All but skeleton law-enforcement troops have been pulled out for some new power play fermenting in the capital.''

"Altitude sickness, and now potential man-eaters,'' Carol said, not having missed one bit of the conversation. "Suddenly I know just why it is I. Bern never got around to opening a branch store in the neighborhood!''

"Actually, there's very little need for you to worry about your safety," Sloane assured her. "There have been no reports of any human deaths from the jaguar, and you'll be out of Peru before the altitude sickness kills you."

"You should have followed Miss Green's astute example and not overdone, and the *soroche* would have been no problem," George said, obviously feeling only minimal sympathy for Carol—if that.

Carol shut her eyes in dismissal of George, and the old man took the hint to return to his own seat.

"Alone at last," Sloane mouthed, making Diana laugh.

CHAPTER FIVE

"THERE!" SLOANE SAID, pointing.

Diana saw the zigzag scar etched on the side of the mountain now coming into view.

"You see before you the Hiram Bingham Road," Sloane said. "Named after Professor Hiram Bingham of Yale, who discovered the ruins of Machu Picchu on July 24, 1911. It's five miles of road built right into the side of a mountain that rises more than a thousand feet from the canyon bottom, where we are now, to the ruins of Machu Picchu up on top. There's a total of thirteen turns."

"Thirteen is an unlucky number," Carol announced, stirring to join everyone in looking out the window.

"Thanks for reviving long enough to deliver that long-awaited bit of good cheer," Diana responded.

"Just please don't tell me I'm going to have to walk up that mountain," Carol said. If so, she was obviously prepared to stay on the train.

"Luckily, you are no longer required to walk or take donkeys. They've shipped in *camionetas* just to serve the tourist trade."

"*Camionetas?*" Diana asked.

"Small buses. Usually VWs."

"Thank God for the Germans!" Carol said.

"Actually, I rather think a donkey would be more fun," was Diana's comment, eliciting a smile from Sloane and an are-you-crazy groan from Carol.

"Well, ladies, if I don't get the chance to say any farewells during the hassle of detraining, let me thank you now for your company." Sloane was addressing both of them, but he was looking at Diana the whole time. Diana was feeling a definite pang of regret, realizing she had actually been hopeful he would be going on to the ruins with them. She was admittedly going to miss the edge of excitement this man had an uncanny way of adding to her life.

"But surely we'll see you on top?" Carol said, not concealing her own hope that she would be saved any further, possibly incriminating contact with the man.

"I'm afraid I'm staying here at the bottom," answered Sloane. "I'm meeting friends for a few days of hiking."

"Be sure to watch out for man-eating jaguars, won't you, Mr. Black?" Carol said, beginning to pick up her things. "I hear they're running rampant."

The train was almost at a complete stop.

"Thank you for your concern," Sloane said. He was speaking to Carol's back, though, because she had already taken advantage of a break in traffic to slip into the aisle, where Al was busy trying to herd his group forward.

"I'm afraid our little charade didn't much fool your friend," Sloane whispered to Diana, flashing her a wide smile, when Carol was out of earshot. "She's very perceptive."

"More likely I'm just a poor liar."

"That could be it, too," he good-naturedly admitted.

The car was almost empty.

"Well, Miss Green, it has certainly been nice meeting you—again."

"And it's been...well, interesting meeting you—again."

"If that's the best I can hope for," Sloane responded with a chuckle, "I suppose it will just have to do." They both got up, Sloane letting Diana slip by into the aisle ahead of him. "You know, I'm rather tempted to ask for another farewell kiss," he added in a low voice.

Diana could feel him close behind her, his warm breath tickling the sensitive nape of her neck. She turned her head slightly. "If you got a kiss for every time we've said goodbye lately," she said teasingly, her eyes sparkling, "I would have ended up kissing you more than I have some of my steady boyfriends."

The train was now completely empty. As they neared the exit Diana felt Sloane's hand on her shoulder, lean fingers pressing gently but firmly into smooth flesh, and realized that she had actually hoped for it.

"Diana," he said. Just "Diana," but it sent strange little shivers up and down her spine. She turned toward him, once again impressed by the pure physical size of him as she looked up into his eyes, seeing those penetrating black pupils surrounded by their brown starbursts.

"I really did believe you when you said you wouldn't call Sipas from the hotel in Cuzco," he told her. "Really, I did. But I had to make sure, cover all the angles, don't you see? It's so very important for me to locate that downed aircraft."

"I thought it was obvious I'd already forgiven you," she replied softly, a tremor running through her at the urgent way his eyes were searching her face.

He cupped her chin in his right hand. His palm against her skin was sensuously rough with calluses.

"In a way I wish I had met you at another time, in another place... certainly under far better circumstances," he went on.

"On the other hand, it's probably far better this way," sighed Diana, wondering if she really believed what she was saying.

"Perhaps," he admitted, sounding no more convinced than she.

His eyes locked hers in a questioning gaze, although Diana didn't think she knew the question—or the answer. She did know there was a mysterious magnetism that seemed to draw her deeper into those hypnotic brown-specked black eyes, causing her to lean toward them: and Sloane took full advantage by reaching out to intercept her and enfold her in his arms. His lashes, lush and long, brushed her soft cheek as his lips touched and then settled firmly on her mouth.

She felt the resulting undercurrent of danger that accompanied their kissing, just as she had felt it at the hotel in Cuzco the first time he had kissed her: an almost erotic combination of longing and fear, pleasure and panic. However, having successfully faced the danger once before, she felt more confident in dealing with it now, which might have been why she made no immediate move to pull away.

He was, after all, leaving her life forever once he left the train, removing with him the threat, whatever it was, he mysteriously offered. And Diana felt an obligation to herself to store up as many memories as possible of the disturbingly unique responses this man, like none other before him, seemed capable of triggering inside her. At the same time she wasn't sure whether she was relieved or disappointed by her intuition that there might never be another man in her life who could affect her the way Sloane did.

As his lips lingered longer and longer, always moving in a gentle caress that added more and more to the exquisite fire flushing her cheeks and warming her body, Diana's common sense finally warned her that she had let herself back onto very dangerous ground.

Oh, she knew there was no way too much could happen here; after all, they were in a train car, and soon Al or Carol would be coming back to check on what was keeping her so long. When her tour group left Machu Picchu later that afternoon, however, Diana would be staying on for a whole week without Al or Carol there to check up on her welfare. And although Sloane had said he was shortly going off into the jungle, there was always the chance, perhaps through that same quirk of fate that had thrown them together before, that he might show up at the hotel on the mountain. Possibly misconstruing the reasons behind Diana's harmless compliance now, he could mistake her behavior for an invitation to attempt future liberties—if and when he ever felt them available. Which was certainly not to be encouraged at any cost!

Telling herself she had been wrong ever to assume she was capable of handling the type of challenge this man represented, she placed both of her hands on his chest—how hard and exquisitely muscled his body felt against her flattened palms—and firmly pushed him away.

"We really must stop meeting like this," Diana said nervously, attempting levity in the hopes of discharging some of the skinprickling electricity that had built up between them.

"Yes, it's frustrating as all hell, isn't it?" His comment only confirmed that he had mistaken her response for something far more serious than Diana told herself it really was—or was ever intended to be.

"I really must be going," Diana said, wondering if she could possibly be blushing again. She hadn't blushed in years—until recently. "Carol will undoubtedly think you've kidnapped me, or something equally horrendous!"

She turned, moving quickly along the aisle to the door and stepping out into the bright Peruvian sunshine. Sloane followed directly behind her.

"Do you see my group anywhere?" she asked, suddenly panicking inside at the prospect of being abandoned with a man who presented a thrilling kind of danger than had nothing whatsoever to do with his association with the criminal element.

"Isn't that your guide puffing in our direction?" Sloane pointed.

"Yes!" At that instant Diana was torn two ways, wanting Sloane to go, and yet . . . .

"Miss Green! Miss Green!" Al Scalipas called, his voice filled with the everyday frustration of a tour escort finding another passenger who has insisted upon venturing from the prescribed program. "We're loading now, and I *would* like to get you settled in on top as quickly as possible."

"Yes, of course," Diana said, extending her hand to Sloane, who took it and gave a farewell squeeze. "Good luck, then, Mr. Black, and a successful journey." She knew it was quite doubtful she could ever really have had a relationship with a man offering the variety of threats that Sloane Hendriks seemed to offer. He might be a criminal—though she no longer thought so; he might be an adventurer—in more than one sense of the word!

"You, too, Miss Green," he said, "wherever that journey may decide to take you."

Al led Diana back to the group. "Diana, thank God!" exclaimed Carol. She looked as if she were going to say more, but suddenly became too occupied in surviving the funnel of people who sucked her and Diana into one of the small buses and then squashed them inside like sardines.

The bus moved quickly into the first of the thirteen hairpin curves. Nineteen minutes later it came to a stop on top, and amid a squeal of excited voices the tourists began to swarm at Machu Picchu.

Al took a head count, satisfied that everyone in his charge had arrived. "All of you may as well eat now," he said. "Our official guide for the ruins is reserved for one o'clock. It's a quarter to twelve now. Diana, if you want to come into the hotel with me for a minute, I'll see about getting you settled."

Carol headed for a table on the small veranda, not yet taking in the stupendous view, while Diana followed Al into a building that doubled as a general store, restaurant, tourist center, tavern and—she gazed hopefully around her—a hotel.

"Take a couple of minutes to look over your room, and if you have any questions I'll try to anwer them before I leave," Al said after Diana had signed in at the front desk. He then intercepted a beer headed for Mr. Davis's table, wanting no one drunk and stumbling too near any precipice.

Diana went to her room, which, while not as elegant as those in a Hilton Hotel, was at least clean. There was a bathroom of sorts, and a bed. What more could a girl want—a girl who had but moments before, on the next to last turn coming up the mountain, thought for sure she had just seen her final day on earth?

Diana told herself that, yes, she was Diana Green; yes, she was in a hotel room at Machu Picchu, Peru; no, she hadn't gone to heaven or hell when the bus had skidded and nearly gone over the edge of the cliff, to the accompanying hoots and howls of the amused daredevil driver.

After freshening up, she went to find Carol on the veranda, stopping Al long enough to inquire about her luggage. She had left her largest bag at the hotel in Cuzco to be picked up on her return. She had brought a small bag with her to Machu Picchu, and she supposed Al had stored it somewhere on the train.

"Everyone is a little busy right now," Al said. "As soon as there's a free moment, though, someone will see that your bag gets to your room."

Diana gave him the envelope she had prepared. It contained a short note of thanks and a couple of traveler's checks that she had signed over to him for all of his bother. After that, since there wasn't really much to say, she headed for Carol.

"Have you ordered yet?" Diana asked, pulling out one of the chairs and sitting down.

"You find a rejuvenation station somewhere?" Carol asked from behind half-closed lids.

"Do you want to use my room, such as it is, to freshen up a bit?"

"Sounds marvelous!" Carol said. "As a matter of fact, it's the best offer this girl has had all day."

Diana gave her the key. "Want me to order you something to eat?" she asked Carol.

"Sadist!" Carol accused, managing a weak smile before disappearing into the building.

Diana ordered *carapulca,* after the waiter explained, in surprisingly good English, that it was made of small pieces of chicken and pork, seasoned with a dressing of lard, onion, *ají, ajo* (Peruvian garlic) and cumin seed, with sautéed potatoes added. The dish was served with boiled yellow potatoes and a garnish of hard-boiled eggs and olives. Diana figured if her digestive tract hadn't adjusted to the altitude by now, it never would.

Carol was looking surprisingly better by the time she returned to the table. "Why do you suppose I came out here expecting to find you with that man?'' she asked, sitting down.

"What man?''

"Come off it, Diana,'' Carol chided. "No matter what you may think, I wasn't born yesterday.''

"Mr. Black, you mean?''

"Very well, Mr. Black, if you prefer to keep up that ludicrous charade. But let me tell you that, whatever name we call him, he's the same one who brought Captain Sipas barging into our hotel room in Lima, isn't he?''

"How could you possibly have come to that conclusion?''

"You meet a guy in a restaurant in Lima, right? He's attractive. First thing you do is tell me about him. That's natural. So you meet this Mr. Black at the hotel in Cuzco. He's about as attractive as any guy is going to get, and yet you don't give me even a hint as to his existence until the matter is forced out of you by his sudden appearance on the train.''

"I was asleep when you got in.''

"I was awake enough this morning.''

"You weren't feeling well.''

"Diana...Diana...Diana,'' Carol charged, shaking her head in obvious dismay.

"That unfortunate incident in Lima is over and done, anyway,'' Diana insisted. "Lima is miles and miles away.''

"Not so far away that Sipas couldn't get here just as quickly as we did,'' Carol reminded her.

"You won't try to contact Sipas, will you, Carol?" Diana asked, suddenly very concerned over that definite possibility. "I mean, Sloane has given me his story, and—"

"You mean Mr. Black?" Diana had blown the ruse, weak as it was. "What you mean is that *Mr. Black* gave you his story, don't you?" Carol persisted.

"Oh, Carol, I believe him. I really do believe him."

"Look, Diana, all I'm worried about is whether or not you know what you could be letting yourself in for. Come tomorrow I'm going to be on my way out of Peru, but you're still going to be here. As for Sipas, I don't care if I ever set eyes on him again; but if I thought this Sloane character was getting you into something over your head, I'd rush to the nearest telephone."

"He's not, Carol. Believe me, he's not." Carol continued to look unconvinced. "I'm a reporter, remember?" Diana said. "I'm used to prying the truth out of people. I really feel what Sloane told me was the truth. In time I'm sure I could convince you, too."

"You're not letting your head be ruled by your heart, are you, Diana? And don't give me that Carol-whatever-are-you-talking-about look! I'm not blind."

"I don't know what you're insinuating, but it certainly isn't anything like that!" Diana said, trying to sound genuinely indignant but not succeeding to either her or Carol's satisfaction.

"Just what were you two doing while a whole trainload of people managed to unload and get lined up outside?" Carol asked. Diana felt herself blushing. "He's handsome, Diana. He's damned handsome. I see that. He's also as charming as all get-out. But, honey, I've been around a little in my time, and there are plenty of con artists in this world who are good-looking, good conversationalists and good in the sack."

Diana was positive she was turning red. She wasn't all that certain why, since she had heard blunter talk around the police stations in Seattle, as well as in the newsroom of the paper.

"I believe him," Diana managed finally. "I really do. Besides, I'll never be seeing him again." She got a particularly wistful feeling when she realized that was true. Sloane Hendriks, for better or for worse, was really gone from her life, leaving a surprisingly large vacuum considering how little he had supposedly meant to her. "He really is going into the jungle with friends."

"Honey, bad pennies always have a habit of showing up when you least expect them, or are you telling me you expected him to show at the hotel in Cuzco and then on the train?"

"He's not a bad penny!" Diana protested, feeling it necessary to come once again to Sloane's defense. At the same time, there was no denying that what Carol was saying had run through Diana's thoughts.

"So at least I've said my piece," Carol finished. "You're a big girl now. I can only point out certain things and hope you've got the good sense to consider them."

"And you won't try to call Sipas?"

"Are you still scheduled to head home when you said you were?"

"Yes."

"Then, two weeks from this very day I want you to call me and let me know you got home safely. Right? And if I don't hear from you I'll do my damnedest to find out what happened. Okay?"

"Okay," Diana agreed, leaning across the table and giving Carol a small kiss on the cheek. "And thanks."

"I do wish you the best of luck, honey. Really, I do," Carol told her, grimacing at the sight of the food being delivered to their table. "Am I seeing things, or are you actually planning to eat that great pile of food?" she asked.

"I'm hungry," Diana said.

Carol ordered tea and tried not to look at Diana eating. Even the thought of food made her stomach go slightly queasy, and she was more than happy when the waiter began clearing away the dirty dishes. Then, hearing Diana asking about *mazamorra morada,* she tried unsuccessfully to block out the waiter's voice as he explained in excellent English—of all times to find a local who could speak English clearly, she moaned inwardly—that it was a very popular jelly dessert made from boiled purple maize, sugar, cloves, pineapple, quince, apples, peaches and dried fruit cut into pieces, all cooked and then sprinkled with lemon juice and cinnamon. Diana, seeing her friend's pained expression, relented, deciding to save dessert until later.

"Oh, don't give up your gorge on my account," Carol insisted when the waiter had left the table.

"I probably shouldn't overdo anyway," said Diana.

Carol couldn't help laughing.

They were finally able to turn their undivided attention to the view. And there was certainly no one, anywhere, who would have denied that the view from their terrace vantage point was stupendous.

They sat facing the chasm that dropped to the Urubamba River below them. The river was a ribbon of brown and frothy white as it churned through the twisting rapids of the canyon that bound Machu Picchu on three sides. To their right was the top of the Hiram Bingham Road. To their left were the ruins, situated on a shallow depression between two peaks. Of Machu Picchu (Old Mountain) and Huayna Picchu (New Mountain), the latter was probably the more recognizable from the pictures in the travel brochures. It rose vertically from the bottom of the valley, reminiscent of Rio's equally famous Sugarloaf.

Everywhere was the prevailing color green. Green leaves on the trees and bushes; green grass on the hillsides; algae in still pools; green moss on the ruins; green, green, verdant green somehow more startlingly green in contrast to the blue of the sky and the tan of the Urubamba River, to the whites of passing fluffy clouds and the yellow serpentine twists of the Hiram Bingham Road, to the varying shades of granite gray in the rocks and the stones. The scene was breathtaking, making Diana feel dwarfed and insignificant by comparison. She was saying as much to Carol just as Al arrived at their table.

"We're about ready," he said. "Diana, do you want to join us?"

"I think I'll just sit for a while," Diana answered.

"Well, I have only the next hour to see this, not a whole week like some people I know," declared Carol, getting stiffly to her feet. "So I guess I had better get my you-know-what in gear."

Al moved off to the next table, pointing out to Mrs. Kelly just where the group was gathering off to one side of the patio.

"You will stick close for proper goodbyes, won't you?" Carol asked.

"I promise to wave before they shove you into your *camioneta* for the mad ride down the mountain."

Carol hooked the strap of her purse over her shoulder and headed off toward the small, waiting crowd of Circle-SA tourists. Meanwhile Diana, finding it pleasantly warm in the afternoon sun, called the waiter over and asked for a glass of *chicha morada*.

When he brought her order, he told her she must be sure to try *chicha de jora* sometime. It was made from yellow maize, fermented but not distilled, and the recipe dated from before the Incas. Diana asked if the drink contained alcohol, and the waiter told her it contained a little, but that she wouldn't get too drunk if she waited for a couple more days before sampling it. She was staying on for a while, wasn't she? She said yes, and he frowned at the other tourists who were scrambling over the distant ruins. "You can't see Machu Picchu in a couple of hours," was his comment.

Diana smiled, nodding in agreement before losing herself in contemplating the view.

Suddenly she realized there was someone standing by her table, and glanced up, expecting it to be Sloane. Undeniable disappointment came over her when she saw it was George Culhaney. He asked if he might join her, and she indicated the chair across from her.

"You are looking on an Incan fortress never seen by the eyes of the Spanish conquistadors," George said as he settled himself comfortably. "This city stayed hidden from them, up here away from their prying eyes, shrouded in clouds that still keep the place completely covered during the rainy season.''

"Fantastic, isn't it?" Diana agreed.

"What a remarkable people they must have been," George reflected aloud. "The Incas. The people who created cities on mountaintops. The word 'Inca,' you know, comes from the Quechua 'king' or 'prince.' It was a term applied originally only to the supreme chief. Then came the Spanish in the sixteenth century, who applied the word to the entire ruling class of Indians, including the nobles and the priests. Today we use the term as a catchall for the whole race of men who ruled what is now Bolivia, Peru, Ecuador, northern Chile and parts of Argentina. And where is that great nation today? Gone. Vanished with cities that are still as lost as this one was before it was found.''

Diana could tell where the old man's mind was wandering. He was no doubt picturing how it had been to stand once in a verdant jungle in front of a lost city he would only lose again.

"The Incas were conquered by a bastard swineherd," George said finally. "For that's what Francisco Pizarro was, you know: the illegitimate son of Gonzalo Pizarro. He spent his boyhood earning his living as a swineherd in Trujillo, Spain. Of course, had he arrived in Peru when the Incan nation was at its prime, his troops—only a few hundred in number, by the way—would have stood about as much chance as Napoleon at Waterloo. But he landed when the empire was weakened by a long civil war. So he conquered, kidnapped the Inca Atahualpa, held him for a ransom and then killed him. He looted. Oh, the treasures the Spanish sacked from this country, it's enough to stagger the imagination! Gold—literally tons and tons of it. And emeralds, some the size of goose eggs. . . . ''

George was still sitting there, though long gone silent, when Carol arrived back with the rest of the group.

Without allowing his people even a brief respite, Al began herding them over to where the line was forming to board the *camionetas* for the ride back down the mountain.

Diana and Carol excused themselves from George, who seemed hardly cognizant of anything going on around him, his gaze vacantly fixed not on the ruins at hand but on some portion of jungle off on the distant horizon.

Carol laughed when Diana produced her going-away gift: the pile of five photographs bought from the boy on the train. But she didn't laugh when Diana gave her the picture of Sloane. Diana was thankful that Carol simply tucked the latter into her purse with the others, without any comment. Frankly, she was a little disgusted with herself for taking the precaution. She should have either trusted Sloane or not trusted him. Still, in a strange country it was always best to do whatever one could to assure one's safety, since more than one traveler had disappeared off the face of the earth without a trace.

"Two weeks," Carol said as the bus pulled up and almost ran over her right foot. "That is, if I survive the trip back down the mountain."

"Two weeks," Diana promised.

Carol disappeared into the bus with a squash of other people, and Diana moved to the other side of the vehicle to see her friend mashed tightly against a window. The two waved to each other as the bus headed back down the Hiram Bingham Road.

Diana went back to the veranda, where Al was rounding up the lagging George Culhaney. Seeing Diana, George came over for final goodbyes; the old man seemed, at least for the moment, to have returned once again from wherever it was his inner reveries had taken him. "You will find the place quite different after the tourists have left it," George promised. Then Al took his arm and guided him to a place in the diminishing transportation line.

Diana ordered another *chicha morada* while more and more buses reached the bottom to disgorge their passengers and start back up the mountain for those people still waiting. The train arrived from Santa Ana, and at a distance the people looked like brightly colored ants as they began boarding. Diana thought she could pick out Carol, and she waved, imagining her friend waving back.

The train was soon moving toward Cuzco, leaving Diana startled to discover she was the only one left on the veranda. She asked the waiter about the other guests at the hotel. Some are out hiking," he told her. "Some are in their rooms resting. No one much likes to see the *turistas* swarm."

When there was no further sign of the train in the canyon, Diana went to her room, where she found her suitcase waiting.

Later, feeling surprisingly refreshed after a short nap, she put on a clean dress, applied a little makeup and combed the tangles out of her corn-colored hair. Examining herself in the mirror, she decided she looked better than she had in a long time.

She left her room, determined to have a small glass of *chicha de jora* that very evening.

The hotel guests had obviously come out of hibernation; several tables were occupied in the progressing darkness. Already most of the canyon was lost in shadow, the Urubamba no longer even distinguishable in the gloom, the blue sky faded to misty gray, the twilight muting even the yellow of the Hiram Bingham Road. The greens, though, were still there, only a deeper shade: thick velvet mantling the hillsides.

Diana strolled out on the patio, looking for the waiter...and found Sloane Hendriks instead. Immediately she experienced a resurgence of emotions she had assumed were safely dormant. Sloane somehow unlocked them from those recesses to which Diana had relegated them, doing so without her will, simply by his being there.

"Diana?"

He had seen her immediately and was quickly on his feet and moving toward her. She gave him both of her hands, slightly embarrassed that most of the people on the veranda had turned in their direction. She felt that dangerous spark of electricity passing from his fingers into hers, fearing what easily combustible tinder it might find somewhere inside of her.

"This doesn't mean there's another goodbye kiss in the offing, does it?" Diana asked, her throat gone dry.

"But this is marvelous!" Sloane said. "Absolutely marvelous! And I was just thinking what a shame it was I had no one with whom to share the beauty of a Machu Picchu sunset."

"You're certainly waxing poetic this evening, aren't you?" Diana said as Sloane, dropping her left hand but still holding her right, led her from the veranda and toward the ruins.

"I thought you would be miles away by now," she said.

"So did I," Sloane said, just an edge of chagrin creeping into his otherwise cheerful voice. "There's been another delay, but I'm waiting now for final word. And what better way to wait than with you? Whatever, by the way, are you still doing here?"

"Working," Diana said. "One of my better-researched travel pieces is scheduled to come out of my stay here."

"And the rest of your group?"

"Gone," she answered, thrilling with the realization that all of her previous chaperons had left her at this man's mercy.

"Even Miss Wiley?"

"Even Miss Wiley," was her response. At the same time she wondered why she hadn't at least pretended Carol was still standing guard in the wings.

"You never once mentioned you would be staying over," Sloane accused good-naturedly.

"I didn't see much point, considering you were supposed to be long gone by now."

They walked near the small gate giving access to the major pathway into the ruins. There was a gathering of Indians around the gate, but no one stopped the couple, the man on official duty merely opening the barricade to let them stroll through, nodding a greeting that said, without words, that he still remembered what it was like to be young and in love.

They passed the rest station made from one of the ruined smaller buildings. During the hours of the daily swarm of *turistas* all of the benches were usually filled, because there was such an excellent view of the terraced ruins.

Diana watched a lacy wisp of mist cling to the top of Huayna Picchu and then be whipped away by a breeze sweeping up from the canyon.

Sloane stopped and with his free hand pointed skyward. "Condors!" he said. Diana could pick out the large-winged birds gliding on the late-afternoon updrafts. "Usually the typical tourist leaves too early to see them."

"They look enormous!"

"They are, many with wingspans of ten feet or more. They're really vultures, you know, sometimes known to eat so much at one sitting that they can't even fly until their meal is partially digested. If attacked while stuffed, they're particularly vulnerable."

Diana found Sloane's voice pleasant, and she hung on every word as he next pointed toward the summit of Huayna Picchu. "See the terraces way up there?" Diana did see them, surprisingly for the very first time. They were small parallel lines high up on the face of the steep mountain.

"The Incas farmed even those hard-to-reach spaces," he told her. "They terraced as a means of avoiding erosion, hauling fertile soil up from the valleys, lugging it up the slopes in baskets and other containers, because the soil up here wasn't rich enough for their crops to thrive.

"Marvelous people, the Incas!" he continued. "Machu Picchu was built on a route that connected the torrid regions of the Antis Indians, after whom the Andes were named, to Cuzco, capital of the fabulous Incan Empire. It was only one of several outposts built, many believe, as a last-ditch attempt to save the fading empire from the advancing Spaniards. To the north there were other latter-day cities of importance, like Vitcos and the legendary Vilcabamba Grande."

Something told Diana Sloane's knowledge was the result of genuine interest. He wasn't delivering a tired discourse that had become dull around the edges.

They paused at yet another vantage point giving them an exceptional view of the multiple layers that made up the city, virtually thousands of narrow stairs connecting one level to another. Sloane extended his arm and began a slow sweep of the vista.

"The main temple, the sacred square, the temple of the three windows...and the Intihuatana, or 'stone to which the sun was tied,'" he explained, pointing out the stone. "Carved from a single block, it's one of the few left intact in the country; most of the others were pulled down and broken up by Spanish missionaries, who said they were monuments to a pagan god."

"Why *didn't* you become an archaeologist?" Diana asked. "It's obvious that you're keen on the subject."

"Yes, well, that is a rather long and complicated story."

"I seem to have plenty of time available this evening, unless, of course, the hotel has festivities planned of which I'm currently unaware."

"I'm not really sure the story bears repeating," Sloane said.

Diana didn't press, but she was curious. A reporter's instinct told her the best way to get this particular story was not by rushing in and pushing for it; yet it wasn't the reporter in her that wanted so desperately to hear it.

"Actually, it was all just a fanciful daydream," Sloane said. The path intersected a stairway and he sat down on one of the steps, where Diana quickly joined him. It was quiet and growing darker, the mountains acquiring a faint nimbus and the valleys becoming completely drenched in darkness. "In the long run I think I'm infinitely better suited to my present profession than I ever would have been to archaeology."

"You're not retired, then, like Mr. Culhaney?"

"Lord, no!"

"So what do you do for a living, besides go chasing after airplane wreckage in the wilderness?"

"I raise coffee, mainly."

"Coffee? Really?"

"Does that surprise you?"

"A little."

"Why? Whatever did you think I did for a living?"

"Professional criminal?" Diana suggested jokingly, and Sloane laughed.

"I guess I assumed you were somehow connected with flying," she said. "I mean, it sounded as if both your father and brother had been involved in that field."

"My father was one of those men who are

always looking for the pot of gold at the end of some rainbow,'' Sloane said, picking up a small stone and tossing it. It bounced three times on the steps and then skipped out over the edge of the precipice into silence.

"His father and his father's father were all a rather nondescript lot, from what I've been able to gather. All hardly eking out a living doing odd jobs here and there. My father was too young for World War I, but World War II sucked him up in the draft, and he went off to fight the Germans. When it was all over he had the skill to fly an airplane, a game leg, a few thousand dollars and an awareness that there was more to the world than the cattle ranches of Montana.''

"Your people were American?''

"Still are. Only *South* American. My father took out Brazilian citizenship.''

"Your mother?''

"She came with him,'' Sloane answered. "But she didn't last long in the places my father dragged her. I used to blame him, you know. Although Jack—usually when he was drunk— was always insisting that it wasn't the old man's fault. 'She wouldn't let him leave her behind, Sloane,' Jack would say. 'She said if it was a choice of dying with him or without him, she would take the dying with him any day.' So they both ended up dead in Brazil.''

"I'm sorry.''

"Oh, we all die—someday,'' Sloane remarked stoically.

"I still don't understand about the coffee," Diana said, diplomatically hoping to move the conversation away from its morbid vein. Around them the ruins grew more ghostly beautiful as the evening faded into darkness.

"My father got his hands on a secondhand airplane and began flying supplies into the Brazilian interior. On the way out he would fly whatever cargo was available: men who had given up and were heading home, men who had made it big and were heading home, letters for home. . . ."

"Indian artifacts?" Diana added when Sloane's voice trailed off into silence. Above them she could sense the condors still circling, although it was too dark to see them.

"Yes, Indian artifacts," Sloane agreed finally.

"Coffee, too?"

"No, not coffee," Sloane said with a laugh, standing. "Come on, we had better get back before we end up tripping over something dangerous in the dark."

Diana was disappointed when he still hadn't cleared up the mystery of when the Hendriks family had got involved in coffee. She was even more disappointed that Sloane hadn't allowed her a more intimate glimpse of his past, because there was something tremendously enjoyable about receiving each new clue, anticipating it as being *the* vital key to unlock the total mystery of the dangerous fascination Sloane Hendriks held for her.

He took her hands and pulled her to her feet, but not *just* to her feet. His guiding movement brought her up into his arms, where she was once again made aware of the hard, muscled body concealed beneath his clothing. She looked up into his face as he drew her even closer. He kissed first her forehead, then her nose, then opened her yielding lips with the pliantly demanding pressure exerted by his own.

In an instant the whole gamut of those conflicting emotions that had plagued Diana during their two previous kisses came flooding back to her in a tidal wave of confusion that left her mentally floundering in Sloane's arms. It was just this sort of kiss—and this sort of confusion—she had feared the last time he had held her in the empty train car. She had broken that kiss before she led Sloane to any false conclusions. Yet she had aided and abetted this kiss by having admitted she was now alone, without protection of traveling companions.

It concerned her that she might have subconsciously been plotting for this to happen, her thoughts having been all the silent incantation needed to conjure Sloane Hendriks on the spot. Such fear was only multipled when she realized that, despite the way she resisted wrapping her arms around his neck, she was no more convinced than ever that he was capable of making any kind of commitment to her, or to any woman. She still felt incapable of surrender to any man not prepared to offer at least an equal emotional investment in their relationship. She suddenly feared she might seem merely a tease, giving the illusion of offering something to Sloane that, considering the circumstances, he simply couldn't have. With that disturbing thought in mind, Diana knew she had to be honest enough with herself and with Sloane to end this whole masquerade before it became even more difficult to do so.

It was Sloane, however, who suddenly broke the kiss, his eyes focusing on the darkness deepening amid the ruins over Diana's shoulder.

"Sloane?" Diana asked, easily sensing something was wrong without having to be told.

"We have company," he said, loud enough that his observation obviously wasn't meant for Diana's ears alone.

Diana didn't know what exactly he mean by "company," but she immediately suspected the worst.

"Don't panic!" he told her, his strong arms keeping her still despite her initial reaction to break free. "Go stumbling off in the dark and you're liable to break your neck if you're not careful!" She immediately saw the wisdom in that bit of advice, realizing how close she had come to doing just what he warned against.

"Okay, we know you're there," Sloane said into the darkness, his hold on Diana relaxing, but not releasing her. "Do you want to come out, or do you want me to come looking?"

"I'll come out, Sloane," a voice said. It was

so close, Diana thought the man was standing right next to her.

Feeling Diana's surprise, Sloane's arms went tighter. "Jacos, you bastard!" he spat, his anger evident.

"You might have humored me with a little longer show," Dan Jacos said, emerging far enough from the shadows for Diana to see him finally. He was the man to whom Sloane had been talking in the picture Diana had given Carol. Another example of the exotic types inhabiting Sloane's dangerous world, he needed a shave, his mahogany face—Diana couldn't tell if his coloring was natural or if he had been a long time exposed to the sun—covered with blue black bristle. His dark bush jacket, possibly once white, had definitely seen better days.

"I wish I could have kept hidden a couple of minutes longer," he went on in a slight accent. "The preview was certainly getting hot, and—"

"Watch your mouth, Dan, or it's going to come up missing a few more teeth!" Sloane said in warning.

"Well, the least you can do is introduce me to the young lady," Dan said. "You certainly seemed to have got far enough, fast enough, for—"

Sloane released Diana with such suddenness that she almost fell for loss of his support. His right arm reached out, his large hand taking a fistful of Dan's shirt at its collar.

"I said, you will keep that filthy mouth of

yours shut!'' Sloane's voice had become even more threatening.

"All right, all right," Dan said, finally seeming duly chastised. "So I made a little mistake. My apologies if I've offended either you or... your *lady*."

"Sloane?" Diana asked tentatively. Her initial panic over, she now felt dislike for Dan Jacos simply because the danger he presented canceled the pleasurable danger that she had been experiencing in Sloane's arms prior to the untimely interruption.

"It's okay, Diana," Sloane assured her. "Dan and I have some business to discuss. I'm sure he'll be glad to wait here until I walk you back to the hotel." He tightened his grip on Dan's shirt. "Won't you, Dan?"

"It's about the plane?" Diana asked.

"Knows about the plane, does she?" Dan observed, his voice a little less subservient than before. "My, but she does work fast, doesn't she?"

"It only seems that way to you because there isn't a girl within miles who'll even give you the time of day," Sloane said, releasing his hold. Then he turned to Diana. "Come on, I'll walk you back to the hotel while Dan waits patiently like a proper little messenger boy."

Back at the veranda Sloane saw her safely seated at one of the empty tables. "Well, here's hoping Dan has brought me the news I want to hear," he said, standing beside her.

Diana reached out her hand, almost unknowingly her fingers wrapping partly around his leg to keep him from leaving, nails digging into the soft denim of his jeans. Having seen Dan Jacos, she was afraid for Sloane. Dan didn't seem the type who would easily accept a put-down, or was above lurking in wait in the darkness until he could come out at Sloane from behind.

"Do you have to go back out there?" she asked. The fact that she would probably have been concerned for the safety of any man who had an appointment to meet Dan Jacos on a dark night didn't completely account for the small voice inside her whispering that it wasn't just any man, but Sloane, whose well-being really concerned her.

"I can take care of Dan," he said, having read her concern, and gave her a reassuring smile. "I have some cash he wants, and he knows he won't be getting it until he delivers."

"You're leaving now, then?" Diana asked. "I mean, you'll be going with him now into the jungle for the plane?"

"It will depend on what Carlyle has in mind," Sloane answered. "Dan is nothing more than a highly paid go-between."

Diana realized Sloane was simply going to disappear from her life just by taking a few short steps into the darkness of the Peruvian night. Not even she could explain why she had let this man enter and exit from her life three times before, but didn't want him to leave it again. If she did have her suspicions, she certainly wasn't ready to admit them to anyone, least of all to herself.

"Please...don't go," she said, knowing he wasn't about to listen to her. He had important things to do, such as getting on with the adventure of a jungle trek that, if successful, would see him removing an undeserved blotch from his family honor. He would think her concern nothing more than an inconsequential irritant, something to be brushed off with a patronizing smile. He had no qualms about facing danger out there, and Diana, knowing he was a danger to her if he stayed, was foolish not to let him go, bidding him good riddance.

He looked at her, gently running the edge of his index finger along a curl in her hair. People may have been watching, but Diana didn't care. "There's something between us that you and I both feel, isn't there, Diana?" he said softly, his voice almost a physical caress. Diana got gooseflesh that had less to do with the coolness of the night than with the sense of impending loss she felt in her bones.

"It does keep getting harder and harder for the two of us to say goodbye," he said, his smile deepening his dimples.

"I..." she began, wanting to cover those dimples with kisses.

"Shh!" he said, placing the tip of his fingers to her lips. "Whether it's true or not, you must at least allow me the pleasure of the illusion."

"Don't go, Sloane," she said. "Please."

"I must," he said. "If I could stay, I would. Believe me. But too much hangs in the balance here, Diana. Far, far too much to turn back now."

She realized suddenly that she was still gripping his leg with such force that it must be hurting him. She released her hold, embarrassed by its urgency and intimacy. "I'm sorry," she said.

"Oh, don't be sorry, Diana." He bent swiftly to brush her hair with his lips. "I'm the one who is sorry. More sorry, at this moment, than you'll ever know." He turned, took five lengthy strides...and without a backward glance was swallowed by the darkness.

Sometime later, Diana didn't know when—it could have been a minute, it could have been an hour—a waiter came. "It's probably just the altitude," he told her when she said she didn't feel like eating.

"Yes," she said, pushing back her chair and coming to her feet. "You're probably right." She made her way to her room and went to bed.

CHAPTER SIX

EVEN IN THE NIGHTMARE she told herself it was a dream, but that did nothing to bring her out of it. She stayed where she was, laid out on a crude, cold slab of stone in a jungle that was growing thicker and more tangled even as she watched it.

Her wrists and ankles were tied by liana creepers that entwined her arms and legs as securely as they cocooned the more massive trunks of the trees grouped around her.

She was wearing the same thin cotton nightgown she remembered having worn to bed. It had slipped down over her right shoulder, revealing part of her breast.

Sloane came out of the forest and saw her, walking over to look down at her. He smiled and smoothed a lock of hair out of her eyes. His lips didn't move, but she knew what he said: "I wish I could help you, my darling, but I have an airplane to catch." He leaned to kiss her forehead.

When he pulled away, he was not Sloane but Dan Jacos. Dan smiled, two front teeth missing. Beneath his rolling eyes, his tongue lolled out of his mouth.

And then he was gone, leaving Diana to sense

an even more menacing threat lurking just out of eyesight. She could hear its softly padded feet caressing dead leaves and living mosses. "The largest, fiercest, most interesting of all the wild-cats of the New World," someone said.

Diana looked up to see George Culhaney straddling a tree limb above her. Ignoring the book open in his lap, he looked at Diana. "You did ask me to tell you about it, didn't you?" he questioned. "Well, here I am, so please try to listen."

His finger ran down the page and found a spot. "'Six, sometimes seven feet long, of which one third or more is tail,'" George read. "'In color, from a ground of dirty white to almost black. Not unlike that of a leopard, except its spots cover more ground.'"

He shut the book with a bang and came to a standing position on the limb. His dexterity belied his seventy-seven years. "I really must go now, Miss Green. It's coming, you know. It's just left a dead goat on the railroad tracks."

Suddenly it was pitch-dark and Diana couldn't see anything, but she could hear it breathing as it came for her. She tried to scream, but there was something over her mouth.

There was something, something. . . .

"Easy, damn it! Easy!" someone was saying in the darkness. "I'm not going to hurt you. . . ouch, you silly bitch!"

She struggled, realizing she was tangled in the blankets of her bed. She was in her hotel room;

someone was in her room with her, on the bed with her, holding her down.

"Just take it easy, damn it!"

It was a man's voice, a man's hand over her mouth, its calluses bruising her lips. Sloane had calluses on his hands. "Sloane?" she asked, her words coming out muffled.

"There, that's better," the voice said. It wasn't Sloane's voice. "Now, I'm going to take my hand away, and if you make any sound whatsoever I'm going to deck you, understand?"

She nodded her head, yes.

"No funny business!" the disembodied voice emphasized as the hand slipped away.

"What do you want?" Diana asked, her voice a hoarse whisper.

"I want to talk."

"Talk?"

"Yes, Miss Green, talk. Does that surprise you?"

There was a slight movement on the bed, and the reading light was switched on.

"You!" Diana said, finding her fear more acute now that she knew Dan Jacos was in her bedroom.

"You do remember me, then, do you?" he asked, as Diana nervously took a handful of blanket and hoisted it to her chin. Dan seemed amused by the small attempt at modesty. "Had I come here to rape you, Miss Green, you would have been raped by now, believe me," he said.

"How did you get in here?" she asked, trying to control her fear and anger, working herself up to a sitting position while keeping the blanket pulled up tight against her throat.

"I picked the lock," Dan said smugly, getting up from the bed, either satisfied Diana wasn't going to become hysterical or—more likely—thinking this move was the best way to keep her from becoming so. He sat down in the chair facing her, mainly in shadow because of the lone light in the room.

Diana felt like someone being interrogated in the glare of a spotlight, and she didn't enjoy the feeling. "You said you wanted to talk."

"About our friend."

"What friend?"

"Come now, Miss Green. How many acquaintances do you suppose the two of us have in common?"

"Sloane?"

"I do like fast women," Dan said, his statement rife with double entendre.

Diana lifted her blanket even higher. "What about Sloane?" she questioned.

"He needs your help, but he's too much of a gentleman to ask for it. All that masculine pride or whatever. I, on the other hand, am no gentleman."

There was certainly no way Diana would argue that point! "What kind of help?" she asked.

"I'm presuming, after your little comment

earlier this evening, that you're aware of this airplane your lover boy is looking for.''

"He's not my lover boy!" Diana exclaimed with an emphasis that was really unwarranted.

"That's too bad," Dan said. "Because it would have helped no end if you and he *had* been involved."

"Why don't you simply get to the point, and then out of here," Diana suggested, her flesh crawling every time she remembered how she had been awakened.

"Well, the way things now stand, Mr. Hendriks isn't going anywhere, except back to Brazil."

"I thought it had all been arranged...about the plane, I mean."

"So did Sloane, and so did I. Unfortunately, Mr. Carlyle has decided against it. Did Hendriks bother to tell you what Carlyle is rumored to be sitting on out there?"

Diana didn't answer, thinking it might be more than a little indiscreet to confess any knowledge of Carlyle's business affairs, especially to someone like Dan Jacos.

"Well, suffice it to say that the fewer people Carlyle has crawling around out there at the moment, the better off he's going to be. That includes his bringing in any extra visitors, like Sloane, who might or might not be who they *say* they are, doing what they *say* they're doing."

"All Sloane wants is to verify that the plane is

there," Diana said. "I hardly see how that can be any threat to Carlyle."

"*You* know that all Sloane wants to do is verify that the plane is there. *I* know it. However, we're not the ones who have to be convinced, are we? And Carlyle needs more convincing."

"I don't know what any of this has to do with me," Diana protested.

"I'm thinking Carlyle can be persuaded to let your boyfriend in—if you would decide to tag along."

"Me?" Diana asked, thinking she must have misheard. "You're out of your mind! Even if I said yes to such a preposterous proposal, whatever makes you think Carlyle would do an about-face?"

"Because he's going to figure Sloane will have his hands too full taking care of you to give anybody else's business a second thought. What man in his right mind, after all, is going to bring his girl friend along with him if he's on a dangerous undercover mission into that kind of country? If, however, it's only the plane Sloane is after, he might have time for other, shall we say, innocent activities."

"Just what kind of country are we talking about, Mr. Jacos?" Diana asked, ignoring his last comment. She refused to believe she actually found Jacos's proposal appealing, telling herself that he was suggesting something too impossible to be taken seriously. However, her innate reporter's curiosity wanted to see how this man's obviously twisted mind had figured anything so outlandish could be workable.

"Granted, it's not the ordinary place any beau would take his ladylove, Miss Green. However, if a woman did care for a man, well, it just might be conceivable she would volunteer to help him realize his all-important goal. Which had me hoping that little kiss of yours was as serious as it was beginning to look before it was prematurely interrupted."

"There's a flaw here, Mr. Jacos. A flaw quite aside from the major flaw of having assumed there was anything serious between Sloane and me. You have the woman in this scenario painted as a simple helpless creature whose very presence is going to have Carlyle assuming Sloane's every extra minute will be occupied protecting her. She could just as easily be Sloane's partner in trying to ferret out Carlyle's activities, couldn't she?"

"Maybe that might have been a possibility if she were anyone but Diana Green, bona fide tourist," Dan said smugly. "But by now Carlyle knows it's highly unlikely you and Sloane have been teamed up by his competition."

"Why?"

"Because it wasn't the competition who arranged for Sloane to be at your hotel in Cuzco and then on your train here to Machu Picchu. It was Carlyle."

"Do you mind explaining that again?" There

had to be a logical reason for all of their meetings, and maybe Carlyle was behind what Diana had considered an uncanny string of co-incidences. She wanted to know the truth even if she would have preferred her meetings with Sloane to have been fate alone.

"After your first meeting with Sloane in Lima, Raphael Sipas, Carlyle's chief competi-tor, tracked you down. You do remember Cap-tain Sipas?"

Diana figured Sipas wasn't the only not-to-be-easily-forgotten person from this trip: Dan Jacos had now added himself to the growing list.

"Well, Miss Green," Dan continued, "if Sipas had found you other than the tourist you were supposed to be, you wouldn't be here right now."

Sloane had made essentially the same com-ment to Diana back in Cuzco, and the reminder was as chilling as ever. But this time she was not to be swayed from her questioning of Dan's out-rageous scheme.

"I thought we were talking about Carlyle, not Sipas," she prompted him crisply.

"Carlyle has his sources in Sipas's camp. He therefore knew when Sipas cleared you of any knowing involvement. He then figured the best place to hide any object was in a place where the searcher had already looked for it. It followed that if Sloane was with you, it wasn't likely Sipas was going to find him, simply because he had already checked you out. Put another way: Sipas thinks you are merely a tourist, so he won't bother with you anymore. That means that if Sloane is with you, he's safe from Sipas.''

"Carlyle used me as a cover for Sloane?"

"Very good, Miss Green!" Dan exclaimed in mock marvel at Diana's coaxed perception.

In the imperfect light Diana could see only half of his smile, and it looked grotesque. "Why all the bother if Carlyle was going to get Sloane this far and then call it off?" she asked, bits and pieces of the puzzle still not fitting.

"What Carlyle is sitting on out there is going to have to be moved to clear a profit. Doing so successfully, safely and secretly is going to take a good deal of money. It seems to have taken Carlyle this long to realize that the money Sloane is offering isn't enough to compensate for the greater risk of letting him come nosing around."

"Sloane is paying?" Diana asked.

"Paying a good deal of money by your standards and mine," Dan said. "The way I hear it, he's mortgaged everything he owns to raise the necessary capital. Of course, the total is piddling as far as Carlyle is concerned, which is probably the reason he's finally decided to say no."

"But why should Sloane have to pay at all?" Diana asked, frankly surprised by this latest bit of news. "It's not as if he's out to salvage the

cargo that—from what I understand—Carlyle
has already made off with. All he wants is to
verify that the plane did go down, find and identify the remains of the pilot. Besides, once
Sloane's father made full restitution to the
original shippers, the proceeds Carlyle got from
the resale of the cargo should have gone to
Sloane.''

"Honey, in this business it's finders keepers,
losers weepers."

"But having Sloane pay out more money is
extortion!" Diana protested, indignant that a
man out merely to prove the honor of his family
should have had to mortgage himself to the hilt
to do so.

"Call it what you will, but I call it shrewd
business, and Sloane, a man who I'll admit has
no lack of intelligence, obviously doesn't mind
playing by Carlyle's rules."

"Where's Sloane now?"

"Sacked out in a room down the hall. He
wants me to try Carlyle again tomorrow, but I
think I'd be wasting my time if I couldn't come
up with some new twist."

Diana would have asked what was motivating
Dan, except she thought she already knew.
Sloane had told her the man was a highly paid
go-between—in this case paid by him. Sloane, in
fact, seemed to be the only one of the lot who
wasn't busy trying to cheat someone else.

"If—I repeat, *if*—I decided to consider your
ludicrous proposal, just what reason are you

planning to give Carlyle for my sudden willingness to tag along?''

"Love, Miss Green. Remember? Just think about it for a moment. It's perfect, even if you insist the notion is ridiculous. It even gives a logical explanation for your staying over at Machu Picchu. By the way, just why did you stay over?''

"If it's any business of yours, which it isn't, I've always wanted to see this place,'' Diana said, deciding to give him as little information as possible. "I wanted to take my time seeing it without dropping over from *soroche,* as every other tourist herded through here seems to be doing.''

"The way I see it, the romance angle will fit nicely, anyway.''

"Well, the way I see it, I'm the only one who's not getting anything out of this,'' declared Diana. At the same time, at the back of her mind she realized that if she did decide seriously to consider this madness, she might be able to salvage some of Sloane's money for him in the process. Helping Sloane suddenly seemed important to her—especially now that she'd met the shady type of character he was forced to associate with in his mission to clear his family name. "Sloane gets his airplane, you get your payments for services rendered, so where do you suppose we might drum up some motivation for Diana Green? Since we're not talking love here, are we?''

"I suppose Diana Green wouldn't be motivated by pure and simple greed, like the rest of us?" Dan asked, his tone indicating he certainly didn't think she was going to be an exception to the rule.

"I want fifty percent of your payment," announced Diana, assuming the same cool facade she had managed when the police had used her to make several illicit drug buys during the lead-up to the eventual narcotics raid in Seattle.

"Wait a minute!" Dan protested.

They finally agreed on forty percent—*if* Diana decided to make a definite commitment. She told him she would let him know one way or the other by the next afternoon. Before she made any decision, she wanted to find Sloane and talk to him.

As it turned out, Sloane found Diana first; his banging on the door jarred her from a night's sleep that had been none too sound after nightmares and Dan Jacos. She glanced at the travel alarm on her bedside table and groaned: it was barely seven o'clock. Sloane obviously had all intentions of getting in, too, even if he wasn't going about it via the stealthier method utilized earlier by Dan.

"Come on, Diana, open up! I know you're in there!"

There was no mistaking his voice; Diana had heard its full range, from loving caress to cutting edge. He was obviously angry now, a muscled giant of a man fuming just beyond the door. Shivering in her thin nightdress, she felt a strange combination of elation and fear as she took hold of the knob, preparing to open the thin door—the only thing that separated her from the unexpected violence now waiting in the hallway.

Sloane shoved in past her, did a quick turn and let his eyes shoot her with arrows.

"I want to talk to you, you little fool!" His voice was menacingly loud with ill-concealed rage, and his hands gripped her naked shoulders. "Just what in the hell do you think you're trying to pull?"

"I want to talk to you, too," Diana said with an effort to remain calm in spite of her confusion. Sloane's powerful physique was trembling with a controlled rage so tangible that she thought she could actually feel the heat of it against her skin. To confront such awe-inspiring force was a fearful and stimulating experience, a special excitement known perhaps only to the native hunter who dares, armed only with spear or bow, to challenge the snarling beast on the animal's own territory.

"Oh, you were actually planning on talking to me, were you?" Sloane asked sarcastically. "How very, very considerate of you. I was rather under the impression you and Dan had already done all the talking—without me."

Now knowing the reason for his rage, Diana was caught up in her own conflicting emotions, wondering whether he was angry because he mistrusted her motives, or because he actually cared that she had considered exposing herself to the perils of a jungle trek for his benefit. If the first, she would be hurt and angry to think he still couldn't trust her by now. This, after all, wasn't Cuzco, where he really couldn't know for sure that she wouldn't pick up the telephone at any minute and call Sipas. She had certainly proved her trust by now, and if not, it was doubtful she ever could. If, on the other hand, he was concerned for her safety, his rage born of that caring, then that was a different story altogether; one that could make Diana feel a unique kind of thrill.

"Listen, Sloane, I—"

"You listen to me!" Sloane interrupted fiercely. "There is no way—no possible way—I would agree to your coming with me out into that wild country. So you can just forget this little scheme you and Dan have cooked up!"

"Sloane, I—" she began again, but once more he didn't let her get a complete sentence in edgewise.

"You must have been out of your mind to let Dan talk you into it in the first place!"

"Just one damned minute!" Diana said loudly, and shook herself free from his hold. She resented his apparent inability to credit her with some common sense. "It may surprise you to know that Dan and I merely discussed the idea. I certainly made no commitment."

Sloane gave her his best I-don't-believe-that-for-a-minute look.

"And, if—*if*—I had even momentarily considered the possibility of going, it was only because I figured it was a shame you had come so close, only to be stopped short by some grave robber's paranoia," she said.

"Thinking only of me, were you?" Sloane taunted, that dangerous edge creeping into his voice. "Willing to journey into the unknown wilderness, face unknown perils, for love, huh? Well, you'll just have to excuse the sarcasm, but I was led by Dan to believe your motives were a little less humanitarian and a bit more mercenary in nature."

So there it was, finally out in the open, and Diana felt a sickening feeling inside of her. He was angry because he didn't trust her, didn't seem capable of seeing that she would never even have contemplated, however briefly, this kind of mad undertaking if she hadn't felt a certain something for Sloane and for what he was risking so much to accomplish. It made no difference that Diana could see exactly how it must have sounded when Dan told him she had agreed to the plan only after bargaining for forty percent of Dan's share. What was important was that Sloane had believed it, swallowed the idea hook, line and sinker without bothering, even now, to give her a chance to explain.

"I suppose there would be little point in saying I had all intentions of turning my share over to you?'' Diana managed to inject into the sudden calm. Sloane sat down on the chair and faced her, obviously exhausted in the aftermath of blowing off so much steam. "I thought it was ridiculous for you to have to pay through the nose to men who probably wouldn't know an honorable cause if it hit them on the head.'' She was still smarting under the knowledge that he didn't have the insight to believe in her innocence without having to be told.

"Why, I wonder, do I *want* to believe that?'' he said, his voice low. He was slumped forward in his chair, his long legs apart, his large hands gripping his knees. He looked tired and appealingly vulnerable, nothing like the raging bull he had been moments before. "Is it because I'm chump enough to want to believe you were motivated by certain feelings—for me—that had nothing whatsoever to do with Dan's offering you a cut of his share?''

"But it's true,'' Diana insisted quietly, knowing their future relationship—whatever that might be—would hinge on his knowing the truth when he heard it. There was, after all, no one else who knew the truth but her.

There followed a long pause, a very long one, in which Diana thought for sure her heart had stopped beating. She did so desperately want Sloane to believe her, truly believe her; to know that what she said was the truth, no matter what Dan Jacos had told him to the contrary.

"I believe you,'' he said finally, getting up

slowly from the chair. He stood looking at her for a long moment and then walked over to her.

He'd said what Diana had desperately wanted to hear him say, and she was so struck with the wonder of it that she didn't even know he had crossed the floor to her until she felt his strong arms around her, pulling her in tightly against him.

"I apologize for being a fool," he said, his sun-bronzed face rubbing against the softness of her silky blond hair, his lips so close she could feel his warm breath on her ear.

She forgave him because, while she had been hurt by his initial doubt, there was the most exquisite kind of pleasure to be enjoyed in for-giveness. It was foolish of her to expect their relationship, brief and intense as it had been so far, to run smoothly; nothing was perfect, not even the emerald, which, she had learned, often displayed its most beautiful and desirable shades in stones that were flawed but no less valuable because of it. Perfection, even in nature, was usually the rare exception rather than the rule.

"You are far too intelligent to get yourself roped into something so mad," Sloane said. "I was stupid to believe you would even have con-sidered such an imbecilic plan."

"But I did consider it," Diana told him, anxious that he should understand how the feel-ing she had for him had forced her into examin-ing the feasibility of Dan's proposal. Sloane, however, pushed her to arm's length and released her. She immediately missed the warm feel of him, the intoxicating smell of him, the way his voice seemed to vibrate deep in his chest whenever she was held tightly against him.

"I suppose Dan didn't bother going into any details about what kind of country you would be going through, did he?" Sloane asked, beginning to pace the floor. "Well, did he?"

He stopped to face her, his arms folded across his chest. The clothes he was wearing were the same as from the previous evening, and Diana wondered if he had slept in them—or slept at all.

"Well," he went on, "let me clue you in on what you could have expected—just for starters. Insects. Creepy, crawly vermin that get caught in your hair and dig in. Disease: hepatitis and dysentery. I suppose you didn't think to pick up any antimalaria tablets on the way here. Or did you foresee the possibility of getting a hundred or so miles off the beaten track? Then there are the bigger dangers: snakes, wild pigs, wildcats, ocelots, pumas; and I'll bet Dan didn't bother telling you about the jaguar that just killed a villager last night, not more than five miles from here, dragging the body two miles and hanging it in a tree for the condors."

"You're saying that to scare me?" she whispered, wishing he would just take her back in his arms and hold her.

"Damned right I'm trying to scare you!"

Sloane answered loudly. "I'm trying to scare the wits out of you. This isn't a little overnight camping trip you and the Ladies' Aid might be planning in the woods outside Seattle, Washington, Diana! In this country there are still people wandering around who don't know what a white woman looks like. And nine times out of ten it's not those natives but the supposedly more civilized inhabitants who would be the first to put a bullet in your back—or worse."

He was getting worked up again, Diana could tell. He had apparently got his second wind and was bent on destroying the thoroughly enjoyable, but still tenuous, peace they should have been savoring after the battle. The satisfaction gained from that peace was simply too precious for Diana to let it be spoiled now.

"Why don't we discuss it later?" she suggested. "Maybe over lunch, when we've both had a little more time to think about it intelligently. Right now I'd really like to get washed and dressed. I do have a story to write and some photographs to take of the ruins."

For a moment he looked as if he weren't going to leave, and Diana would have welcomed that decision if they could have found a subject of conversation safe for the both of them. Sloane, though, as well as Diana, must have realized the danger inherent in his staying, because he went to the door, stopping just before he opened it.

"Lunch, then," he said, leaving her to her

confused thoughts on the whole matter of Sloane Hendriks.

As Diana stood before the mirror in the tiny, cramped bathroom splashing her face with cool water from the tap, she noted that faint dark circles had appeared beneath her eyes—evidence of the night's unsettling experiences. She noted, too, the suspicious flush in her cheeks. Hurriedly she completed her toilet, put on pants, shoes and a silk shirt, gathered up her camera equipment and went out onto the hotel veranda.

"Buenos días, señorita," the now familiar waiter greeted her. As far as the weather went, it was indeed a good day, the mountaintop already clear of mist, the sky blue, the sun bright lemony as opposed to the blinding white it would become later in the afternoon. The whole panorama was a patchwork of variegated greens.

Diana ate breakfast and then picked up a pocket guide of Machu Picchu from the attendant at the main gate. She followed the guide maps, reading about the history of the place and keeping a record of her photographs so that she wouldn't have any trouble identifying her shots later. She read with interest how one theory of the city's origin was that it had been a great religious sanctuary overseen by the sacred Virgins of the Sun. Other scholars postulated that Machu Picchu had served as a final refuge from the Spanish for the Incan women, after the sacking of Cuzco. Whatever the truth may have been, the intriguing fact remained that the majority of skeletons found on the site were female.

The lighting was excellent, and Diana quickly went through two rolls of 35mm black-and-white film, positive she had enough good pictures to satisfy her editor. She would supplement what she had with a few black-and-white shots of tourists scampering like ants, plus a couple in color: mood shots at sunrise or sunset.

She had just checked her wristwatch, noting it was almost eleven, when she saw Sloane coming toward her wearing a knapsack.

"Lunch?" he asked when he reached her. With a nod of assent, she allowed him to take her hand and lead her back the way she had come.

"I thought we might picnic in a spot with a view, somewhere beyond the usual endurance of the *soroche*-weakened tourist," he suggested. "Past experience tells me we need go only a little beyond the Sun Dial and the Moon Calendar. Think you're up to it?"

They chose a spot on the edge of the escarpment, overlooking the Urubamba River. While Diana made herself comfortable, Sloane unpacked the knapsack, producing hard-boiled eggs, dried fruit, bottled water and sandwiches of thinly sliced chicken.

"Now, then," he said, handing Diana a paper cup, "I'll just sit here while you tell me how it really went with Dan last night." And she told him, glad that he let her finish without interruption. "That's how I figured it," he admitted finally, making sure the shell from one of his eggs dropped into the paper bag he had brought along for their garbage. Diana was touched by the conscientious gesture.

"Welcome back to a more rational state," she teased.

"You actually should have been flattered by my first reaction," he said in apparent seriousness.

"Flattered?"

"Sure. Do you think I would have carried on quite as much if I hadn't cared about Diana Green? If I hadn't given a damn, I would probably have jumped at your offer."

"And I figure you should have been flattered that I even considered the possibility of letting such a trip come off—money or no money," Diana countered. "I wouldn't have considered going off into no-man's land to help just anyone."

"Touché!" he said, offering her more cool water from the bottle. They sat in silence for a moment, just enjoying the spectacular view. A pleasant electricity seemed to be passing between them.

"What happens if Carlyle still refuses to let you in?" Diana was compelled to ask, because she was genuinely interested in Sloane and felt almost physical pain at the idea that he might yet have to turn back.

"I'll go home, I guess," Sloane replied with a slight shrug. "I certainly wouldn't give good odds on locating the plane on my own; too many people having tried and failed before me. I have a chance only if Carlyle guides me."

"Isn't it enough to know the plane is there?" she asked.

"The point is, I don't know it's there until I see it, do I?"

"You have proof that the Indian artifacts turned up in Lima."

"But that doesn't prove that they were salvaged from a downed plane. Holsteen could conceivably have sold them, it being purely luck that they surfaced at all. Art objects, especially those of dubious ownership, are often traded under the counter for years on end within the rarefied community of some closemouthed collectors."

"Didn't you say Dan told you the artifacts came from the downed plane?"

"That's what Dan *said*. That's what Carlyle *said* the one and only time I ever met him personally."

"Why would they lie?"

"What this all boils down to is that Carlyle might have lied to me just as a ruse to get my money. Who knows, the plane may not be in the jungle at all but in the hangar of some deserted landing strip where Holsteen parked it twenty years ago."

"Ask Carlyle for photographs."

"Of the plane, you mean? Photographs can be faked. Even if I asked him to go so far as to bring me an actual piece of the aircraft, what would that prove? He could just as easily have it ripped off the airplane where it now sits hidden. But if I see the plane for myself, I'll know; and there's little chance of his faking a wreck to make it look as if it happened twenty years ago—certainly not in the fast-growing Peruvian jungle."

"Is it true you might not have a home to go back to when this is all over and done, no matter how Carlyle decides to go?"

"Dan has a big mouth!" Sloane said contemptuously.

"He said you had everything hocked," Diana persisted.

"Yes...well, that part is true enough, but I wouldn't have been able to hold my head above water much longer anyway. We had a big freeze three years ago and another one last year. Utter disaster for the coffee crop. I had the choice of borrowing to try to squeeze by for one more year, in the hope that good weather would let me keep a little ahead of the game, or of borrowing for the sake of an adventurous quest for family honor. I obviously opted for the latter, so here I am."

"And if you don't get to meet Carlyle, and have to go back to Brazil, do you have enough money left to save...is it a plantation?"

"Do you think that whether or not I save my

plantation—yes, it is called a plantation—is any of your business, Diana?'' Sloane asked. Then, before she could think he took her sincere interest as nothing more than a snoop's nosy prying, he said, ''Oh, hell, the answer to your question is no, but don't go shedding too many crocodile tears. What I'm losing isn't all that grand, take my word for it. Oh, there's a lot of good acreage, most of which I never did have the money to develop properly. There's a big house, a few horses, a few other head of livestock, and that's about it. So, you see, it's no big loss.''

However, just the way he said it led Diana to suspect he cared a little more than he wanted to let on.

''You never did tell me how your family got involved in coffee.''

''Didn't I?''

''Think we have time to go into it now?''

''We have time, unless you have your heart set on going back to join the tourists in swarm at the hotel.''

''We have time,'' she said, suddenly unable to hear enough of whatever he was willing to share with her about himself.

''There were some important gemstone finds made along the Rio Negro, one of the rivers in Brazil that drains into the Amazon basin from the north. Suddenly there were all sorts of people willing to pay my father good money to fly them to the Rio Negro faster than those who were moving in by water and on foot. Most people ended up paying more money for their flight in than they were ever able to get out of the area once they got there, so dad piled up a sizable nest egg and bought himself a coffee plantation as someplace to hole up in his old age. However, when the plane crashed a few years later, he turned the place over to a man called David Journer as partial compensation for Journer's share of the missing cargo. When my brother died, and then my father soon after, David Journer took me in—a teenager still wet behind the ears—and did damned good by me in the bargain. Then when David died he left me everything he had, which included the property he'd got from my father. End of coffee story.''

"It seems a pity you're going to lose the plantation a second time," Diana said, her heart going out to him, "especially if there's a genuine possibility that Carlyle might go for the trip with me along."

"That is not a viable option, even if Carlyle would accept the premise!" Sloane said with firm finality. "Nor has it ever been!"

"You've held me in your arms. Did I feel to you as if I were made of easily broken porcelain?"

"No," Sloane said, a tightness playing at the corners of his full mouth. "But you didn't feel like hard stone, either. And the jungle we're talking about has swallowed up stone cities without a trace—many of which it hasn't coughed up to this day. It's not likely to be any less merciless to a beautiful woman made of mere flesh and bone.''

She would have liked him to tell her exactly what he had felt each time he held her, each time he kissed her. She knew that a large part of any attraction was the mystery of it, but in other relationships people had time to slowly explore and savor such mysteries. Diana felt a sense of urgency regarding her and Sloane, a sense of time running out. They had had so little, and she constantly felt he would disappear for good, whether into the jungle of Peru or into bankruptcy in Brazil. She therefore needed and wanted specifics though she was afraid of what they would be if she heard them.

She felt now, had really always felt, that there was something about Sloane that, even before she had known anything of his past, hinted of an inability to tie himself down. What he had told her of himself only seemed to verify her initial intuition. Yet there was a definite feeling building in Diana, becoming more intense each time Sloane even went so far as to caress her with a look, no physical contact necessary. Diana had fought that feeling less and less successfully from her first meeting with Sloane in Lima to this moment with him in Machu Picchu.

What scared her the most was the gnawing suspicion that she was slowly being drawn toward this man only because she knew she would never have him. She needed stability; he offered nothing more than a fleeting taste of exotic adventure.

"Shall we walk a bit?" Sloane suggested, putting the remains of their picnic into the knapsack. "Or did you do enough walking this morning?"

"I'd love a walk," she said, coming to her feet and brushing dirt from the seat of her slacks. They strolled leisurely, keeping mainly to areas too distant from the hotel to attract any short-stay tourists.

Only once during the next couple of hours did either again mention Dan Jacos. "I've noticed he made himself rather scarce this morning," Diana said.

"That's because I sent him back to Carlyle to try one more time," Sloane told her.

At two o'clock they headed back to the hotel, since that was about the time the train pulled in from Santa Ana, and the swarm began converging on the buses for the ride down the mountain. By the time they reached the veranda the last bus was leaving its dust on the Hiram Bingham Road.

They sat on one of the tables nearest the chasm, the same table Diana had occupied to watch Carol travel down the mountain only the day before.

Sloane ordered them each a *chilcano,* a drink made of pisco—the brandy Diana usually enjoyed mixed with syrup, lemon juice, bitters and egg white in the form of a pisco sour—and ginger ale. They sat in comfortable silence, glad to be isolated from the frantic activity taking place at the bottom of the mountain, wishing they could be equally isolated from certain feelings for each other that seemed to be coming unleashed.

"And isn't this a picture of romantic bliss?" Dan Jacos remarked, startling them both by pulling up a chair and sitting down at their table. He looked just as seedy as he ever did, his cheeks and chin black with at least two days of unshaved beard. He was sweating. "I'm out breaking my back while the two of you just sit around drinking up the booze." He nodded toward their drinks. "How about ordering me one of those?"

Sloane had immediately gone tense, Diana could see the lines of strain pulsing along his powerful jaw. When Sloane made no effort to summon the waiter, Dan lifted an arm and did so. "I'll have what they're having," he said. "And just add it to Mr. Hendriks's tab." Sloane grudgingly nodded his approval, and the waiter disappeared into the hotel for the drink.

"Well, isn't anyone going to ask me how my meeting with Carlyle went?" Dan asked, leaning back so that his weight tilted his chair up on its rear legs.

"You have something to say, then say it!" Sloane said, his patience with Dan having already worn thin.

"You go in in three days," the other man announced, smiling triumphantly.

For a brief instant, looking at Sloane with his usually controlled facade melted away by ecstatic relief, Diana got a glimpse of just how much clearing his father's name must mean to him. His adventurous setting right of his father's reputation seemed the only possible reward Sloane could gain from all this.

"On the condition that Miss Green be a member of the party," Dan added.

Diana thought the worst was going to happen. Sloane's expression went ugly, his dark eyes narrowing, his nostrils flaring as his lips pulled back to reveal white teeth in a ferocious grimace. Dan almost tipped over backward in a move to take himself as far as possible from Sloane's reach. With obviously controlled temper Sloane rose slowly to his feet, pressing his fingertips on the edge of the table with a force that made his knuckles go white.

"You and your Mr. Carlyle can very well both go to hell!" he said in a voice made even more forceful in that it came out low and guttural rather than in a raging roar. He turned on his heels and began stalking away from the table toward the ruins.

"You ungrateful bastard!" Dan screamed after him. "I had to talk my head off to get him to agree to that. It's this way or no way!" He glanced across the table to Diana, wiping sweat from his forehead with one soiled sleeve of his bush jacket. "He's going to blow it for all of us, baby!" he said. "Damned if he isn't!"

Diana got up from the table and started after Sloane. His long stride and powerful legs, plus his head start, had let him cover a sizable distance by the time she caught up with him. She grabbed his arm, but he kept on walking.

Diana was breathing hard. Although she had pretty well acclimatized by now, the running had been demanding. Just when she thought she was going to drop, Sloane stopped.

"Thank God!" she said breathlessly, leaning against a ruined stone wall that came as high as the small of her back.

"That bastard!" Sloane exclaimed furiously, not needing to tell Diana who the object of his anger was, because she knew. "I should have wrung his neck on the spot!" Then he seemed to realize for the first time that Diana was panting. "Are you all right?" he asked, his words filled with concern.

"Fine," she said, feeling a little light-headed. "I just have to catch my breath, that's all."

They stayed where they were, Sloane lost in his own thoughts, Diana slowly recovering from her overexertion. "So what will you do now?" she managed finally. She could thoroughly sympathize with Sloane—all chance of his finding the plane now seemed hopelessly at an end—but there was another aspect of the situation that was to her somehow more disturbing. Now Sloane's only reason for being at Machu Picchu had suddenly ceased to exist. If he wasn't leaving her to go into the jungle, he *would* soon be leaving her to return to his coffee plantation in Brazil. Diana would regret seeing him go, not because she was willing to admit that he had already become a vital part of her life, but because she would have liked a bit more opportunity to decide just what kind of a part—if any—he might have played in her life in the future.

"I promised myself I would have Dan try to convince Carlyle one more time," Sloane said, giving Diana reason to hope his departure would be postponed for at least a few hours. "Just one more time, since I truly would like to believe in miracles, even though I should have given up on them long before now."

"Listen, Sloane, I've had a little time to think about all of this, and I—"

"Don't even say it!" he interrupted, raising a hand as if to physically stop her flow of words.

"But if it's the only way...."

"I told you, it would never be a viable way."

"Not even if I were willing to go?"

He placed a hand on each of her shoulders, looking down on her, showing her a face that registered such a range of conflicting emotions that she couldn't easily read any of them.

"I appreciate your offer," he said. "Really, I do. You don't know how warm it makes me feel inside to know you would be willing to expose yourself to danger for me. But it is simply out of the question, as any man of good sense would quickly tell you."

"Is it because I'm a woman, or because you simply don't want to be obligated to anyone?" she challenged. While she could appreciate his concern, she couldn't help feeling a little hurt and angry that he wouldn't let her help, especially since she seemed to be the only one who *could* help.

"We've been over this before, haven't we?" he accused, his hands tightening on her shoulders. Through the cool silk of her blouse Diana could feel his lean fingers pressing into her, burning into her flesh like a brand, and found herself longing for those fingers to spread their magic imprint. But she realized she must resist the intimate feelings that threatened to overwhelm her until she could make him see where she stood.

"Well, I think we might discuss it a bit more," she said. After all, it was one thing if he was trying to force her into accompanying him, quite another is she was volunteering with a full knowledge of what she might be letting herself in for. "It's not as if I haven't been exposed to danger before. When I did my undercover research for the article on drugs, I—"

"This is not Seattle, Washington!" Sloane exploded, giving her a shake. "If you thought you were exposed to danger by having a few addicts firing off popguns, you haven't seen anything compared to what this jungle can dish out!"

"It seems to me the degree of danger becomes

relative once exposure to it means risking one's life," Diana argued defensively. "What I did in Seattle could have got me just as dead as meeting a jaguar in the jungle. In fact, I would venture to guess the odds were less in favor of my being killed by a jaguar."

"That just might be a bad guess. Listen, I didn't mean to belittle what you did in your job back home," Sloane apologized. "It's just that back there, Diana, you were dealing with something you at least knew about. You know absolutely nothing about surviving in a jungle."

"And I suppose you don't know enough for the both of us?" she asked in challenge.

"I see no point in risking anyone's life in a matter that concerns only me and family—what was once my family."

"Risking anyone's life? What about your own?"

"My own life is mine to do with as I see fit."

"And my life, I suppose, isn't mine to do with as I see fit?"

"Diana, please don't twist what I say, because you very well know what I mean."

"What you mean is that you're a quitter, isn't it? You've come this far and now you're just going to chuck it all." What she found herself helplessly fearing was the possibility that he simply didn't want to go into the jungle—or anywhere else—with her.

"You call it whatever you damned well please!" he said, his hands going more clamp-like on her shoulders. "But hasn't it ever occurred to you that a man who has lost a mother, brother, father and his family's good name, a man who will soon be losing the very house he lives in, just doesn't want to take the unnecessary risk of losing the only other thing he now holds dear?"

"What good is your life if—"

"*My* life?" Sloane asked incredulously. "*My* life? You think I'm actually talking about *my* life? Diana, you are such a fool!"

CHAPTER SEVEN

DIANA WOULD HAVE PREFERRED to see Sloane, but was quite prepared for Dan Jacos as he stood in her hotel-room doorway. "Come in," she said. "I've been thinking."

"I hope so, baby," Dan responded. "Otherwise you and I are going to be out some big bucks."

He had a one-track mind, but Diana saw no point whatsoever in setting him right, especially since she had aimed him in the wrong direction in the first place. "I have a plan," she told him.

"I'm ready to try anything," Dan said. He had gone to the bed, sitting on it and bouncing up and down on the springs.

"Stop that!" Diana commanded irritably. He took a chair, but she remained standing. She thought that even if Dan had initially come up with the plan to convince Carlyle of Sloane's harmlessness, he hadn't the faintest notion of where to take it from there.

"Tell Sloane I'm going whether he likes it or not," she declared.

"You alone?" Dan gave a loud disbelieving laugh. "Lady, I thought you had a plan. That isn't a plan, that's lunacy! We need something workable, not some fanciful daydream you picked out of the air. And the way I see it, there is no way Sloane is going to believe you're prepared to go off into the jungle on your own."

"Are you quite through?" Diana asked.

"You mean there's more?"

"The truth is, I have every intention of going," Diana said. "While I'll hardly be able to pay you the exorbitant guide fee Sloane was offering, I'm sure we can come up with a satisfactory figure."

"And what about Carlyle's fee, honey? You think he'll drop it for you just because you're a lady? I can tell you, he's about as apt to do that as a snowball is to survive in hell!"

"I'll make arrangements to get Carlyle his money," Diana assured him with more confidence than she really felt. Of course, she had her savings to draw on, but that sum was liable to do very little for Carlyle except send him into belly laughs. A better potential source of funds, however, was the newspaper. If she could get the go-ahead to develop a series of articles on the black-marketing of archaeological finds, tailoring it to a U.S. audience by comparing robberies of U.S. Indian-grave sites, she figured the paper could be convinced to cover her expenses.

"The way I see it, my going should certainly meet with Carlyle's approval," she said. "As you mentioned, it's highly unlikely he would suspect me of being out to undermine his illicit activities.''

"You don't know anything about the jungle," Dan pointed out, eyeing Diana as if he suspected she might have gone off the deep end.

"One has to start somewhere," Diana insisted. "Besides, I'm sure, for a price, I can find someone willing to jungle-sit with me for a few days.''

"Sure," Dan replied, giving a lecherous smile. "Maybe even me, huh?" Diana certainly hoped Sloane would be around to save her from that fate worse than death. "What I don't get is why you would risk going at all if you're not getting paid for it.''

"Money, you will discover someday, Mr. Jacos, is not everything there is in the world—by a long ways.''

"So maybe you think more of Sloane than you let on, huh?''

"I can hardly see where that could possibly have anything whatsoever to do with you.''

"I thought that kiss you were giving him in the dark was a little more than your everyday garden variety.''

"And I think I'm not the least bit interested in your speculations—whatever they might be.''

"You can snap all the pictures of that old wreck you want and bring them back to Sloane—oh, don't worry, I saw that fancy camera you were dragging around this morning and I've a pretty good idea that's what you have in mind—but it's not really going to make one hell of a difference. Sloane has been saying from day one that photographs aren't the proof positive he's looking for. He has to see it all with his own two eyeballs.''

"Yes? Well, how do you think he's eventually going to feel knowing that my photographs *might* be genuine, and he missed the opportunity to see the real thing with his own two eyeballs?''

"Smart lady!'' Dan said, ready with appreciation. "Make him look as if he's a coward, huh? Make him look as if he's nothing but a chicken when it comes right down to the bottom line? Him holding back while the little lady is willing to make it there and back? That threat just might work. Yes. . . it just might.''

"Why don't you go get Sloane and find out?'' Diana was suddenly anxious to get Dan out of her room.

"Okay, baby, we'll give this a try,'' Dan agreed, getting up and heading for the door. "As I said, at this point I'm game to try just about anything.''

When he was gone, Diana locked the door behind him and leaned against it. Dan made her nervous. She sensed he was somehow more animal than human. Even the way he moved was as she imagined a nocturnal predator would move: soft of foot and hungry as hell.

When neither Dan nor Sloane had turned up

by supper, Diana extended her meal until she was one of only three people left on the veranda, then gave up and went to her room. She realized there could be any number of reasons for the delay; still, she had hoped to get the confrontation over with as quickly as possible.

It was well after midnight when she finally went to bed. She slept fitfully, expecting to wake up any minute and find she had company. But by 5:00 A.M., when she got up, there was still no sign of them.

"My God, you look like death warmed over," she said aloud to her reflection in the bathroom mirror. She did her best to improve her appearance and dressed for the chill of early morning: blue jeans, flannel shirt, cashmere sweater, tennis shoes.

She carried her camera equipment to a deserted lobby. Beyond the closed door, darkness shrouded the mountaintop. Diana sensed something out there, waiting for her. Something once only a figment of her imagination, featured in her nightmares, now making its bid to bridge the gap to reality.

Don't be absurd, she told herself, fishing into her camera bag for the small flashlight she carried. When she opened the door, her face felt the gentle massage of mists whirlpooled in the morning breezes atop the mountain. She shivered, feeling *it* out here, having no idea what *it* was. Crossing the veranda and finding the main pathway to the ruins, she felt comforted by the faint glow beginning to gray the blackness of the eastern sky. Soon the day would be dawning.

The Incas had worshipped the sun, and Sloane had pointed out to her the symbolic Intihuatana there at Machu Picchu: that stone to which the people who built this mountain fortress believed the sun was tied. She momentarily contemplated locating the Intihuatana now, and trying to set up a shot to catch the rising sun as it topped the sacred stone, but decided against wandering too far into the unfamiliar predawn blackness. Reaching the main entrance, which was without an attendant at this early hour, she slipped over the uncomplicated barricade.

Suddenly she was sure she had heard a noise. She stopped, her ears tuned for sound like those of a frightened deer sensitive to unseen danger. She was amazed at her high degree of apprehension and wondered just who or what she was expecting to meet.

Dan Jacos? Now, there was someone who could make her blood run cold. Having Dan Jacos out there—watching her—would have been more than enough reason for anxiety. She really had no intention of going anywhere with him alone, especially not into the jungle. She merely had hopes that her ploy would persuade Sloane not to give up his own plans out of a false notion that Diana was too weak to keep up. It was a trick, a kind of blackmail, but she didn't care. She wanted to help Sloane.

Sloane? Her present feelings for Sloane were certainly not the kind to inspire the gnawing fear she felt now. Sloane offered her a unique and special kind of danger, more exhilarating than frightening. She pulled her thoughts back to the moment. The noise she had heard could have been anything: the wind toppling a small stone that had teetered on the edge for centuries, waiting until now to fall; a small animal, more afraid of Diana than she had any need to be afraid of it, startled by her footsteps in the darkness; an interaction of cold nights and hot days on stone that chose that particular moment to bleed sounds into the stillness.

She reached the small building that was thatched to provide a rest area. Here Diana extended the legs of her camera tripod. She chose a lens and screwed it into her camera. She had checked her film before leaving her room, but she checked again, then attached the motor wind. Fixing the camera to the tripod, she sighted far enough to the east to catch the dawn, far enough to the north to catch the ruins perched precariously on the edge of the precipice.

Finished except for the light readings and lens adjustments necessary during actual shooting, she took a breather, sitting on one of the empty benches, watching Machu Picchu slowly materialize from the blackness like a picture appearing from the seeming blankness of photo paper submerged in a chemical bath. There was no denying the splendor of the spectacle, made even more startling by the fact that the people who had constructed this marvel of urban engineering had left no written record.

At one time the Incan Empire had numbered more than twelve million people. Its roads had been longer than those of the Romans, and often superior to them. Its economic and social systems had apparently been refined to the point of genuine communal living. But the glory of the Incas was all gone now, the jungle having swallowed its people, its roads, its cities, leaving only enticing teases like Machu Picchu to offer more questions than answers. The thought filled Diana with sorrow, though the tragic destruction had happened so long ago.

Dawn appeared over and through the serrated edges of the Cordillera de Urubamba, telegraphing flashes from distant ice peaks in the east. Diana became occupied with capturing as much of the magnificence as was possible on film. When her roll was completely exposed, she dismantled her equipment and sat for a few minutes, sampling a view that was constantly changing as the rising sun spilled its light and shifted the shadow. She found her previous uneasiness was being dispelled with the darkness.

As she prepared to head back to the hotel, she was surprised to find Sloane standing less than six feet away. She was delighted to see him, and though she wondered how he continually managed to sneak up on her, she didn't connect him now to any fear she had experienced earlier that morning.

"How long have you been standing there?" she asked.

"On this spot? Only a couple of seconds. Watching you? Since you left the hotel."

"Actually, I was expecting you to come around before now," she said.

"Yes, I suppose you were," Sloane responded with no trace of a smile. "However, I told myself that this time I would save myself any need for apology by waiting until my initial reaction had passed. So you see before you a man with no intention of raging on like a wounded bull. I've come prepared to listen to whatever rationalizations you can come up with for your latest slip into madness."

Diana smiled nervously. "I'm glad you decided to enter our discussion with such an open mind," she said.

"When a rational man comes upon a woman who is teetering on the brink of disaster, his first reaction is to reach out and save her, not to take the time to discuss her reasons for being there."

"Very well, then, I won't even try to bore you with my rationale. What it boils down to is, will you join me on *my* trek into the jungle or not?"

"You're determined to go no matter what, I suppose?" Diana didn't answer. "You know,"

Sloane continued after a moment, "when I finally got over my first heated reaction to this latest scheme, I remembered how—last time— you said I should be flattered rather than angry. So I convinced myself I was flattered. It is a very endearing quality, I said to myself, this seeming willingness on your part to unselfishly sacrifice so much just for me. I think I loved you at that moment. Genuinely, unabashedly loved you."

Love. Had he actually said he loved her? Was it love, then, that Diana had been feeling for him? Did love encompass all those conflicting emotions that had been running rampant through her since their first meeting? Was it love that had suddenly given her the ability to consider her own safety something willingly sacrificed if it meant Sloane would finally see an airplane ditched in the jungles of Peru over twenty years earlier?

"Are you laughing?" he asked.

"Laughing? Why should I be laughing?" she replied, made extremely uneasy by a question so startlingly out of context.

"Why not laugh?" Sloane said, leaning back against the wooden balustrade that was all that was separating him from the abyss. The rickety guardrail made Diana nervous. "Isn't it just a little amusing," he said, "how I let my wishful fantasies cloud my visions of a woman who was in reality only ruthlessly motivated by her career and not by any genuine concern for me?"

Diana knew what was coming. And while she

could validly argue, in her own mind, how thoughts of benefits to her career had evolved from her desire to help Sloane, and not vice versa, would he ever believe that?

"Cat got your tongue, Diana?" he asked dryly, his strong arms folded across his chest. "Think I was so taken by you that I wouldn't see how you had cleverly decided to use me?"

"I never had any intentions of using you," Diana said simply, knowing he disbelieved her.

"Not even to get a story on Peruvian grave robbers?" Sloane persisted. "Oh, I know you didn't tell Dan that's what you have in mind, but you're not completely stupid. You know what Carlyle would think if he heard how his typical American tourist, from her typical Circle-SA tour, had metamorphosed into a nosy reporter, don't you?"

"Why would my newspaper be interested in anything Carlyle is doing out in the middle of some isolated Peruvian jungle?"

"Because what's happening here is merely a microcosm of what's happening everywhere, what *has* happened everywhere for a very long time, whether we're talking about Northwestern American Indian baskets, Aztec burial gold or marble statues of Greek gods netted by fishermen in the Aegean Sea. Every country with an archaeological heritage is being sacked daily by unscrupulous men who see greater profits in selling to the highest international bidder than in preserving national treasures for future generations within the countries of origin. In the mad scramble to get a fair slice of the steadily dwindling pie, it's possible that even some of the major museums put out scandalous sums to purchase objets d'art whose journey from dig to final showcase, more often than not, has at least one Dennis Carlyle or Raphael Sipas lurking behind it. And you're going to tell me this golden opportunity for on-the-spot research, for a story of such potential universal appeal, completely slipped by you in your anxiousness to do your good deed by me?"

"I'm not denying I *saw* the story possibility."

"At least you're honest, Diana Green. When backed into a corner, that is."

"However, I didn't see it until looking for something to convince you I was serious in my desire to help you."

"I find that concession to my bruised ego more than a little touching," Sloane said, his upper lip drawn in a stiff line. "I would prefer, however, to take my knocks like a big boy. So you can save your efforts while I go do a few things that are definitely necessary before we can start this little jaunt you've so cleverly arranged for us."

"You're coming, then?"

"I may be an old-fashioned romantic, Diana, but I'm still helplessly compelled to at least attempt saving that woman teetering on the brink of disaster, no matter how preposterous her reasons for being there. But then I suspect, what with you being such a skilled newspaperwoman, you pretty much had my emotions pegged accurately from the very beginning, didn't you? Congratulations on some super moves, Diana. I only wish I could have been a more proficient game player."

He stepped away from the balustrade. "By the way, I wouldn't wander around too much after dark once we're on the trail," he said. "It's really not all that safe for you to be doing it even here at Machu Picchu."

"Please don't try to scare me, Sloane."

"Scare you, Diana? I'm no longer out to scare you. We've passed that point, haven't we? Now I merely want to give you certain valuable tips for your survival. I wouldn't take much satisfaction in seeing you dead, even if your suicide were engineered through your own folly."

"Despite what you apparently seem determined to think of me, Sloane, I don't consider it folly to want to help you find that airplane."

"Give up your idea for this news story of yours, Diana, and see how quickly I'll be content to leave that plane to continue rusting in the Peruvian jungles without me."

Diana looked away, her gaze sweeping the greenness visible among the gray of the ruins. "But then you really don't care what I feel, do you, Diana?" he continued quietly, hurting her to the quick. "You're merely pretending it's primarily my needs, and not your desire for a good news story that motivate you—"

"I do care what you feel!" Diana protested vehemently. Actually she could have confessed more, but it seemed to be the wrong time, even if her procrastination did make her feel exceptionally sad. She knew she had been given more than one opportunity by Sloane to admit her growing depth of feeling for him, and she knew she hadn't taken advantage of them, possibly because she still remained fearful of attempting any expression of emotions she wasn't one hundred percent sure she could define to herself.

"We'll go into the jungle, Diana. You and I. But know right now, we're going there not for me but for you. And if you die out there, Diana—and don't dismiss that possibility for a minute—I'll go to my grave hating you for having wrecked something between us that might have been infinitely better."

Diana's heart leaped into her mouth at Sloane's words, but she wanted to remain calm: she *had* to remain calm.

"Very easily said," she replied, "but how do you think you would one day feel toward a woman who could have got you access to that plane but hadn't jumped at the opportunity?"

"I would feel she was intelligent enough to know that anyone who would risk losing something forever by insisting it be put to that kind of test was a pretty poor excuse for a man." He didn't wait for her, but turned and headed back to the hotel.

When Diana finally caught up to him, out of

breath from hurrying with her camera equipment in her arms, he was standing on the edge of the veranda with a small group of the other hotel guests.

"Ah, you're right, there she is now," a little Englishwoman said upon sighting her. Diana had seen the woman on several occasions, but they hadn't progressed beyond a nodding acquaintance. "We were counting our numbers, my dear, and we came up missing two. Then Mr. Hendriks turned up and told us you were safely on the way."

"Is something wrong?" Diana asked.

"Seems we had a visitor last night—or early this morning," Sloane explained, directing her attention to the damp ground not far from where her footprints had been registered earlier that morning. "He left his calling card. Several of them, as a matter of fact." There in the mud, as big as handprints, were the pugs of a very large cat.

"Jaguar, wouldn't you say?" someone was asking as Diana looked up to see Sloane disappearing into the hotel.

DURING THE NEXT TWENTY-FOUR HOURS she didn't see Sloane or Dan—or any further traces of the large cat. When the small toylike train again began spilling its living contents onto the canyon floor the next afternoon, Diana watched. At one o'clock she wandered off with a tour group of Americans from a luxury liner that had docked on the Peruvian coast for a couple of days. It was a fairly large group, but Diana still managed to feel as if she stood out like a sore thumb, since, having formed their own little cliques, the tourists completely ignored her.

At two o'clock Diana melted into the line waiting for the buses, soon uncomfortably squashed between a fat man and fat woman in the back seat of a *camioneta*.

At the train depot there was still no sign of Sloane or Dan; Diana found a seat on the train and, in answer to a comment from an older woman sitting across from her, remarked that, yes, Machu Picchu was something grand. Then she sat back and closed her eyes.

"I have a splitting headache," a male voice groaned in one of the seats behind her, and a woman's voice offered comfort in reply while dust trails on the serpentine Hiram Bingham Road told Diana that the buses were still moving in both directions on the mountain.

She asked herself why she had come down the hill to the train depot and got on the train, thinking it was perhaps because this train could take her to Cuzco, where planes were available to take her to Lima, then to Los Angeles, and then home. Home....

Didn't that sound far away at the moment? *Wasn't* it far away, for that matter? Yet coming down the mountain was the first step of that long journey, taking the train the second, taking the plane the third...how simple it would be to leave Machu Picchu, Sloane, Dan, Carlyle, the jaguar and a jungle that devoured whole cities piecemeal! She was actually contemplating leaving, going home, getting a night of uninterrupted rest, reaching a place where she could walk without fear of being stalked by an animal intent on hanging her body in some tree for the condors.

The train whistle blew, startling Diana out of her reverie. Opening her eyes, she saw seats filled with tourists in one state or another of *soroche,* while beyond the window the last *camioneta* had reached the bottom and was spilling out passengers who obviously seemed to think the train was preparing to leave them stranded in the middle of nowhere.

But Machu Picchu *was* somewhere. It was a place on a mountain that daily brought hundreds of tourists. It was a place whose familiar picture, gracing travel offices around the world, was known to millions of other people who had never been there and probably never would have the opportunity to appreciate its magnificence. On the other hand, where Diana was going with Sloane there would be no roads; no pictures had been taken of it to hang on travel agents' walls. Few people had even set eyes on that little corner of the jungle in which an airplane had gone down and in so doing wreaked dishonor on the Hendriks family.

The train whistle blew again, and Diana felt

the metal cocoon around her shiver slightly like a runner tensing for the starter's gun. It would be so easy just to stay on board. She had money in her pocket with which to buy a ticket from the conductor; she had her passport, her international certificate of vaccination and her credit cards; she had her plane tickets from Cuzco to Lima, Lima to Los Angeles, Los Angeles to Seattle, the departure dates easily juggled by any airline representative to fit a new schedule.

She would surely be able to find suitable accommodation somewhere until all flight arrangements could be made, and no one was apt to miss her at the Hotel de Turistas until after she was long gone, since her room had been paid for in advance. As for the clothes, other personal items and camera equipment in the room, she could easily notify the hotel staff to send them on after her; the unused portion of her hotel bill would more than cover the cost of the extra effort on their part.

The train gave another noticeable shudder, and Diana got up to head quickly along the aisle for the exit, getting off just as the wheels began their actual movement on the tracks. From the platform she watched the train shudder into its snail's pace, knowing it still wasn't too late for her to get back on board, standing right where she was as the train grew smaller...smaller... smaller.

"Why didn't you go, Diana?"

She wouldn't answer his question because she

didn't have the answer; anyway, not one she was willing to tell him. What she suspected was that her impulse to remain at Machu Picchu was related to her having felt, if just for an instant, the sense of being on the verge of some wonderful discovery, only to have it kept from her, much as George Culhaney's joy in finding a lost city had been robbed from him by attacking natives. And as George was driven year after year to this area in his attempts to recapture his all too brief moment, Diana, too, could sense her own secret world quietly waiting for her just out of reach in the verdant denseness of that jungle.

George might have failed in all of his attempts, relegated finally to annual visits to stand on the edge of the escarpment and but fantasize what was lost to him forever, but Diana might end up being just as unsuccessful in her attempts, but there was surely much more to be lost in *not* trying than in at least making the attempt. Sloane might not now believe her motives for going with him were other than career oriented, but at least there would be the time available in which to try to convince him otherwise. And convincing him was suddenly so very, very important to her that maybe, one day, even she would be able to admit to herself just why that was so.

"Do neither you nor Jacos make noises like normal human beings?" Diana asked accusingly.

"You were thinking of leaving just now, weren't you, Diana?" Sloane said, ignoring her question by asking one of his own. "Why didn't you? Did you decide your story on archaeological thieves was just too juicy to pass up?"

"No, I decided if I didn't stick around you'd never set eyes on that damned airplane of yours!"

For a brief moment he looked as if he might believe her, the lines in his face softening, the loss of tension making him appear even more handsome. He raised a hand as if he were going to stroke his fingers gently along her left cheek.

"Oh, Diana, you should have been named Circe, sorceress who beguiles and confuses men's minds," he sighed, and she wanted him to touch her, wanted the sensuous feel of his work-roughened fingers sliding along her cheekbones, her jaw, her neck, her. . . . "Come on—" Sloane turned sharply "—there's no reason why I should have to lug all of your gear up the hill."

"What gear?"

She followed him to the front of the small depot, where he stopped long enough to call out in Spanish to one of the drivers leaning against a *camioneta*. The man yelled something in reply, and although Diana couldn't make out much of the exchange, she got the gist of it: Sloane had arranged a lift back up the mountain.

They went into the depot, walking over to one corner where a boy was standing guard over several packages stacked on the floor at his feet.

Sloane fished into the pocket of his trousers and pulled out a handful of coins. *"Muchas gracias,"* he said, transferring the coins from his large hand to the boy's smaller one, then he turned to Diana.

"I hope the boots fit," he said. "I had one of the hotel maids check your things for sizes."

"You bought me boots?" Diana asked incredulously, watching Sloane bend down and pick up several of the packages, which he handed to her.

She found herself responding like a robot, her arms outstretched while Sloane stacked them with wrapped merchandise. When he had successfully managed to pile all of the goods into her arms, leaving nothing for himself to carry, he seemed exceptionally pleased with himself and smiled at Diana over the boxes before heading for the door. She followed him wordlessly. This was a harmless little joke, this toting of packages, and she was sport enough to take it in good spirit.

The ride up the hill, like all of Diana's previous rides over this particular terrain, found her on the edge of her seat, the minibus on the edge of the roadway. With all of the room in the world, the drivers seemed to prefer driving with at least one wheel hanging over the void.

On each sharp turn Sloane seemed purposely to avoid even usual body contact, and when in a flurry of dust the *camioneta* arrived at the top, he was quick to open the door and get out.

"Why don't you go drop that stuff off in your room and we'll have dinner," he suggested, checking his wristwatch. "It's getting late."

Late? Diana couldn't see her watch, but she doubted it was much later than three-thirty, and said as much. "But that gives us only a little more than twelve hours, doesn't it?" he answered. "I suggest you enjoy the comforts of a private room and soft bed while they're still available to you."

In her room she opened the packages one by one and was surprised to find boots, underwear, socks, slacks, a bush jacket, belt, scarf, small carrying case and waterproof duffel bag. Then she went to find Sloane.

He had already ordered them *pachamanca*, proceeding to explain how the dish derived its name from the Quechua *pacha,* meaning earth, and *manca,* meaning pot. It was cooked in the ground in a manner similar to that used by natives of the South Seas. Washed stones were placed in a hole dug to a depth of close to two feet, followed by firewood. The wood was ignited and kept burning for two or three hours; then the hot ashes and embers were shoved to one side with a stick, while pieces of meat wrapped in banana leaves—lamb, in the case of Diana's and Sloane's meal—were laid on the hot stones. This was followed by corn on the cob and white potatoes, all wrapped in leaves. The food was covered by more leaves, another layer of hot stones and finally more earth. Everything was left to cook for two hours, after which it was unearthed and served.

"Better set your alarm for three-thirty in the morning," Sloane said, spearing a piece of the lamb with his fork. "We have to leave here by four, and Dan informs me that Carlyle isn't going to wait around for us if we fail to rendezvous with him on time. Put whatever toiletries you're going to need into the small carrying packet, and stuff everything else in the waterproof duffel. Someone will be keeping watch on your room here to see that anything you leave will be safe until you—or someone else—comes to claim it."

CHAPTER EIGHT

DIANA STRETCHED to turn off the alarm, surprised she had been able to sleep at all. She cut off the whirring drone that was vaguely reminiscent of the *turistas* in swarm. The room was dark, and chilly outside the covers. Subtropic or not, it was never very warm at eight thousand feet after the sun went down.

She threw back her blanket. Her eyes were already growing accustomed to the dark, so she didn't turn on any lights until she reached the bathroom. When she looked in the mirror, she thought the glass must be faulty. There was simply no way she could look that fresh at this ungodly hour!

After she had washed her face and brushed her hair, she sorted through her toiletries, deciding what she needed: soap, lip balm, a squeeze bottle of Visine, her toothbrush and toothpaste, her brush, her comb.... She didn't realize until later, too late in fact, that she had forgotten to bring a mirror. The essentials went into the small carrying packet, which in turn went into the top of the duffel bag she had packed the night before.

She dressed, amazed at how well everything fit, though the boots gave her a bit of trouble. For a moment she had visions of Sloane purposely having given her the wrong size. But the trouble was merely in pulling them on. Once she stood up in them and took a few steps they actually felt comfortable.

She turned to the full-length mirror on the bathroom door. "Trick or treat," she said, looking suspiciously like some *memsahib* off to board an elephant for a tiger hunt. She decided she rather liked the way she looked—ready for a step into the unknown, ready for adventure.

At his knock Sloane was let in, wearing faded denim pants and jacket, light blue shirt open at the collar, black riding boots, no hat. He looked so casual yet so remarkably handsome.

"Your things ready?" he asked. Then, spotting the duffel bag, he easily hefted it onto his right shoulder before leading the way out of the hotel.

By the time Diana realized she was really on her way, she was at the upper end of the Hiram Bingham Road, becoming confused when Sloane led her past it. "Aren't we going down?" she asked.

"No trains stop at this time of the morning," he said. "You and I will have to look for other transportation."

There was an exceptionally thick mist, and the occasional gust of wind glossed Diana's face with moisture. To her left the Hiram Bingham

Road was shrouded in fog beyond its first bend. The Urubamba Canyon was filled with fluffy clouds to the extent that neither the Old Mountain nor the New Mountain was visible. Segments of the ruins appeared and then disappeared as if mere spectral illusions damned forever to materialize and disintegrate at random.

Diana could see no moon, but she suspected one was up there, since the darkness wasn't pitch-black despite the hour. She could tell they were heading uphill by the way her feet hit the ground, and every so often she thought she could detect smooth stones under her feet. Bushes and plants were dark shadows, dripping moisture, and already she felt soaked to her skin even though her clothes had been treated to shed water.

"Careful," Sloane instructed. "Watch your step." Rocks underfoot became dangerously slippery, and Diana began counting her steps. One...two...twenty...one hundred...two hundred.... A compulsion to count things was called arithmomania. Where had she read that?

What seemed like a good hour later, Diana glanced ahead to see the fog lift momentarily, revealing a segment of stone ruin. She was confused, disoriented, sure that Machu Picchu should have been below her and off to the right. "The upper guard post," Sloane informed her, stopping beside the large stones that fit neatly together without mortar.

Diana leaned against them, breathing harder than she would have liked. "Why put a guard post here?" she asked. "Were they expecting invaders to drop from the sky?"

"The road ran up here," Sloane explained, "the ancient Incan way. The Incas didn't reach Machu Picchu by coming up from the bottom of the Urubamba Canyon as the tourists do today; they traveled along the spine of these mountains. This same road took them to other Incan fortresses and settlements: Choquesuysuy, Corihuayrachina, and Runcuraccay."

"How long did it take you get to the point of being able to roll all of those off your tongue without stumbling once?" Diana asked laughingly.

Sloane smiled. "Years," he said, then told her she was going to have to wait there alone for a couple of minutes.

"You're leaving?" Diana asked, hoping her question hadn't come out quite as frantic as it had sounded to her own ears. She didn't relish the idea of being left alone in a swirling mist that belonged in a Dracula movie.

"Just for a minute," he assured her. "But be sure to stay put, or your last step is liable to be a mighty long one!"

As Sloane walked into the shifting gloom, Diana felt an irresistible urge to follow. She surveyed the fog, trying visually to penetrate it; looking toward where she thought the hotel should be, but seeing nothing; looking toward the main ruins and again seeing nothing. She was standing in a draft as if poised on the lip of a cliff, which for all she knew at the moment was possibly the case.

Sloane, after what seemed an eternity, materialized from the mist. "Expecting somebody a bit more sinister, were you?" he teased, extending his right hand, which Diana gladly took. He gave her a gentle pull, and she came away from the wall to a spot very close to him. In the V of his shirt Diana could see the crisply curling black hair at the top of his muscled chest. She shivered, and not from the cold. "This way," he said.

Diana stumbled, fell against something soft. The softness moved. She let out a sound that was too breathless to be a scream, stumbled again, collapsed, found herself suddenly supported entirely by Sloane's strong arms.

"Diana?" She heard her name coming from what seemed miles away, and wondered if she had stepped off the edge of the chasm, was even now on her way down, Sloane's voice carrying after her on the wind. "Diana?" he asked again, having knelt down to let her body drop to the ground with his.

"It's alive," she heard herself saying. "It's alive."

"I should hope so," Sloane answered. "It wouldn't be doing us much good if it were dead."

Diana came to her senses quickly, something

about the calm, cool and pleasant timbre of Sloane's voice telling her that her supposed peril had been nothing like what she might have imagined. She sat up, hoping Sloane's hands wouldn't be too quick to relinquish the position they had taken high on her waist.

"I slipped," she said, knowing her statement to be superfluous.

"And almost knocked one of our burros off the cliff," Sloane added, sounding and looking amused.

"What burros?" she asked, struggling to her feet with his assistance. There they were: two burros in the fog, watching her as if she were some new hybrid recently introduced to their private domain. Motioning Diana over to one of them, Sloane helped her mount.

LATER, WHEN THE SUN BEGAN TO RISE, it was a huge red ball, its rays filtered by the same mists that magnified it to ten times its original size. It seemed as though it were being drawn upward as wispy curtains of moisture skittered back and forth across its face, occasionally releasing shafts of pale sunlight that slashed the air with beams reminiscent of those in religious pictures.

All around them the mist was in movement, heated by that fiery orb the Incas had worshipped, lifting each second to reveal some new rocky crag, another swath of green jungle, the peak of some distant snowcapped mountain. Diana tried not to look down. She knew it was a long way to the bottom; had known that even before the canyon walls began to appear, because even filled to its very brim with foam-like fog the canyon had still exuded an ominous impression of great depth.

"How far down?" she asked Sloane as the burros carefully picked their way along a narrow pathway. Although even as she asked the question she wasn't sure she really wanted to know the answer. She wouldn't welcome any information that would make her more frightened than she already was.

"Through here, maybe three thousand feet," Sloane said. "Just stay on the burro and the burro will stay on the path." Diana tried to act as if she weren't a bit unnerved by the idea that all there was between her and the bottom of the chasm was one four-footed animal and a few thousand feet of uncluttered air.

Somewhere, not close, a rock fell into the void, bouncing a couple of times on solid stone, then slipping into the silent emptiness existing before that final, unheard collision far, far below.

Diana gasped in childlike wonder at a rainbow that momentarily formed within the elevating mist. Sloane, who was seated on the lead burro, turned back to look at her and followed her gaze. "Cuycha, the Rainbow," he said, "venerated by the Incas as the servant of both the sun and the moon."

"Beautiful!" Diana exclaimed in wonder.

"There is much that is beautiful in Peru," Sloane said. "When the fog lifts further you'll be able to see the snow on a good many of the highest peaks of the Cordillera de Urubamba, and the lush green of jungle growth in the valleys. It's a place of extremes, a place in which civilization often seems never to have penetrated at all, although many peoples actually thrived here."

The burros manipulated another turn in a pathway that had begun to narrow considerably. More mist dissolved, more canyon appeared, its bottom still unveiled. The hole might well have been bottomless.

The path began to widen by the time the last of the fog disappeared from the canyon to reveal a river trailing the deep groove: a thin sliver of silver reflecting the rising sun. "Is that still the Urubamba River?" Diana asked.

"Yes," Sloane replied. "And if we turn around and follow it back, we will eventually reach Machu Picchu. Shall we turn around, Diana?"

"No," she answered.

The path widened further, and after the tightrope the trail had been, it suddenly now seemed to Diana like a superhighway. Less concerned for her immediate safety, she became aware of a few aches and pains that had until then gone unnoticed. Her back hurt, the insides of her legs were sore from chafing against the sides of the burro, and she had a stiff neck. She would have asked if she could get off and walk, but dismounting still might have meant her or the burro's going over the side of the abyss.

The trail assumed a steeper incline, and Diana could finally see where it topped the cliff. In a few more minutes she had hopes of feeling safer still.

"We'll be able to get off and stretch up here a bit," Sloane said. "We'll also be able to eat." Hungry now, Diana remembered with a pang his comments over the *pachamanca* the night before to the effect that it was liable to be their last good meal for quite a while.

The chill in the air hadn't been completely warmed away when Diana's burro gracefully exited from the narrow end of the pathway to step out on top. With the drop of the gorge behind her, Diana looked upon a rolling landscape of lush greens interspersed with massive upthrustings of dull gray granite.

Sloane pointed toward southwestern snowcapped mountain peaks. "That's Huayanay, the larger one's Salcantay, the Wild Mountain," he identified them. Diana doubted she would ever get over the surprise of finding snow so near the equator.

"This is the Cordillera de Vilcabamba," Sloane said, and what Diana saw looked about as hostile as anything she had ever seen, the lush greens of the jungle seeming no more hospitable than the gaunt upthrustings of rock.

Sloane guided his mount down the slope

toward one large stretch of jungle, and Diana's burro followed. It really made little difference how Diana fooled with its reins, the sturdy little beast merely followed the leader. "How about my walking for a while," Diana suggested. "I could certainly stand a change of position."

Sloane stopped and dismounted, and Diana's burro stopped, too. Sloane came back to help her down, pushing his large hands up beneath her arms and lifting gently—too quickly completing his task and pulling away. She ignored the pang of regret that his quick withdrawal caused. Once out of the saddle, she felt as if she had spent days riding waves on a barrel. She leaned against Sloane's body as her feet hit the ground.

"Stiff?" he asked.

"Yes," she admitted.

"Come on," he said. "We'll get the kinks out, then we'll have something to eat."

The sun climbed higher, and Diana was glad for its warmth as they continued to the edge of a wall of jungle greenery that looked completely impenetrable until Sloane quickly found his way through. They were soon swallowed on all sides by banks of waxy green leaves, the thicker underbrush eventually giving way to an area reminding Diana of the inside of a huge tent supported by bark-covered poles. Above her the upper limits of those poles merged to form a thick canopy that cast a deep shadow upon the forest floor. Diana immediately missed the sun.

She heard water, birds, monkeys and even a few unidentifiable creatures, seeing none of them. She had never really thought about the special sound of the jungle before, but now she knew it was like nothing else.

"There's a stream up here," Sloane said. "We'll stop on the other side of the bridge."

Getting to the other side, Diana soon discovered, would require her walking across a contraption of swaying vines and rotting hunks of wood. She had seen such things in the movies but didn't think they really existed. "You and I obviously have different conceptions of what is, and what is not, a bridge," she said. "By my definition, that is *not* one."

"I'll help you across and come back for the animals."

"Send me across to test it out, so to speak?"

"I said I would *help* you across, not *send* you across."

"And you're quite serious about this being a bridge?"

"Actually, it's one of the best we're liable to find."

Sloane tethered both burros to a tree. The stream, which Diana had assumed would be available for the soaking of her tired feet, was nowhere within reach, but rumbling in a frothy boil through a deep cut that was a good thirty feet across.

The walls of the gorge went straight down to the water, offering no apparent footing or handholds. If the bridge collapsed, it seemed apparent to Diana there would be no coming back up—even if she survived the fall.

The roar of the cascades was even louder on the edge of the gorge. "Shall I carry you across?" Sloane asked, his lips sliding back over his teeth in an easy smile, his dimples deepening.

"I'll carry my own weight, thank you," Diana said firmly, knowing there were countless women who would probably look upon crossing this bridge as nothing all that hazardous, but she wasn't one of them. Although she would never have admitted that to Sloane.

"Just don't look down," Sloane warned, motioning her to take a position on the end of the bridge. "I'll be right behind you. Just hold on and don't step into any of the holes, will you?" Which Diana found a bit inconsistent. If she didn't look down, she would be a little hard pressed to locate any of those holes she was supposed to avoid.

She grabbed the handrails, which were nothing more than twisted vines stretched parallel across the chasm. Sloane moved up close behind to where Diana could sense his reassuring presence. He leaned his head over her shoulder to press his mouth close to her ear.

"Think we could move it a little faster?" he suggested jokingly. Diana took a few tentative steps, and the bridge weaved as a result. For a moment a terrifying dizziness took hold of her.

Sloane stepped in closer, which comforted her, so she shuffled forward.

"Hole coming up at six o'clock!" he told her. She looked down to see her right foot about to cover nothing but the drop to the water. Reflexively she stepped back, bringing herself in even tighter against Sloane's body. He placed steadying hands on her shoulders to give her support, and Diana once again became aware that his touch was offering her a kind of danger apt to be far more hazardous to her well-being, especially in the long run, than any of the treacherous holes in this dilapidated bridge.

Assuming that merely by breaking physical contact with Sloane it would be possible for her to eradicate this special danger she was feeling, she moved forward with a speed that had her across the bridge in less time than she could have thought possible. "Good going!" Sloane congratulated her, having followed close behind, his strong hands on her shoulders again, his head bent forward so that she could feel his breath sifting her hair.

Diana turned, looking up into his dark smoldering eyes, knowing that while she had successfully challenged the obstacle offered by the bridge, her sense of apprehension hadn't diminished, but rather seemed to become more intense with each passing moment.

She contemplated pulling away, except that pulling away from Sloane on the bridge had accomplished nothing. Besides, the best way to

conquer fears was often to confront them head-
on, as one could sometimes dissolve the phan-
toms of nightmares simply by turning in
haunted dreams to face them.

In more than one way, so many aspects of
Diana's past few days had been of the unreal
fabric of which dreams were made. On the other
hand, this was a real man she was touching, as
she uncontrollably reached out to trace her
fingertips gently along his square jawline and
down his muscle-corded neck. These were real
arms being slid around her with a gentleness
that belied the pure animal strength of which
Sloane was capable.

They stood unmoving on the rim of a gorge
filled with a roaring to match the frantic sounds
of Diana's heart, two people simply enjoying
the pleasures of a closeness that momentarily
didn't need the intrusion of spoken words to
enhance it.

It was there, couched securely within a world
that, at least for the moment, had been telescoped for Diana to include only herself and the
man tightly holding her, that it finally dawned
on her: she had discovered love.

Yes, she loved Sloane; it was as pure and as
simple as that. Seeing it so clearly, Diana knew
she had been keeping that revelation concealed
inside of her as securely as the surrounding
jungle kept veiled its lost cities. She loved him,
even though he was about as far as anyone
could be from the type of man she had once

imagined would spark the fire inside of her. A fire that was now blazing to holocaust proportions.

Recognizing her love for what it was offered a sudden solution to many of the little mysteries that had cluttered her life since first meeting Sloane in the Lima restaurant. Oh, how clear it all became when she was able to put everything in its proper perspective, finally seeing it with vision no longer clouded by her refusal to believe that love had found Diana Green in this unique and frightening way.

It was no longer a mystery why she had felt the way she had every time he had ever kissed her: at the hotel in Cuzco, in the empty train car, in the ruins of Machu Picchu. It was love that had made her so upset in Cuzco when Sloane confessed to monitoring her phone calls and paying someone to spy on her. It had, after all, been quite shattering for her to learn that the man for whom she was even then beginning to care deeply was not returning the trust that was a natural part of her own blossoming affection. And once she had got over her initial hurt at his betrayal, she had magnanimously forgiven him...because she loved him. Love had made her happy to see him again on the train ride to Machu Picchu. It had made her sad when she thought he had once again left her for good at the train depot at the bottom of the Hiram Bingham Road.

How easy it was in retrospect to understand

why she had known such ecstatic pleasure when she walked out on the veranda of the Hotel de Turistas to see Sloane sitting there, feeling her hands in his when he came to greet her with that look of genuine pleasure on his handsome face. She could even explain the extreme reluctance with which she had watched him return to Dan Jacos in the blackness of that one Machu Picchu night, believing he was finally gone from her life forever. Love had given her reason to rearrange her life and make it possible for Sloane to come out here on this mission to clear his family name.

This special something happening to her was not to be denied any longer. And surprisingly, she didn't feel uneasy when she realized she could no longer deny that Sloane loved her, too. Admitting his love could make even more of the pieces fit: his genuine concern for her welfare leading to his attempt to persuade her not to expose herself to the dangers of the jungle on his account, and his finally agreeing to go on this trip with her only when he had thought Diana would need his protection.

He had clearly been speaking about her when he had said he didn't want to love the only thing now dear to him after losing his mother, brother, father and, potentially, his plantation. What exactly had he said? "*My* life? You think I'm actually talking about *my* life? Diana, you are such a fool!"

If he loved her, maybe she had been wrong in

assuming he would be incapable of ever making a commitment. However, whether she had been right or wrong in that estimation, she wanted him to know where she stood. She wanted him to know she was willing to make the commitment if he was. It would no longer be her fears that would deny them all that could be possible between them.

"I love you," she told him.

His arms tightened, pulling her in against his muscled chest, letting her become even more acutely aware of the delicious feel of him. His mouth touched her ear wetly, the sensual caress of his tongue setting Diana's blood boiling as she responsively arched her neck for the downward progression of his hot kisses. "Diana," he groaned, his hands sliding down along her back, pressing her even closer against his hard male body. She turned her head slightly, feeling the brush of his thick hair on the smooth skin of her face just before his lips came to meet hers in a kiss that exploded pleasure inside her.

His collapsing weight brought her to the ground, spilling them upon green moss like lovers spilled sensuously upon green velvet sheets. His eyes devoured. His body demanded. "I love you," he said. "If you only knew how much I love you."

"And I'm only here because I love you, too," Diana breathed, aware of his want as he pressed down atop her, and wanting him in return. "What I'm doing out here is *only* because I love you. Oh, Sloane, please tell me you believe that!''

"Diana, Diana," he said, his voice husky, almost muffled as his lips roamed excitingly along her neck. "I've been such a fool. I'm sorry, so damned, damned sorry...."

With a reckless abandoned fury he pulled her pliant softness even tighter against the unyielding hardness of his powerful body. He shifted completely on top of her, his strong thighs pressing hers open while the crush of his chest and stomach forced the air from her lungs to leave her in panting breathlessness. She clamped her hands on the back of his neck, feeling the passion-tautened muscles straining there before her fingers slid upward to become lost within the tangle of his silky black hair. "I love you, I love you," she moaned.

His strong and sinuous body slid downward along the seeming frailness of her own, igniting fiery pleasure wherever it passed, his kisses raining hot and erotic sensations on the arc of her neck as he fumbled to unfasten the buttons of her blouse. His callused hands, rough against her soft skin, peeled back the material to expose the creamy swell of her breasts. She gasped as his hand found the willing softness of one breast, caressing, teasing, arousing in maddeningly delicious circles, his other hand dropping to describe equally sensuous designs on the inner curve of her thigh. Still she entwined her fingers in his hair, caught between a will to push his face away and a desire to draw it even closer. She was caught up in the feel, the touch and the taste of him. All of her senses were forged into a heat that was partly hers, partly his, partly the result of the incendiary magic that was happening between them. She wanted the fire to continue, wanted Sloane to continue onward to that dangerous moment when she would be either lost forever or melted with him into one body— one perfect harmonious unit.

His hands raked over her skin, molding her curves as a sculptor molds sensuous lines in wet clay. She felt his touseled hair and tempting kisses trailing her neck, her breasts, en route to forbidden places his hands, now at her waistband, threatened to lay bare. She wanted him...and she sensed with all her heart that he wanted her, too.

But suddenly Sloane pulled away from her, coming to his feet, making himself distant by a space not merely measured in physical units. "It was better for me to continue believing there was no chance of your loving me in return...you know that, don't you, Diana?" he said, his words almost an accusation. "In fact, I really wish I didn't know now that you love me."

"How can you say such a thing?" Diana responded, stunned, although intuitively she knew and feared what was coming next. She felt exposed and self-conscious as she tried to re-arrange her clothes and prop herself up in a position that spoke less of the passion still fluttering within her. "How?" she repeated.

"Because nothing can ever come of this, Diana," he said, his words stabbing her to the heart. He had to see the hurt branded in her eyes! "At least not the way things stand at the moment." He sounded as if he genuinely regretted what he had suddenly injected between them.

Diana was frightened to near illness at having been so close to surrendering herself, mind and body, to a man who was willing to give himself as completely to her as she had been prepared to give herself to him.

"You see before you a man who, if he doesn't soon have some sudden change of fortune, is going bankrupt within the year. That hardly leaves me in a good position to propose marriage to anyone, wouldn't you agree?"

Diana couldn't believe he was rejecting her for something as ridiculous as his present lack of money. Love, after all, should go beyond material things. Love should transcend all.

"But you'll find other work," she insisted, wishing with all her heart that he would come to his senses.

"I'm rather like my father when it comes to repaying bad debts," Sloane said. "Which means, not only do I stand to lose everything I presently own, but I'm probably going to end up devoting a good many years to making things right. Getting my affairs back to a condition in which I could even begin to think of marriage is not likely to happen overnight."

"And if it wouldn't matter to me?" Diana asked, realizing she was once again in the predicament of having, but not being able to have, the man she had finally admitted to herself and to him that she loved.

"It would matter to me, though," he said. He took her hand in his, kissing her fingertips, then nibbling on them gently. "I couldn't expect you to wait as long as it might take, and I wouldn't like myself very much, knowing you were growing old somewhere while I selfishly held on to you. You're too young, and too pretty, to be saddled with someone who couldn't possibly give you the kind of life he wanted to give you—the kind of life you certainly deserve."

Diana was silent, knowing any attempt she made to speak would only end up coming out as uncontrollable sobs.

"How do you think I would feel, watching you wither daily, turning prematurely old from a hard life as my mother did," Sloane continued, "and being able to do absolutely nothing about it? I couldn't take that, Diana. I won't take it, as a matter of fact!"

"But I love you," she insisted, trying desperately to stop the flow of tears that were starting despite all of her efforts to control them.

"You see how weak this man you love, and who so desperately loves you, really is, Diana?"

he said finally, bitter sadness evident in each and every word. "I should have kept on resisting the temptation to hold you close, knowing that if and when it came to this moment, I would be standing the chance of losing you before I even had my chance to have you. Simply because I can't afford to have a relationship with any woman who is looking for a firm commitment, and you aren't the kind of woman who would settle for less than one hundred percent from any man, are you, Diana?"

She knew he was really asking her if she would be willing to take advantage of what little time they had here and now, tossing aside all thoughts of tomorrow. Yet, as tempting as that might be, Sloane was right in thinking that Diana wasn't the kind of woman who would be satisfied with second best. Oh, there was now no denying she wanted Sloane, wanted him in the worst possible way. However, she wasn't sure she was ready to sacrifice certain long-held moral standards, as tempting as it might be to simply cast them to the wind.

She knew she wanted this man as her husband, her legal partner, until death do them part; so how could she now settle for a man who would be with her for only a couple of days and then disappear from her life for good, possibly taking some vital part of her with him? The potential dangers of such a short-term relationship were too numerous for her to even begin dealing with in her present state of mind.

Apparently as far as Sloane was concerned she had answered his question merely by not answering it, because Diana immediately saw the way a mask seemed to lower over his features, blanching his face of all visible emotion.

"We'll be walking on dangerous ground these next few days, won't we, Diana?" he said in a voice that made her shiver because of a timbre that, though calm in delivery, still hinted of turbulence. "Because you and I both know that I'm not as strong at resisting temptation as I might have wished to be. My succeeding temporarily, a battle won, doesn't mean I've won any wars. So while I've had the strength to save us this time, Diana, be forewarned. It's going to take the both of us to make sure that what was begun here isn't one day going to be brought unwittingly to its natural completion because of some moment left too long unguarded between us."

Diana could only agree. It wasn't just Sloane who had fought a battle and nearly lost.

He went back across the bridge for the burros, and Diana's sense of accomplishment in having successfully braved the bridge remained only until she saw the ease with which the burros moved across. The two animals mastered all obstacles in record time, Sloane not having to crowd up behind them once. "They've had a little more practice at this sort of thing than you have," he said, apparently sensing Diana's deflation.

He rummaged through one of the saddlebags, coming up shortly with a large and wicked-looking machete. Walking back to the end of the bridge, he delivered a whack that neatly sliced through the anchoring Gordian knot of vines.

"Sloane?" Diana questioned, coming hurriedly to her feet. She was shocked, not understanding immediately why this bold action was necessary.

He delivered another mighty cut that sent the whole suspension system into major convulsions. Suddenly the bridge slipped away entirely, unwinding against the opposite wall of the narrow gorge.

"There are other ways to cross," Sloane said. "But not anywhere close. Carlyle wants this bridge down behind us to hold up anyone who might be following."

"Do you think we're being followed?" Diana asked nervously, watching Sloane walk to his burro to put away the machete.

"I don't know if we are or not, but I figure Carlyle has every right to protect against that contingency. Since he has spies in Sipas's camp, he would be foolish to assume none of his own men could be bought."

Sloane now surprised Diana by pulling out of the bag a belt with gun and holster. "I presume you have no questions as to why I'm giving you this, do you?" Sloane said. "It's to protect you from annoying animals. Two-legged or four."

Diana knew he was referring to what had happened between them, but it was an extreme thought, a ridiculous one.

He walked directly over to her, turned her around impersonally so that her back was to him, and fitted the gun belt on her as if she were a large doll. He let the holster hang to her right side, reaching around her middle to fasten the large belt buckle, kneeling to adjust the thigh thong. He moved quickly, too quickly, leaving Diana yearning for more of his touch. "There," he said, getting up. "Turn around and let's take a look."

Diana turned. "Not bad, not bad," was his comment. Folding his arms across his chest, he stepped back even farther, cocking his head as if he were a painter out for proper perspective on a subject he was about to immortalize on canvas. He walked back to his burro, fishing into the baggage for another gun and holster, which he strapped to his own hip. Diana decided he had to look far better with a gun on than she did.

Pulling out two bullet clips, Sloane motioned Diana over to a rock, where he sat himself down. She sat beside him as he put one of the clips in her gun. He seemed exceptionally bemused as Diana gingerly returned her gun to its holster; by the time her guard flap was back in place, Sloane's gun was loaded and at his hip.

He was soon up again, heading for Diana's burro, where he unhooked her camera from the saddle horn on which she had hung it. Holding the camera up, he snapped her picture. "Something for your children and grandchildren," he said.

Having forgotten her compact, Diana hadn't been able to look in a mirror since she had left the hotel, and she could well imagine just what kind of a picture she made. "Come on, we'll snap a good shot of you over here," he said, motioning toward the edge of the gorge.

Diana had never been all that fond of herself in pictures, even those snapped under ideal conditions, and these conditions certainly weren't ideal. However, she could just sense that Sloane wasn't going to take no for an answer, so she got up, albeit reluctantly, and headed in his direction.

"If you lean here—" Sloane indicated the place where the end of the bridge had once been anchored "—then I can shoot you with the bridge hanging in the background."

"I presume you'll be doing all of this 'shooting' with a camera," Diana joked, noticing how he allowed her a slight smile for her attempt at levity. She leaned where he told her to lean, and smiled when he told her to smile.

Finished, Sloane hung the camera around his neck as if he were expecting another great shot to present itself shortly. He went back to his burro, and this time his search of the saddlebag produced two small plastic bags full of... "Raisins and nuts," he said, jiggling the contents. "High energy. High protein. Sorry that it can't be ham and eggs, but we're roughing it."

He tossed Diana one of the bags, which she caught, then he unhooked a canteen from the saddle and headed to a nearby rock, where Diana joined him. She opened her breakfast bag, scooping up a small handful of nuts and raisins. The nutty-sweet combination was delicious. Or, more likely, Diana was hungry enough to appreciate anything.

All that day they trekked through the jungle. The slow but steady progress of the burros had so regular a rhythm that several times Diana almost dozed off—which didn't surprise her, considering that she had risen in what had been the middle of the previous night. But she didn't fall asleep. It would have been dangerous, and besides, it would have robbed her of Sloane's presence. Not that they spoke much. Around them the jungle was alive with its own sound: the twitter of birds now and then interrupted by a raucous screech, the babbling of monkeys, the swish of ferns and leaves as they passed, the dull, plodding thud of the burros' hooves. Into the verdant jungle whose noise was somehow even more still than silence, Diana rode behind Sloane, wordlessly following wherever he led.

CHAPTER NINE

THEY CAMPED THAT NIGHT in a cave. Just before Sloane moved the last large rock in front of the entrance, Diana heard the sound. The two burros, tied off in one corner just beyond the light of the camp fire, heard it, too, perking up their ears and moving skittishly. "Jaguar," Sloane said, as calmly as if he were discussing the weather.

"It sounds hungry," Diana said, as if she were an expert at telling whether a jaguar's stomach was empty or full just by the sounds of it after nightfall.

"We can take some consolation in that they seldom attack a man unless provoked," Sloane said. "Or a woman, either," he added, and smiled. "They really prefer monkeys, capybaras or deer. Maybe an occasional sloth or tapir."

"And the one out there somewhere, killing villagers and goats?"

"There's always the exception to any rule, isn't there?" Sloane replied, stirring the smoldering embers. There was enough ventilation in the cave to make a fire possible, even with the main entrance partially blocked. Streaks of soot on the ceiling gave indication that the place had been used as a sanctuary on more than one occasion in the past.

They ate something from heavy plastic bags, the bags having first been boiled in a pot of water over the fire. The food tasted rather bland at first, but it improved with the addition of a little salt; the tea tasted better, and the dessert—a few pieces of dried fruit—was best of all. Diana washed the tin utensils, stacking them on a flat stone near the fire to dry, while Sloane spread their sleeping bags, placing them several feet apart.

During the night Diana, imagining all sorts of large animals sniffing around just outside the cave, glanced over to where Sloane was asleep and looking exceptionally boyish in the feeble light cast by the last of the fire's burning embers. Comforted by knowing he was there, saddened because he wasn't snuggled close beside her, she curled on her side, shut her eyes and went to sleep.

When she awoke in the morning Sloane was already outside, having led the burros to a nearby stream and packed the implements used for preparing supper the night before.

"You awake, Diana?" he called, entering the cave. She could see daylight behind him at the entrance, and looking at her watch, she saw it was almost eight o'clock.

"I'm awake," she said, sitting up and stretching, sore but deriving a decided pleasure from her aches and pains, as if they were evidence of things accomplished.

"Sleep well?" Sloane asked.

"Pretty well, yes."

"I've got some water boiling outside," he said. "Shall I bring you in a cup of tea or instant coffee?"

"No, I'll get up and get it," Diana responded. A cave wasn't exactly her idea of a place in which she would care to loll away the morning. "I'm afraid I'm going to need help, though, in getting this sleeping bag of mine rolled up."

"Why don't you go get yourself something to drink, and I'll take care of it?" he suggested.

"If I'm hoping to survive in the great outdoors, I had best take time to learn a little something about survival, right?" she said. "Now, I have no immediate plans of going off and shooting meat for supper—that's frankly a bit beyond me, at least for the moment—but I can certainly get the hang of taking care of my own bedding. Even my mother quit making my bed when I got old enough to do it myself!"

He showed her how to roll the sleeping bag into a ridiculously small tube. It all was pretty basic stuff, something countless kids knew how to do, but Diana, city born and bred, couldn't recall a time she had ever been camping.

Sloane carried her bag outside, Diana following as far as the fire and the boiling water. While Sloane fastened the bedding in place on one of the burros, she poured water over a tea bag and then set her cup on a nearby rock to brew. They had picked an idyllic spot for a campsite, she decided, looking around her appreciatively. The cave, of course, had been ideal protection, the outside setting quite beautiful. Oh, it certainly wasn't as breathtaking as the scenery along the trail that skirted the Urubamba Canyon, but it held up quite nicely.

A small stream cascaded over an eight-foot embankment to form a nice-sized pool, overflowing one lip and gurgling merrily into a small indentation that carried it off into the dense tangle of underbrush on one side. The jungle had changed again from large trees to dense underbrush. Among the plants Sloane had pointed out the previous day, Diana now recognized a quinine-yielding cinchona and a wild rubber tree.

Sloane finished what he was doing and walked over to Diana, standing just in front of her, looking down with a strange expression on his face. Diana had never denied he was handsome, finding he had a nice balance between masculine good looks and boyish innocence: a combination that had probably held him in good stead with more than his share of women, many of whom were probably equally made weak by his deep dimples. How she so desperately yearned to just reach out and touch his firm jawline!

"Diana," he said, extending both strong,

sinewy arms and clasping her delicate hands in his rough ones. He pulled her to a standing position, and she found herself hoping that he had reconsidered the stupidity of thwarting their love with obstacles that surely could be worked out between them if he would just allow them to pool their resources and try. He touched her hair with his right hand, his fingers combing gently through her long blond strands. He was so close! Surely he wouldn't be so cruel as to offer them both up to temptation—unless he had second thoughts regarding the commitment she so desperately needed and desired from him.

"You had better cut your hair," he said—not exactly what Diana had been expecting.

"My hair?" she echoed faintly, assuming she must have misheard.

"Look," Sloane said. Diana looked, saw and gasped. There were two of them, small and black...and crawling! There was no doubt in her mind about where Sloane had got them, either.

"Hold on, Diana!" Sloane said, obviously surprised at her vehement reaction. He dropped the bugs and took hold of her as she started moving away from him. "They're harmless."

Harmless or not, they had been secreted in her hair, and Diana had known nothing about them. Suspecting there were others up there right that moment, she was obsessed with a need to go exploring for them with her fingers, but was afraid of what she might find there.

"Diana, for Pete's sake, please don't get hysterical on me!" That was very easy for him to say, since he hadn't found bugs in *his* hair. "I was going to suggest yesterday that you cut it." Diana started to cry, embarrassed that she couldn't keep from it. "Really, Diana, you'll look just as good with short hair," Sloane consoled her. "If we check it nightly we won't even have to cut off all that much."

He pulled her closer, cupping his right hand behind her head to pull her face in against his hard chest. She could hear his heartbeat beneath his shirt, and after a while began to feel a little silly. It was ridiculous of her to be making such a fuss over a couple of bugs when she had gone marching merrily into the jungle while jaguars screamed in the night. Still. . . .

"Diana, are you okay?" Sloane kept asking in continued concern.

"I'm fine," she managed finally.

"Are you sure?"

"Really, I'm fine," Diana said, once more in control and feeling better for having had her cry.

"Sure?"

"Sure."

"Good!" Sloane said, giving her an affectionate squeeze that almost made Diana start crying again from frustrated longing. Then abruptly the two of them jumped apart as if they had been caught playing doctor and nurse behind the woodpile. Dan Jacos was standing less than ten feet away, seeming to come out of nowhere. But, then, Diana's little performance had pretty much monopolized her and Sloane's attention.

"She was just a bit upset because she thought no one had decided to show," Sloane said. "You *are* a little late, you know."

"I had to make sure you weren't followed," Dan said.

"And?"

"It looked okay, but you never know. Carlyle says something is coming off. He smells it in the wind. He almost canceled you out again, buddy, even with little Miss Green in tow. I had to talk my head off to make him keep to his part of the bargain."

"Is he meeting us here, or is he somewhere up the line?"

"Carlyle, you mean?"

"Who else?" Sloane asked irritably.

"Well, actually, Carlyle sends his regrets, but...."

"We made a deal!" Sloane exploded.

"Hold your horses, buddy!" Dan held up his hands as if he expected a physical assault. "He knows you two had a bargain, and he's prepared to live up to his end of it. However, instead of giving you a personal tour, he's sent me along to stand in for him."

"You? You know where the plane is?"

"You might as well know, I was with the group that went in shortly after one of our scouts reported cargo still in the wreckage, but no way would I have taken you in without Carlyle's okay. Now that you've got that, and now that Carlyle is busy taking care of some things that are far more important to him at the moment than pointing out a few scraps of junk to you, I'm afraid you're stuck with me."

"You and Carlyle had better not be trying to pull anything funny," Sloane warned, his voice having a decidedly dangerous edge to it.

"The only thing funny around here is the fact that you seem to think Carlyle has the time to spend traipsing through the jungle with the likes of you," Dan said, shaking his head in disbelief. "Buddy, you and this mission are small potatoes to Carlyle. You're lucky he even bothered sending me."

Sloane glanced from Dan to Diana and then back to Dan again.

"And you'd better remember, on this trip, to keep your hands to yourself at all times!" Sloane warned him.

"Ah, love," Dan said theatrically. "Isn't it grand!"

"You had also better mind your own business!" was Sloane's response. "That is, if you're planning to go back to Carlyle in one piece."

"And you had better tell your girl friend here to get her hair cut. The way it is now, she's a walking invitation to every bug within a hundred miles that walks, crawls, hops or flies."

Diana reconfirmed right then and there that she didn't much like Dan Jacos.

The three moved slowly into a jungle that accounted for nearly two-thirds of the country's total area but held barely ten percent of its population, mostly crowded on the riverbanks in the cultivable land. It was a territory of vast canopied rain forest, stretching from the Madre de Dios River in the southeast all the way to the Putumayo River bordering Colombia in the north; a territory described by the locals and the fifty-odd known Indian tribes in the region as El Infierno Verde, the Green Hell.

Curtains of green vegetation filled with constant hum, buzz, squeak and screech of birds and insects were a backdrop for butterflies whose fluttering hordes made up pulsing clouds of yellow, blue, red, black and gold. Orchids of breathtaking beauty—some odorless, others spilling heady fragrance into the hothouse humidity of the air—dangled in profusion from palm, mahogany and Peruvian cedar. The damp closeness of the air was made more so by the claustrophobic effect of the jungle greenery pressing in from all sides.

It appeared a world isolated, a unique space on the planet revealing its wonders for the very first time: an illusion. "Over there!" Dan said, and pointed. Diana's gaze picked out a short stretch of mossy stones almost hidden by the long grass beside a stream. "Part of the old Incan highway system." He shifted their attention to more stones off to the other side. "Possibly what's left of a Unu Kancha, a religious temple for worship of the water. The Incas worshipped rivers, streams, waterfalls, even rainfall."

It was obvious to Diana that Dan, as well as Sloane, was acutely familiar with the civilizations that had been this way before them. With each step she came to appreciate him more fully as a man knowledgeable of his particular environment—but that didn't mean she liked him any better.

By later afternoon talking had become a chore; it was an effort even to put one foot in front of the other through the heat and the choking vegetation. "It must be ninety degrees!" Diana moaned, her blouse soaked and sticking to her skin.

"More like a hundred," Dan corrected.

It rained a total of three times in as many hours. Twice Diana hurriedly slipped into the plastic slicker Sloane had provided, but by the third deluge she didn't bother; the rain actually felt good as it bathed skin and clothes gone quickly dry in the interim between downpours. At times the water came in such volume it seemed as if it were being poured from giant buckets directly over Diana's head, that illusion intensified when overhanging leaves, quickly drenched, tipped like giant ladles to release virtual torrents of liquid.

By nightfall Diana was wet and exhausted, almost too overcome to eat the cook-in-the-bag beef stew that Sloane forced on her. "You have to keep up your strength, Diana," he said. "You can't get sick out here; it's not as if there's a hospital waiting around the next corner." So Diana ate, not even protesting when he said he would clean up the dishes. She spread her weary bones out in her sleeping bag and immediately went to sleep, aware of nothing until morning.

When she did struggle awake, it took her a while to remember just where she was.

"Diana? Diana? Diana?" It was Sloane's voice, close by.

"Mmm," she responded, enjoying the warm feel of his hand on her shoulder. How marvelous it was to be coaxed awake by his voice and sensuous touch!

"Come on, Diana, and please keep it cool. They're really friendly, and...." Who was really friendly? Her eyes popped open, not blinded by any sun, since the jungle canopy had snared all sunlight as efficiently as any spiderweb ever captured insects.

The first thing Diana saw was Sloane, the next thing was the Indians—five of them, decked out in a combination of native nakedness and modern clothing: two in tattered pants, three in loincloths; three in shirts, two bare chested; none wearing shoes. Their faces were painted with a series of diagonal red-and-blue stripes. She noticed that two were carrying rifles and the others had spears.

"They're not out looking for heads, Diana!"
Dan shouted from his position over with them.
"So don't look so much as if yours is in danger
of getting suddenly disconnected from its lovely
neck." He laughed, and so did all five of the Indians, who had teeth that were either stained or
missing.

"Who are they?" Diana whispered, reaching
for her bush jacket and slipping it on over the
blouse she had been too tired to remove the
night before.

"In Brazil we would call any Indian with such
a spear *tigrero*. *Tigre* being, of course, the
jaguar they hunt; the jaguar being no stranger
to my part of the continent, either." Sloane sat
down beside her. "Note the spears." The calm-
ness of his voice made Diana relax. "Strong
wooden shafts tipped with those tempered metal
blades, each blade about nine inches long with
that forward-curving crossbar at the base. Do
you know the purpose of the crossbar?" Diana
said that she didn't. "It keeps the cat at spear-
point distance once the blade has been securely
thrust home. No hunter, after all, wants to feel
the slashing fury of a wounded jaguar's razor-
sharp claws and fangs."

"What do the Indians want here?"

"They're hunting the jaguar," Sloane told
her. "Seems the big cat has killed two of their
villagers this past week, and last night got a pet
monkey."

"They think he's around here?"

"They *know* he's around here," Sloane said. "They lost two dogs to him this morning."

"Wouldn't we have heard something?" Diana asked.

"Dan and I did hear him," Sloane said. "You were dead to the world."

Diana didn't like the idea that she had been sleeping quite so soundly, completely unaware of a death struggle taking place in a section of jungle close by.

"This cat is a cunning one," Sloane said. "He has obviously had previous experience with both men and dogs, because he refused to make himself vulnerable by allowing the dogs to tree him. He knew how to search out a marshy place and jump from one hummock to another, leaving water in between to throw the dogs off. He also knew that by leaping in a wide arc to one side, over a small brook, he could double back, lie in wait and kill the dogs as they came sniffing his trail."

"I notice they were smart enough to bring along guns, too," Diana observed.

"It's doubtful, though, that they'll mess up the opportunity for a good kill with a spear to use one of those guns," Sloane said. "It's powerful medicine, you know, to face the jaguar with only a spear and kill him. It has become even more so now that the cats aren't as numerous as they once were."

The Indians stayed only a few minutes more, talking to Dan in their own tongue, then quietly leaving. Dan went to the fire, squatting to pour himself a fresh cup of coffee.

"Come on, Diana, let's get your bedroom picked up," Sloane said. Diana noticed for the first time that his and Dan's sleeping gear had already been loaded.

"Give you a little fright, did they?" Dan asked, coming over to Diana while Sloane was off arranging her things on the burro. "I must admit, they're hardly the kind of neighbors you're used to having pop over in the morning, now, are they? Luckily, they're civilized. A few years back their daddies would have sneaked in during the night, fighting like hell over the privilege of taking that pretty head of yours for shrinking."

"Damn it, Dan, keep your horror stories to yourself!" Sloane ordered, coming back from the burro with a couple of cereal and nut bars, which he handed to Diana. "Breakfast," he informed her. She ate the bars and sipped a cup of coffee while Sloane cut her hair, using his hunting knife.

She knew her hair had to be cut, and she actually had no qualms about having it done. One thing about hair—it always did seem to grow out again. It was just that she would have preferred to have someone other than Sloane do the job. Though, with Dan Jacos being the only other potential barber handy, Sloane was the best possible selection. Diana didn't want Dan near her, let alone fooling with her hair.

There was, however, something too sensual about the way Sloane's fingers lingered in her corn-silk strands as he cut them; something maddeningly exciting about the way his finger-tips, in the simple motion of brushing away clippings from the back of her neck, could thrill her. The emotions triggered by his skilled touch sent her mind wondering if she wasn't being just a little ridiculous to hold out for years of shared bliss when instead she might take advantage of what precious little time she had left now. Some people, after all, never did experience the thrill of true love in their lifetime, and here was Diana, throwing away a chance at happiness just because Sloane's love for her might be for today only—with no hope for tomorrow.

Diana was aware of the ease with which some women moved in and out of relationships with far less love than existed here. But it frightened her that she was even contemplating surrendering personal values that until now she had never questioned. But, then, she had never contemplated there being a man in her life quite like Sloane.

She was suddenly very glad Dan was traveling with them. Without his watching now, Diana knew she would have reached up to take Sloane's hand, bringing it to her lips to kiss its broad palm. Without Dan there she might have done all sorts of things for which she might very well have been sorry later.

She found that her mental anguish was reaching such a degree that it actually caused her physical pain. She had to fight back tears, knowing there would be no way she would be able to explain them to the others. Just when she couldn't bear the pain and the pleasure of Sloane's touch for one moment longer, he stepped away.

"There," he said, eyeing his job with evident satisfaction. "Not bad at all."

Oh, the haircut was fine. What was bad was that Diana wanted him so desperately but couldn't yet convince herself that all she would be risking would be worth it.

CHAPTER TEN

THAT EVENING they camped in a cul-de-sac, three sides of which were jungle in a natural weave so tight that Diana would have dared even a snake to slither through. Couched within the dark recess formed by the thick undergrowth, their camp faced outward, their fire separating them from the trail—and from anything that might have chanced a nightly stroll along that pathway.

Night, as always, had fallen fast, and the fire, while shedding light on the immediate circle, had a tendency to make shadows completely beyond its illumination even blacker than usual. Sloane was off with the burros, swallowed by that blackness. Dan, feeding wood to the devouring flames and sitting back on his heels, acquired an unworldly appearance from the flickering tongues of light that were caught and reflected by his eyes.

Diana's attention was momentarily drawn from Dan to a stretch of darkness beyond him. Although she didn't hear or see anything unusual, there was no mistaking the way her more primitive instincts began a sudden pulsation of fear upward along the length of her spine.

"You feel it out there, don't you, Diana?" Dan asked, the sound of his voice doing nothing to alleviate her anxiety. He had taken a candy bar out of his pocket and was peeling back the wrapper.

"Feel what out there?"

"The danger lurking just beyond the light of this camp fire," he said, crumpling the candy-bar wrapper and feeding it to the flames.

"I merely caught a chill," Diana said. "Please don't make a whole production number out of it."

A hunk of wood shifted, causing a shower of sparks to levitate toward a false sky of matted leaves and vines. "In reality the jungle isn't evil," Dan said softly. He had chocolate smeared on his lower lip. Sensing it was there, he licked it clean. "Neither is it good. It's merely a neutral ecological system, balancing itself on the basis of kill or be killed, survive or perish. We, having intruded in the game, must play by the existing rules." He stirred the fire, conjuring more sparks. Squatting on his haunches, bent slightly forward to give his back a hunched posture, he reminded Diana of Rumpelstiltskin from the childhood fairy tale.

"It's a game of chance played by all who enter here," Dan continued. "It's a giant maze, with many hallways, many doors. Select correctly and you go for days on end as safely as strolling down some simple country lane back home. Select wrongly, however, and you can find yourself confronted with jaguars that have sampled human flesh and acquired a taste for it, or with natives suddenly deciding to rebel against encroaching white men's ways in one final reversion to the primitive, or...." He shrugged.

"You certainly do have a way with the English language," Diana said, being facetious in order to hide her inner fury at having—even for a moment—allowed Dan to see she was afraid. She suspected men like him made a point of always searching out the fears of others and using that knowledge to prey on them. "You must have had some teacher!"

"My teacher worked for an oil company," Dan surprisingly volunteered. "He made it a point to be assigned to backward countries like Peru, where he could specialize in teaching all kinds of lessons to poor boys like me." He threw a stick into the fire, watching its brief moment of immunity prior to its becoming part of the general conflagration.

"Where is he now?" Diana asked, admittedly curious. "Back in his own country?"

"You really want to know what happened to him?" Dan challenged in a low voice, turning his fire-filled eyes more fully on her. Something about the way he asked left Diana with doubts about whether she wanted to know or not.

"I'll tell you what happened to him, Diana," he said. "I killed him." Diana cringed reflexively. "There are some things no man should have the right to be able to purchase from another. Where's the justice in forcing a child to become a commodity on the marketplace for survival? What kind of a world is it where a few crumbs of bread can buy you another human being who will do anything—*anything*—when faced with the threat of being dumped back on the garbage heap? And I *mean* a garbage heap, Diana. Do you know what a fruit bird is?"

Diana, still shocked by the insinuated horrors of this man's childhood, could only numbly shake her head no. "Well, *I* was once a fruit bird," Dan continued, "one of many children in many marketplaces who must compete with stray dogs and rats for pieces of spoiled fruit. Of course, on some days my mother used to wake us up before dawn and walk us to a fish cannery on the edge of the city. The battles fought on those days always included sea gulls and buzzards who were just as anxious for the fish heads as we were. Occasionally, though, we would catch a careless pelican, take it home and boil it for supper. But that was very seldom. Children could be killed in fights for a pelican. One of my brothers was."

Diana waited to see if he was joking, her gaze locked with his own. There was no smile on his face. "I was a very hungry child, Diana. Hungry all the time. My belly was often swollen, but it was empty nonetheless."

"I'm sorry," Diana said, knowing it was hardly sufficient.

Dan shrugged. "The Peru of my childhood was a country of swollen bellies, flaccid skin, hair faded to the color of straw. The Peru of my adulthood is very much the same, except my belly is no longer one of the swollen ones. Have you seen Lima, Diana?"

"Yes," she answered, although she thought she might have misheard his question, since it seemed out of context.

"The Plaza de Armas? The Torre Tagle Palace? The Museum of Art?"

"Yes."

"The Bayovar?"

"The Bayovar? No, I don't think so."

"No, I don't think so, either," Dan said. "It's a straw-mat shack settlement on Lima's outskirts. One of many such shantytowns circling the city, but very seldom pointed out to tourists."

"You live there?"

"In the Bayovar? No. The slums change. Actually, the place where I did live is now a quite respectable little neighborhood with clean streets and neat brick houses, running water and electricity. Not at all as it was when my family moved in and began 'mining' the garbage for food. No, nothing at all as it was when I was there. When I was there it was much like the Bayovar today. If you ever go back to Lima, Diana, you must make a point of going to the Bayovar. Peru, after all, isn't just the Plaza de Armas, the Torre Tagle Palace, the Museum of Art." He smiled. "Nor is it just the Tambo de Oro."

He slapped at a bug too small to be seen but not too small to deliver a painful bite, then wiped the sweat off his forehead with his left shirt sleeve. "By coming to Lima, my father lost his *chacra*," he said, "a small parcel of ground upon which we were able to grow a few bits of food when we were in the country. He lost it because someone had told him how much better city life was than eking out a living where he was. So what's a peasant to do in the urban sprawl, huh? He ends up going on the dole. Sometimes he gets bread from 'Food for Work' by quarrying rock and shale for the roads. More likely he gets handouts from the Catholic Relief Service or CARE. A proud man like my father doesn't live long without his pride, Diana. His wife doesn't live long without her man. His children don't live long without their parents."

There was a pregnant silence that Diana didn't have the faintest notion of how to interrupt diplomatically. She couldn't fathom why Dan was telling her all this. She certainly wished he hadn't, because she had actually preferred thinking of him as purely another grave robber, evil personified, with no past or future of interest: a creature who simply *was*. It disturbed her to realize he was more complex than she had ever imagined, and it disturbed her even more than she had allowed herself the luxury of biased judgments that weren't at all the stuff of which any good investigative reporter was made.

"You can start out life in Peru so far down, it takes one hell of a miracle for you even to survive, let alone pull yourself up and out," he went on. "You do what you have to do, whether it's selling yourself or selling a few metal trinkets from old graves. The latter is preferable, wouldn't you agree? Why, after all, shouldn't some Incan bauble be used to purchase a little more time for the living instead of being sealed up in a glass case in the Museum of Anthropology and Archaeology in memoriam for the dead? Ask any of the countless starving of Peru and see to what use they would like to see their ancestors' handiwork put in this, the twentieth century."

There was a slight sound as Sloane reappeared from the darkness. "The burros are a bit nervous," he said. "I think maybe they...." He stopped, apparently seeing something in the expression of Diana's face: something made even more disturbing by the flickering shadows cast by the fire. "Diana?"

"She's all right," Dan said, coming to his feet. "You must tell her that she shouldn't ask a question if she isn't prepared to hear the answer."

She was glad when Sloane didn't press immediately for any details. He proceeded, instead, to get out the packages of freeze-dried food for supper.

Halfway through the meal Dan suddenly stopped eating, his fork suspended in front of his mouth. "Something?" Sloane asked, more alert than Diana had obviously been, his voice a mere whisper.

Diana listened, still hearing nothing. Dan laid aside his plate on the ground by the fire and took his gun out of its holster. Sloane followed suit, and Diana became acutely aware of the weight of her own weapon on her hip. She dreaded even the thought of being put into a position of having to use it.

"Yooooooo!" came a sudden low and distant moan.

"What is it?" Diana asked, getting goose-flesh.

"Shh!" Dan commanded, cupping his right hand to his mouth. "Yoooo...yoooo... yoooo!" he responded. Although now the sounds were recognizably human, they still gave Diana chills.

"Yoooo...yoooo...yoooo!" came the reply.

Dan put his gun back in his holster, motioning for Sloane to do the same. "A friend," he said.

"A friend?" Diana asked incredulously. "What does he want? How did he know we were here?"

"Still asking questions, are you?" Dan chided, shaking his head in mock disbelief and coming to his feet. "I'd better go out and show him the way in."

"In the dark?" Diana asked.

"Your concern is appreciated," Dan said with a slight smile. "But I think I can manage."

In truth, Diana's concern hadn't been for Dan at all. Her concern had been for what might happen between her and Sloane once Dan left them alone. Her concern most of all was for what she might *want* to happen. She felt the heightened sense of excitement the moment he disappeared in the darkness. He had, after all, acted as a barrier between her and Sloane, an unknowing chaperon whose very presence had kept his charges toeing the line.

Diana nervously began picking up the eating utensils, rinsing them in water that Sloane had brought earlier from a stream across the trail. She couldn't look directly at him, fearing that her eyes might offer an invitation her mind and body weren't yet prepared to carry through to completion.

Sloane spread her sleeping bag near the fire, picking up his own bag and carrying it a few feet away, where he unrolled it but didn't crawl in. He sat on it thoughtfully watching the fire in front of him.

Finished with the dishes, Diana went over to her own bag, suddenly knowing what she was going to do. One part of her screaming yes, the other screaming no, she reached down, took hold of one corner of her sleeping bag and dragged it over to Sloane. "Mind the company?" she asked, her voice coming out decidedly breathless.

She was hurt when he didn't give an answer but just looked up at her instead. She had difficulty reading what was in his eyes, and figured he was merely suspicious. He certainly looked that way, as if her move had been a flagrant violation of their agreement, and perhaps it was. However, just because there existed a mere threat they might fall into each other's arms at any minute didn't mean they should have to spend the rest of their time together speaking *over* camp fires, *around* Dan, or *across* burros. They were two intelligent adults, not animals who couldn't control certain basic needs.

"Would you rather I moved back around the fire?" she asked, deciding there was little point in staying if he really objected. Against her better judgment she found exciting the idea that she might incite Sloane to stirrings of desire.

"Suit yourself," he said coolly, hardly the reaction she had been expecting. Diana was suddenly struck by the possibility that he was being cool to her for some reason other than that she had crossed the mutually agreed-upon boundary between them.

She busily straightened her sleeping bag, aligning it beside his, then sat down on it. She didn't know what he was feeling at that moment, but she was feeling definite excitement from having initiated this flirtation with danger. She had almost decided that the two of them had made too much of this impending, cataclysmic "unguarded" moment. Anyway, they certainly weren't showing any signs yet of having to fight each other off, for Sloane had not said anything more but returned his gaze to the fire.

"You think I was playing reporter with Dan, don't you?" Diana ventured finally.

"I didn't say that," Sloane replied, more than a little tenseness beginning to show along his jawline.

"I know you didn't say it, but it's what you're thinking, isn't it? You're thinking that since I couldn't get my hands on Carlyle, I'm grabbing at the next best information source available to me—Dan Jacos. Right?"

"What exactly did Dan tell you?" Sloane asked noncommittally.

"Nothing much, except that he had a pretty tough time of it as a child," Diana said, knowing—if she heard Dan right—that that was a gross understatement if ever there was one.

"Funny," Sloane said, his voice sounding very far away. "I've known Dan for about two years. I've known *of* him for longer than that. In all of that time he could have sprung full-grown from the sea for all I knew of his background. Yet he talks to you after only a few hours."

"I'm a...woman," Diana said. She had been going to say, "a reporter," but had decided against it. "It's sometimes easier for a man to talk to a woman than to another man, especially when he knows that woman is transient in his life."

Sloane didn't reply. He didn't look at Diana, either. "I really wasn't quizzing him, you know," Diana explained. "We were just talking, and what he had to say kind of slipped out. The truth is, he probably didn't even realize he was being quite so candid."

"Damn it, Dan isn't the point!" Sloane erupted, turning accusing eyes on her. "And I'll be damned if I'll keep on pretending that he is!"

"What is the point, then," Diana asked, her heart beating so loudly she thought for sure he could hear it.

"The point—*the* point—is that I am merely human, Diana," Sloane told her. "I hardly think it's fair of you to put temptation in my path, even if—giving you a giant-sized benefit of the doubt—you don't mean to do so."

"What's wrong with a little temptation?" Diana asked lightly with what she hoped was a disarming laugh.

"You are playing with fire, little lady!" Sloane informed her, all seriousness, not a suspicion of amusement in his voice. "So you had better pick up your bag and move it and yourself right back where you both were, unless you're one hundred percent sure you're prepared to burn more than your fingers. And you're not one hundred percent sure yet, are you, Diana?"

"I see no reason why we can't go about this like two civilized—"

"You want me civilized, then you move!" he

interrupted. "And I mean you move damned fast!"

She knew the moment he gave her the ultimatum that she really wasn't ready for what was on the verge of happening, so she came to her feet, gathering the lower part of her sleeping bag on one arm, the rest of the bag left to drag on the ground. In retreat or not, she had ventured closer to the brink than she had ever been before, and she was exhilarated by the experience.

She turned, immediately seeing *it* crouched there in the rim of twilight between the firelight and darkness, its eyes catching and holding the flickering reflection of the flames. The hypnotic sight of it took her breath away, this evil incarnate, worshipped by the Incas as a god, poised long and low in shadows that merged with its inky spots, the contrasting golden hues of its sleek pelt almost invisible. Jaguar: real lord and master of this territory, watching Diana, nothing separating them but a small space that could have been mastered easily with the springing release of tension now gathered in the rippling muscles of its powerful hind legs.

She couldn't imagine how it had got there, the undergrowth around their campsite having seemed impenetrable. Even the normally alert burros had failed to give warning. But there it was nevertheless, obviously more familiar with the intricacies of this jungle labyrinth than Diana could ever hope to be. It was there, holding her with its malicious gaze, filling her with a sense of danger that was sheer unadulterated fear bordering on panic. She felt in the innermost depths of her heart that she was going to die.

"Diana?" Sloane broke the sinister silence, obviously aware that something was wrong. She wished he would be still. The large cat hadn't moved, but that didn't mean it wasn't going to once it sensed it had been discovered by someone apt to do more than stand complacently by like a lamb ready for slaughter. It wasn't likely to wait idly for Sloane to draw his gun and shoot it.

"Diana?" Sloane said again, scrambling to his feet and seeing it, too. "Dear God!" he muttered. And as if proper incantations had been spoken, the beast was gone, vanished as if it had never existed; disappeared, as it had come, without a sound, leaving behind it a stench that was not the spoor of the animal but the exuded fear of the man and the woman who had seen the beast and had not missed the implied message that, though their time had obviously not yet come, the ruler of this domain could have them at any time of its choosing.

Diana groaned, the sound coming from low in her throat and emerging with soblike intensity from her lips. She had seen the revelation, discerned the nuances between danger...and *danger*; and there was little satisfaction in having stood on the brink to which that man-eater had pushed her. She felt unnerved by the experi-

ence, turning for comfort to the only one who
could really give it—the man she so desperately
loved. She still couldn't speak, her words, without coherent thoughts to form them, coming out
jumbled whispers.

"It's all right, Diana. It's all right," he kept
comforting, kept assuring. But it wasn't all right
at all! Death existed at every corner, in every
tree, under every rock. If the jaguar didn't kill
them, what about the snakes that masqueraded
as innocent green vines? What of the cutthroat
robbers of Incan graves? Sloane had known all
along that he and Diana might not survive these
dangerous ordeals, and Diana now saw and
knew that with a certainty, too. Seeing and
knowing, how could either of them continue to
deny what they both wanted? In fact, it was in-
humanly cruel for them to keep in check needs
that had built to the point at which they un-
ashamedly demanded satisfaction.

"Sloane, I..." she began. But his lips were
there to cut off her words and finish the
sentence for her, his body, heated as it was by
their mutual experience of danger, reaffirming
her own undeniable arousal. She moaned in
pleasure in his arms, her fears dissolving as she
savored the hot glide of his tongue and the low,
exciting purr that came from somewhere deep
down inside him.

His firm male lips once more claimed her
open mouth in a passionately devouring kiss
that threatened to draw the very essence from

Diana's being. In truth, this experience was a totally unique one: a world unto itself, sending her senses whirling deliriously to a different plane far more pleasurable than the region of fear they had inhabited in the horrible nightmare of a few moments before.

"Love me, Sloane...love me," she begged him as his mouth left hers to explore the soft and sensuous curve of her vulnerable throat.

"Yes, Diana...yes," he moaned, his lips like butterfly wings against the hollow at the base of her neck.

It was gunfire, not any lack of passion, that brought them apart at that moment when Diana thought for sure there was no longer a force on earth capable of separating them. And with the new danger represented by those shots, Diana's mind was sent reeling under the brunt of evil that seemed so intent on bombarding her from all sides. She was a mass of jumbled sensations. In a daze, she stood, her breasts heaving with the erratic breathing brought on by the combined assaults of danger and of love.

Dan Jacos stumbled suddenly into the firelight, his hair disheveled, his bush jacket torn, looking very much as Diana imagined an apparition from hell would look. "My God!" he said, "that cat has to be as big as a horse!"

Diana did the one thing she couldn't remember ever doing before. She fainted, not even realizing it was Sloane's strong and reassuring arms that were quickly there to break her fall.

Wanting to forget the horrors, possibly wanting to steer attention away from the fact that she had fainted, Diana's first question upon reviving concerned not the jaguar but the mysterious friend Dan had gone into the jungle to meet "He delivered his message and headed home," Dan answered.

"Dan has got instructions that he must leave us for good," Sloane interjected, and Diana immediately felt the impact of the message as tremors broke loose inside her. Having seen what could happen with Dan gone for a few minutes, she could anticipate with pleasurable dread what might happen if he were completely removed from the scene. She only hoped that Sloane would understand when she tried to tell him that certain past moments between them were best forgotten because of—or despite—their unrealized potential.

"What about the plane?" she asked, thinking she could somehow still hold Dan to his bargain. She knew full well what she and Sloane had almost done. If it had happened, there would have been nothing to do about it. The time, the place, the circumstances would have made it right; anyway, Diana would have been able to rationalize it that way—after a time. However, the moment of spontaneity was over, and Diana was helplessly back to her old lucid self, her need for a mutual commitment no longer overridden by extenuating circumstances.

"Don't worry about getting to the plane, Diana," Dan assured her, his look seeming to tell her that, like the jaguar, he could see into the depths of her being to read the real fears that were lurking there. "We'll reach it tomorrow evening."

TRUE TO HIS WORD, they were there the next day at nightfall, Dan pointing out in the fading light those pieces of wreckage that, like many Incan ruins in this jungle, initially could not be detected without a keen eye. "It's scattered over a fairly large area," he explained, "but there's a piece of the wing, and over there. . . ."

Sloane was intensely interested. If he could find positive identification of plane or pilot among these scattered and rusting pieces of a long-ago crashed aircraft, this would be the culmination of his dream, the final erasure needed to clear his family name. Diana was excited, too, since she had always known how much this moment would mean to Sloane: she proudly felt she had had a part in bringing Sloane's dream this much closer to realization.

However, her joy at the discovery was secondary to thoughts of what this moment really meant to her. On the one hand, it meant her hours with Sloane were now undeniably numbered; on the other hand, without Dan in attendance the nights with Sloane remaining to her were liable to hold far too many temptations. Her fears of the latter mounted when Dan sud-

denly announced that her first night alone with
Sloane might be arriving even sooner than expected. "I think I'll head out this evening," he
said, sending lightning bolts of fear directly to
her heart.

"Oh, surely not!" Diana protested, her voice
sounding so loud and strained she knew it
caused the curious looks both men were giving
her. "It would be pure lunacy for you to start
out before daylight, especially with that jaguar
out there fuming over the meal it lost last
night."

She had expected an argument, her mind racing to dig up any other logical reasons—she certainly couldn't tell him the truth—for having
Dan around to help her and Sloane safely
through at least one more night. "Maybe you're
right," he said, his words punctuated by
Diana's almost audible sigh of relief. "I'll make
far better time if I'm rested."

Staying on until morning, though, wasn't
staying on forever, and Diana knew she had successfully postponed the danger but not removed
it. As a result she spent the night more restless
than asleep, trying desperately to come up with
some reason why Dan should stay on. But there
wasn't one forceful enough to counter the fact
that Dan had been summoned to the side of
Dennis Carlyle; and when Carlyle made a de-
mand, it was obvious the members of his jungle
army were quick to obey.

She heard Dan stirring before dawn, and

listened as he went about making morning coffee. Crawling out of her sleeping bag, her bones
still complaining of the previous days' exertion,
she told herself that she might yet be able to
think of a last-minute excuse to make him stay.
In her heart, though, she knew she must now bid
farewell to this man who had played a signifi-
cant role in their expedition, in a different way
from Sloane. Now she knew things about Dan
that made him more to her than just a grave
robber, or just another man she might pass on
some city street. It wasn't, after all, only love
that could bind two people; memories could
bind them, too, and she and Dan had shared
memories.

Sloane stirred. Diana suspected he was
awake, although he made no move to get up,
perhaps able to sense that there should be private farewells between Dan and probably the
only person, man or woman, to whom he had
opened up in a good many years. At that moment Sloane had to know that Dan and Diana
were bound closer than he and Dan could ever
be.

She found Dan stripped to the waist and shaving. His body was thin but muscular. His skin
was laced with scars: one running from the left
side of his chest all the way down to his left hip,
another running diagonally across his flat
stomach. Diana would have liked to know the
history behind each of those memorials of battle, but she knew she never would.

He looked up briefly when she sat down close to him at the fire, his look not one of surprise but one that seemed to say that he, possibly like Sloane, had expected her to be there. "You look better without all the stubble," she told him. He looked younger, too, perhaps even in his thirties. Diana found it slightly shocking that she knew intimate things about this man's past without knowing commonplace things like his age.

He finished with the razor, one of the disposable type with a blue plastic handle, and wiped soap from his face. "Shaving, just in case of a funeral," he told her, causing a feeling of uneasiness to penetrate to Diana's core. She suspected whose funeral he was talking about, too, since, although much had gone unsaid, it wasn't hard to figure out that Carlyle's summons had something to do with the battle soon to be fought in this jungle for a cache of ancient Incan artifacts. "Manguella wouldn't have approved of my looking as scruffy around a lady as I have around you," he said, making it sound like an apology.

Diana would have liked to hear more about Manguella, a name merely dropped in parting, a woman who obviously had had some say in Dan Jacos's life, now relegated to the past tense. Dan, however, wasn't interested in immediately continuing with that line of conversation.

"What are you two going to do when I'm gone?" he asked her, squatted on his haunches like a native, facing her at eye level.

"Find Gary Holsteen's remains, bury them...." Her voice trailed off. She could tell, just by looking at Dan's expression, that his "do" hadn't referred to excavating the wreckage. He knew that she loved Sloane and had known even before she had admitted it. What was it he had told her in her hotel room at Machu Picchu? "So maybe you think more of Sloane than you let on, huh?"

"You think I don't know two people in love when I see them?" Dan asked. "Diana, I was so long without love, I can recognize it when I see it happening even between two birds in the trees." She couldn't answer, not knowing how to. "What happens if one of you dies later today?" he asked. "Just up and dies from whatever cause—snake bite, jaguar attack, bullet wound. What then? What if the two of you blow it?"

She would have told him about her need to have a commitment from Sloane, but somehow she didn't think he would swallow that argument at this point. Her suspicions were soon confirmed.

"Do you know how long I had with the woman I love, Diana?" Dan's voice was challenging, bitter. "Two weeks. Just two weeks. Yet without those two weeks of memories I think it would have been impossible for me to go on...."

He paused reflectively to stroke his lean jaw, his fingers rubbing slowly as if surprised to encounter skin that was suddenly smooth. Then he went on more gently but pointedly, eyes glittering at Diana.

"Some people, when they talk of love, when they speak of relationships, like to mention words like 'forever,' 'eternity,' 'until the end of time.' Take it from me, Diana, it's sometimes better to enjoy the seconds, minutes, days and, if you're lucky, weeks, or else you're liable to find yourself with nothing in the end. And if you think life can be lonely with only brief memories, it's nothing compared to the loneliness of reaching the end of the road without even those. I've known enough men—and women—who have got there to know, so don't cheat yourself. For God's sake, don't cheat Sloane, because what is he going to have when all of this is over and done? Family honor? Sense of adventure? Well, granted those are something, but I doubt very much if they'll be enough."

She wanted him to tell her something about Manguella, but realized she couldn't ask because she was on the verge of tears and words were at that moment impossible. He told her, though, without the question.

"She died not too far from here," he said, then glanced down at the ground between his legs, trying to hide glimpses of emotion that were managing to penetrate his usually unreadable face. Finally he was able to continue. "She and I were a lot alike, Diana. I mean, about learning how to survive. We had both done some things in our lives of which we weren't particularly proud—although I suspect she had had an even rougher time of it than I had. I never did get to know her all that well, you know. Not the way you get to know someone you live with and love for a very long time. We weren't married all that long. Just two weeks before she was murdered."

"Murdered?" Diana's response had been automatic, wrenched from her by shock.

"We were taking a shipment of merchandise out by mule for Carlyle. We were ambushed in a small ravine about fifty miles east of here."

"Ambushed by Raphael Sipas?" Diana asked, her emotions barely under control.

"No," Dan said. "Though Sipas would have been right there had he known anything about that particular shipment. It was soldiers who ambushed us, no doubt having been informed that our cargo of artifacts would be better put to use by some museum."

"Your wife worked for Carlyle, too?"

"Oh, you mustn't blame Carlyle!" Dan insisted, seeming genuinely sincere in his defense of a man Diana had come to loathe without ever meeting. "Manguella and I both knew the dangers. Had we succeeded in getting the shipment out, Carlyle would have rewarded us handsomely."

Diana must have shown her disbelief.

"We did a job for Carlyle," he continued.

"We had the satisfaction of knowing we could do that job well—in most cases. Which gave us pride. I think it was easier for Manguella to die with her pride intact, working at a job she was good at doing. There are certainly less satisfying ways of dying, many of which I have had the misfortune to witness."

He tossed the shaving water on a fire that quickly hissed the soapy liquid to steam. "I only regret that when I die there will be no one to know that Dan and Manguella Jacos made it out of the shantytowns of Lima to find something better with each other."

"I'll know," Diana said, not wanting him to die.

"And maybe that's why I've told you," he said, coming to his feet and looking sadly toward the east.

By then it was time for Dan to go, and he and Diana were joined by Sloane, who apparently sensed they had said all they were going to say. For a moment Diana was afraid Dan would take up with Sloane where he had left off with her, but she should have known better, since it was now obvious to her that Sloane and Dan were strangers and probably always would be, cut off from really knowing each other by a barrier that was even more inconquerable than whatever it was Sloane and Diana had thrown up between themselves.

"Be forewarned," Dan said in parting. "This section of jungle is going to be even more dangerous than what you've already passed through."

When he left he took both of the burros with him, leaving Sloane and Diana their provisions. "It's called commandeering," he said, and Diana, expecting some kind of protest from Sloane, was surprised when he gave none.

"We'll be okay," Sloane told her. Diana had become rather fond of their pack animals, calling one Bunny, because of its ears, and the other one Patch, because of a black discoloration on its rump. Quite aside from that blossoming attachment, however, was the worry of just how she and Sloane were going to manage getting out of the jungle without them. She had no desire to attempt even a fraction of the workload the burros had saved them. "We're going out in real style," Sloane told her. "We're flying."

"Flying?"

"Sounds inviting, doesn't it? Believe me, I have no more desire to make that long trip back on foot than you do."

"But how?"

He walked over to their pile of supplies and produced from it a small black box, holding it up for Diana to see. "We go back to that big clearing we crossed yesterday morning, activate this electronic marvel, and a helicopter waiting for the signal will pick us up in far less time than it took us to get in here."

"Why didn't we fly in?"

"For one, we were playing by Carlyle's game

rules. By giving us a little exercise, he ended up with two more animals to transport his goods. For two, flying in would have alerted everyone for miles, and with the clandestine happenings going on in this area between Carlyle and his competition, there's no way I wanted to red-tag our activities."

They didn't talk about the trial they knew was coming up for both of them at nightfall, although they obviously shared an awareness of it as Sloane prepared for an initial sweep of the wreckage in search of that part of the downed plane containing a registration number. He was looking, too, for what was left of Gary Holsteen's remains, the thought of which made Diana shudder.

"It's now eight o'clock," he said. "I promise to check back with you between one and two. That way you won't have to start worrying unless I don't show up on time. If you see anything before I'm back, keep hidden. If you find yourself in a bind, fire three shots in quick succession. If you hear me firing three quick shots, on the other hand, you and this little black box are to get yourselves back to that clearing and get out the minute the chopper sets down. Got it?"

"What about you?"

"If you hear three shots out of me, it's likely there won't long be a Sloane Hendriks to worry about."

Diana certainly didn't like the implications of that. "What happens if one of you dies later today?'' Dan had asked her that very morning. However, since there were no immediate signs of danger, and since the prospect of flying out had decidedly brightened her spirits, Diana managed to make it through the morning troubled mainly by thoughts of how each hour gone by found her and Sloane coming closer and closer to a confrontation. She was back to having her old doubts; the night was liable to be very unpleasant for both of them, especially if she couldn't make Sloane understand her feelings about the necessity of mutual commitment.

He came back at one-thirty right on schedule, and the two lunched on raisins and nuts. He hadn't yet found the cockpit, but he wasn't discouraged, either. "I'm beginning to get the general gist of the scatter pattern," he told her. "Certain pieces are leading me to certain others."

Diana wished him luck as he set out again, not knowing how he could make head or tail out of anything in that choking maze of greenery. She had volunteered, albeit hesitantly, to help him in his search for Holsteen's remains, but her realization that she hadn't the faintest notion of what to look for, coupled with Sloane's reluctance, had decided them both against it. She picked around their campsite, which was a secluded little nook in a great pile of rocks, and prepared herself for another few hours of anguishing replay of how she imagined that evening with Sloane would go. No matter how many variations she came up with, she was always left with the feeling that she would either successfully resist his advances and regret it later, or succumb to them and regret it later. And then there was the recurring idea that he might not make any advances whatsoever—which Diana found herself considering the most unnerving possibility of all.

To say that the sudden sound of a man's voice sent her into panic would have been an understatement. She knew Sloane's and Dan's voice when she heard them, and this was definitely neither. It was not only unfamiliar, but speaking Spanish, something about the heat: *"El calor es insoportable."*

"¡Sí!" came the reply.

If one man had been enough to send her scurrying into concealment, the second man's presence definitely terrified her.

But where were they? Diana shifted her position. Peeking around a large boulder, she saw them. They looked like characters out of a movie, complete with cartridge belts crossed over their chests and backs. Their machine guns were propped against a rock beside them as they lighted the cigarettes they had stopped to smoke.

Diana felt close to hysteria. What if they saw her? It was highly doubtful they were friendly. Frantically she searched her mind for anything she or Sloane might have left lying around to indicate their presence. The supplies were concealed a few feet from where Diana was crouched, quite out of sight of the two men. The sleeping bags were, too. What was left of the fire luckily wasn't visible to them, either.

Diana unsnapped the leather flap that held her gun secure in its holster. Even if she felt she stood little chance against two men with machine guns, at least any shots would warn Sloane of the danger.

After what seemed an eternity, the two men got up and headed back down the rocks, disappearing into the underbrush. She looked out over the jungle, searching for signs of Sloane, fearing they might have seen him, captured him—or even worse. Then she told herself to be calm, not to let her imagination run away with her, and waited....

By the time Sloane arrived with the gathering nightfall, Diana almost shot him. Because by that time she had endured a whole line of armed men threading their way through the jungle mere feet from where she had been forced to hide in a state of virtual panic. She had thought for sure they were going to discover her.

"Diana?" Sloane asked. He couldn't mistake the fact that something was wrong, quite aside from the drawn gun in Diana's hand. Her expression was obviously that of a woman under terrible stress. She dropped the gun and came into his supporting arms, her body trembling with relief at seeing him alive, at feeling his warm, hard flesh against her own.

Oh, what fantasies her imagination had conjured in the long hours of his absence!

"I thought they had killed you," she moaned softly.

"Who?" Was it possible he didn't know?

"There were so many of them," she said.

He tried to push her at arm's length, but she wouldn't let him. "Hold me...hold me...hold me." Her hands grabbed the back of his shirt, her cheek pressing into his chest.

She hadn't been this frightened when she'd faced the jaguar. No. This was a new degree of fear. Because, she now realized, she had been more afraid for Sloane's safety than her own, even though Sloane was better equipped to survive in these hostile surroundings.

"Diana, it's all right...it's all right," Sloane said, his voice soothing. His right hand came up, gently sweeping her short blond hair. She lifted her face to his, her mouth trembling. Would he still her uncontrollable trembling with a kiss?

He thrust her away with a force that left Diana's fingernails aching from having been wrenched free of their hold on his shirt. He held her extended, only his hands touching her where they were clamped strongly on her upper arms. He looked angry, and she couldn't understand why.

"Snap out of it!" he ordered, his voice like a slap across her face.

She felt her eyes beginning to water. "I

thought you were dead!" she screamed, yanking herself from his grip with a force that made her stumble.

Sloane automatically moved foward to catch her, but she slapped him away. "Don't touch me!" she said. "You don't have to, you know, if you suddenly find it so distasteful."

"Diana...."

"I said, don't touch me!" she commanded loudly, then fell back against a boulder, breathing hard. She tried to wipe the hot tears from her eyes, but they kept coming.

Sloane stood there looking as if he didn't know she was crushed by his rejection. "I'm sorry," she said. "Foolish of me, wasn't it? Losing control, I mean. I should have known you would be all right. Big, strong Sloane Hendriks can take care of himself, can't he? Oh, yes."

He looked at a loss. He took another step toward her, but came no farther. "I'm fine... I'm fine... I'm fine," Diana said, still not able to clear all of the tears from her eyes. Damn it, why couldn't she quit crying? "I see you're fine, too," she said. "Oh, yes, very fine. Why did I even suspect you might be out there somewhere dead?"

He looked as if he were going to say something, but Diana cut him short. "Actually, I wasn't worried about you at all," she said. "I was obviously worried about myself, about poor Diana Green." She put both of her hands over her face, her fingers growing quickly wet in the tears trailing down her cheeks.

"Diana, please don't cry," he coaxed. "Just try calmly to tell me what happened."

She dropped her hands, folding her arms across her breasts in order to contain the savage beating of her heart. She watched him through the blur of her tears. "I thought you were dead," she said simply, the softness of her voice more able to convey her inner turmoil than hysterical screaming would have been. She must have looked as if she were going to collapse, because he rushed over to her, bending down, slipping his arm behind her legs to lift her free of the ground. He carried her to his sleeping bag, dropping with her to his knees. He laid her back on the bag, still keeping her body couched against his own.

"I love you," she said, her arms sliding upward around his neck as if to assure herself that he was real.

"Diana," he said, his voice a low moan, his face burying itself against the soft curve of her throat, his moving lips a sensuous flutter that finally ceased at the spot where her blouse had pulled free of her shoulder. "Oh, Diana... Diana." His lips pressed hers gently, tenderly, Diana's mouth answering with a warm, demanding need.

She closed her eyes, feeling something inside her unfold like petals of an exotic flower teased open by the caressing sun. His kiss became more intense, parting her lips beneath the pressure, his breath becoming enticingly one with her own.

It wasn't only his mouth but his lean, hard body against her that roused her softness into willing response. She felt and tasted the glide of his tongue. She smelled the heady muskiness of him. She heard the passion-choked timbre of his voice as he whispered at the breaking of their kiss, "Diana, I do so...so...want you!"

Diana's hands trailed around his neck, down into the V of his open collar She unfastened the buttons of his shirt, parting the material with her fingers, unveiling the muscled expanse of hairy chest and stomach. Her curved palms cupped his sides, riding playfully along his hard ribs, his sensitive skin. At his belt she found the securing buckle and unfastened it.

He pulled away, but only to remove his boots. He stood, taking off his shirt and dropping his trousers.

Her gaze was entirely held by the startling classical purity of his male nakedness: the graceful symmetry of his muscles and tanned flesh. He came down to her, her renewed touch telling her he was real and not cold bronze, his flesh hot against her fingertips, making her shiver with the miracle of its velvety hardness.

Requesting and receiving permission in a language beyond words, Sloane undressed her, his hands gentle, with calluses sensuously rough against the smoothness of her skin. He leisurely explored her with his tongue and with his fingers, in ways no man had ever done before him.

"Oh, Sloane, yes!" Diana groaned as his hard flesh claimed her soft, the two literally becoming one: pieces of the same jigsaw; the Oriental yin and yang; halves of a coin, once cut and strung around lovers' necks, now completely whole again.

"Love me, Sloane," she whispered, made more alive by his hands, mouth and thrusting body than she had ever been before. "Love me!"

Sloane loved her, his large hands molding her hips, moving with them as Diana responded willingly beneath him.

Finely tuned to each other's every movement, they were willing voyagers caught in a fiery vortex that whipped them, buffeted them, played with them and finally enticed them into a mutual consummation of passion that exploded in a spiraling holocaust.

CHAPTER ELEVEN

"I SUPPOSE I SHOULD THANK DAN," Diana said.

Their sleeping bags had been zipped together, and within the resulting cocoon she was aligned against Sloane, thrown slightly over him. Her left arm wrapped him, her cheek resting so closely against his chest that she could feel his finally quieting heartbeat.

"Well, that's gratitude for you," Sloane said, his right hand combing through the silky blondeness of her short hair. "Where's *my* thanks?"

"Don't be tacky!" Diana retorted.

When her lips moved, they were tickled by his curly black chest hair.

"Then, maybe you would like to tell me how Dan had anything to do with this?" he teased, his fingers passing down along the nape of her neck and onto her back.

"Did you know his wife was killed not far from here while bringing out a load of artifacts for Carlyle?"

"I didn't even know Dan had ever been married," Sloane admitted.

"They had been married only two weeks,"

Diana said. "When he told me that, I got to
thinking how quickly we could die out here.
Hearing that made me conscious of my vulner-
ability, more so than knowing a jaguar might be
stalking, or a snake waiting for me around the
next bend in the trail, or men lining me up in the
sights of their machine guns."

"So you decided you would start cashing in
on my goodness before one of us got knocked
off, huh?"

"You!" she accused, and tried to push away.
She didn't, however, try very hard, succumbing
easily to his efforts to keep her right where she
was.

"I was only kidding," he said, although
knowing his statement was superfluous.

"Well, don't even kid," she said, snuggling
closer.

His body was warm and toasty as the jungle
grew even darker around them.

His right hand brushed Diana's hair to one
side. "Do you know when I first fell in love with
you?" he asked. "At the Tambo de Oro."

"I thought you told me you would have sat
down with any lonesome woman who looked as
if she might be wanting male company."

"Is that what I said?"

"Yes," Diana confirmed, and laughed.

"So, possibly I didn't know it was love
then—but I did know after Cuzco. You can't
imagine how excited I was when Dan told me
Carlyle wanted me on the train to Machu

Picchu, knowing you were scheduled to be on it, too."

"Why didn't you tell me, then?"

"For the same reason I was so willing to convince myself that you wanted to come along on this trip just for a news story. For the same reasons the two of us have discussed before."

Diana didn't want to recall those last reasons—not now when she had so successfully managed to cast them aside, pretending they had been dissolved like ice in the heat of their passion. Sloane, though, seemed determined to broach the subject, undoubtedly feeling it was more honorable and realistic not to delude themselves into thinking their lovemaking had solved their problems. He might have found the plane, might even come to identify Gary Holsteen as its pilot, restoring the good name of the Hendriks family, but he was still as close to bankruptcy now as he had been, and certainly no closer to being able to make a commitment.

"I'm weak, Diana, God, how I'm weak! Weak enough to make excuses for my stumbling in, unheeding of the consequences. What kind of a man is that for you to love? One who hasn't got the willpower or the control to save either you or himself from the heartache we face."

SHE WEPT until there were no tears left, until her sobs were dry and tore at her insides. The darkness drew more closely around them, matched by the darkness slowly closing in on Diana's heart.

It was hours later when, still unable to sleep, Diana heard the distant, alien sounds suddenly punctuating the jungle's night music. "Thunder?" she whispered softly, thinking Sloane might be awake, too.

"Man-made thunder," Sloane answered, his arms drawing her nearer.

"I love you," Diana said, a chill taking root and sunbursting quickly throughout her body.

"I'm getting you out of here tomorrow!" he told her. "I certainly had no intentions of getting you involved in a bloody war...."

The gunfire continued until almost dawn. However, when the two of them got up the next morning, and Sloane began packing, Diana informed him that she wasn't going.

Sloane sat back on his heels, giving her a look she couldn't read, and then continued packing.

"I'm serious," she said. "I did a lot of thinking last night."

"So did I," he said. "And we're getting you out of here today!"

"I know you're strong," she said. "But how far do you think you're going to get carrying a kicking woman over your shoulders?"

He stopped what he was doing, once again looking up at her, his face wrinkled in a frown.

"How far away was that gunfire?" Diana asked.

"It's hard to tell in the jungle," Sloane said. "The underbrush muffles and distorts sounds."

"What if it was as far away as it sounded? What are the chances of the fighting really spilling over into our small piece of jungle?"

"According to Dan, the chances are too damned great!" he said, coming to his feet. "And Dan was certainly in a position to know." He walked over to her, standing tall before her, drawing in his breath in an apparent attempt to intimidate her with his sheer size. "Now, shall we forget this silliness and get going?" he asked.

Diana walked away from him, leaning against a rock, folding her arms defensively across her chest. "I'm not going," she declared.

"Damn it, Diana, why not?" he asked. His previous manly bluff having failed, he was now looking like a frustrated little boy.

"There's simply too much involved here," she said, knowing in her heart that she wasn't referring only to his being on the verge of finding the evidence he sought. She was really more interested in prolonging her time with him, knowing that once he was out of this jungle, he would be out of her life forever. She was actually jealous of even those two weeks of marriage Dan had managed to share with Manguella; Diana and Sloane had had only one night of love.

"What you're looking for has to be around here somewhere close, doesn't it?" she cajoled. "It has to be just a matter of time before you find it."

"Diana, I can always come back now that I know where the crash site is, can't I? Come back when it's safer. Come back when I don't find myself going weak every time I think of what could happen to you."

"But that would make what I've done so far seem worthless," Diana argued.

"How do you possibly figure that?" he asked, genuinely incredulous. He walked over to her, reaching out for her, pulling her into his arms. "Without you I still wouldn't have the faintest notion of where the plane had gone down," he said, his lips moving against the base of her neck, his breath warm and exciting. "Without you there would now be no possibility of my coming back. So please get all of that silly stuff and nonsense out of your head!" He kissed her lightly on the cheek and stepped away.

"What about Carlyle?" Diana asked. She was a newspaper reporter, used to looking at things from more than one angle. "You think he's going to let you come back again—without paying for the privilege?"

"What Carlyle doesn't know isn't going to hurt him, is it?" Sloane pointed out.

"What Carlyle doesn't know but finds out is liable to hurt you, though," Diana countered.

"Diana, Carlyle doesn't own this jungle!"

"Well, you'll pardon me if I seem to see every indication that he certainly has a good deal to say about what does and does not go on here."

"So, if I have to, I'll pay him."

"With what?" Diana asked. "You've already mortgaged everything you own, and don't bother telling me you'll dig up the cash somewhere, because by the sounds of it you won't soon be able to afford any more excursions like this one, no matter how admirable your intentions are."

"Damn it!" Sloane said in obvious frustration. He broke away from her. "You're impossible!"

"And *you're* wasting valuable time arguing with me when you could be spending it out sifting through the wreckage."

Sloane paced three steps in one direction, two in another, then stopped. "Two days," he said. "Just two days. At the end of which, whether I've found anything or not, we put our tails between our legs and get out of here—sooner if the fireworks get any closer."

"Two days it is," Diana agreed, pleased she had bought herself that much time. Two days weren't two weeks, but in two days she might yet convince Sloane that she would gladly marry him despite his poverty. He came back to her, taking her in his arms and kissing her hungrily, his lips lingering, then reluctantly pulled away. He pointed out a distant section of jungle dominated by an exceptionally large tree and told her he had found some indication that what he was looking for might be there.

The minute he walked into the jungle, Diana's

sense of accomplishment at having persuaded him to stay was dampened by the unsettling suspicion that she was being watched, had possibly been watched all morning—maybe even the previous night and throughout the day before. Watched by something so stealthy it could actually pass close by nervous burros without being detected. She wasn't consoled, either, by her intuition that the watcher was animal, not human. In fact, the idea that the beast she had faced by firelight was out there, having followed her to spy on her now, was so fearsome a thought that she felt sick to her stomach at the mere prospect. She had, after all, been lucky once, had gone to the brink, confronted the malevolence and survived. Such feats of magic didn't often happen twice: she and Sloane were still in the jaguar's natural domain, still forced to follow its rules or perish in the violation.

There was sudden movement behind her. She turned automatically and, expecting to see the creature gone airborne in its leap to claim her, found even the hint of her scream choked off by her overpowering fear. What she saw instead was a cause for conflicting emotions: a flooding of relief that there was no adversary, and a surge of concern over the image before her. "Dan?"

He stood there, his hair ratted and filled with broken pieces of twig and underbrush, his face filthy and streaked with nasty gashes, his jacket even more tattered than it had been. His right hand gripped his left shoulder, his fingers gone pink against a blossoming red stain.

"Hello, Diana," he said, so calmly she thought for a moment her eyes and ears were relaying conflicting messages. However, when he collapsed where he stood, she knew this was real and she knew he was hurt.

She rushed over, dropping to her knees beside him. He had fallen into a slightly curled position, and she rolled him to his back. As she did so his hand fell away from his shoulder, revealing fully the bloodstain he had been trying to cover. Hurriedly she took off her jacket, making a pillow to cradle his head. She tried desperately to recall anything she had ever learned about first aid, remembering none of it. Despite her previous escapades, she knew nothing about the treatment of gunshot wounds.

She unbuttoned his shirt—his jacket was already pretty much ripped away—and began peeling back the cloth to reveal his hard, scar-striated body. Seeing the bullet wound turned out to be anticlimactic: it appeared as nothing more than a small oozing puncture in his tanned skin.

Diana glanced up nervously, surveying the jungle, knowing *it* was out there, watching and scenting the life leaking out of this wounded man. She was close to panic, but managed to will herself into remaining calm. She had to think this out thoroughly—except, by the looks of Dan, she really didn't know if she had time.

He obviously needed help that she didn't have the skill to give.

Her mind sorted quickly through her alternatives. Three quick shots of her gun would bring Sloane...and also everybody else in the area; for unless Dan had walked a long way, the chances were very good that the enemy was near. She could stay put, hoping for the best, and possibly watching Dan die when she could have been doing something to save him. She could leave him and go for Sloane, but then the bleeding would be liable to attract every animal around that....

Dan groaned and opened his eyes. His pupils were slightly dilated, but he seemed to recognize Diana, because he actually smiled. "Sorry for being a nuisance," he said. "I just didn't much fancy dying, clean-shaven or not."

If that had been an attempt at humor, Diana was too frightened to laugh at it. "How bad is it?" she asked, hoping he had enough experience with this sort of thing to know.

"Not too bad, I should imagine," he said, his words slurred. He licked his lips, tried to smile, but was obviously in pain. He shut his eyes, and Diana thought for sure she had lost him again, her heart in her throat even after his eyes opened once more. "Sloane will probably know what to do," he said. "I suppose he's busy at the moment foraging through his precious pile of junk, huh?"

"He said to fire three quick shots if I needed help."

"Oh, for God's sake, let's *not* do that," Dan said, giving another low groan in punctuation. "That would really bring the scavengers running."

"I do know where he is," Diana added, thinking that was probably an exaggeration. The only thing she had to go by was a large tree he had pointed out in the distance. "Do you think you'll be all right while I'm gone?"

"That depends upon how long you're gone, doesn't it?" Dan said, a crooked smile indicating another attempt at humor. He probably sensed Diana was near panic, and was trying to put her at ease.

"I'll be as fast as I can," Diana promised, removing his gun from its holster and checking to make sure it was loaded. She handed it to him after helping him to a sitting position. Then off she hurried in the direction Sloane had taken earlier, turning back briefly to see Dan manage a weak wave.

She lost sight of the tree for which she was headed, finding it again, losing it. She could see no sign that Sloane, or anyone else, had ever passed that way before. Branches reached out and snagged her hair and clothing; large tree roots reared out of the ground as if they had a conscious malicious intention of snaring the toes of her boots. She watched for snakes, knowing her hurried progression through the undergrowth would hardly give them an opportunity to get out of her way. She stopped finally, panting, getting her bearings, since there would be nothing gained if she were to get lost. The experiences of the past few days of jungle travel helped her now to pinpoint certain landmarks. Every so often she paused long enough to gauge her position.

Suddenly she was again sensing the hair-raising nearness of the jaguar, actually expecting to see it coming around any bush, crouched in any tree. She was superstitious because of her savored moments with Sloane. Irrationally, she felt that the jungle cat was out to take every advantage of the extra opportunities Diana had given it by stealing two more days in its jungle with the man she loved. Something caught one of her feet, tripping her. She felt herself falling, took a few steps in the hopes of regaining her balance, then went down, luckily into a pile of soft earth.

She had landed not two feet from a rough cross made from broken tree limbs. Hung over the upright pole was a tarnished identification bracelet with a name still legibly engraved on it: Gary Holsteen.

"Diana?" She turned toward the safety represented by that voice, seeing Sloane. Still dirt covered from burying Gary Holsteen's remains, he was obviously very surprised to see her. She scrambled quickly to her feet, running to him, allowing herself to be taken into the secure haven offered by his muscled arms, certain nothing could ever harm her there—nothing.

She told him about Dan, and they immediately returned to find him conscious—if barely. Using water Diana brought from the nearby stream, and some antibiotic powder he produced from a small first-aid kit, Sloane washed and dressed the wound, ripping one of his spare shirts into bandages to bind it.

"I don't think it's too serious at the moment," he told Dan, "and I doubt it will be if we can get you out of here and to a doctor. The bullet is definitely still in there, but I'd personally feel safer turning its removal over to a professional who knows what he's doing when he goes in after it."

"Better make that a doctor who makes house calls," Dan joked, looking and sounding better even if his eyes still had a decidedly glassy sheen. Diana mentioned the device to summon the helicopter. "It's not going to do us much good unless you're planning to have it swing down and pick us up from the treetops," Dan told her. "Because a chopper turning up over any clearing along the way we came in is going to be shot down before it can set down. At this point neither Carlyle nor his competition is going to stand for even the suspicion of reinforcements being brought in for the other side, and there's enough artillery out here at the moment to take on the whole Peruvian army and air force, with a damned good chance of winning."

"There's more than one clearing in the jungle," Diana assured him. "If not back the way we came, then somewhere else farther on."

"I hope it's within easy walking distance," Dan said, "or I don't think I'll make it."

"You'll make it," Sloane encouraged him, giving him a pill to ease the pain and allow him some sleep.

"You making any guarantees?" Dan asked, handing back the tin cup from which he'd been drinking water.

"You walked this far with that bullet in you," Sloane pointed out. "What's a few more miles?"

"You're all heart," Dan said, settling back. Diana adjusted the jacket still folded under him, and stayed with him until he seemed to be asleep. She went over to Sloane, who was looking back toward the spot where Diana had known such relief in looking up from Gary Holsteen's grave to see Sloane standing there.

"Congratulations, by the way," she said finally, getting the impression, and saddened by it, that he didn't even seem to know she was there.

"Congratulations?" he echoed, not turning toward her but keeping his gaze focused on that distant stretch of jungle. She tried to pinpoint what held his interest, seeing only that same large tree that had earlier acted as her guide in finding him.

"It was your father's plane?" she asked,

although she felt her question superfluous. "The identification bracelet proved it, didn't it?"

"Oh, yes," he said, hardly showing the enthusiasm she would have expected from a man who had just devoted so much time, energy and money to removing the stigma from his family name. Unless, of course, he was as saddened as she was by the knowledge that his success had only hastened the pain that was destined to accompany their moment of final parting.

He turned toward her finally. "I have to go back out there, Diana," he said, although she couldn't believe what she was hearing. "At least for this afternoon. There's little sense in leaving until morning anyway, not with Dan in the condition he's in at the moment, and when we go into deeper jungle, looking for a safe clearing, we'll need all the daylight hours we can get."

"Why do you have to go back out there?" Diana asked, thoroughly confused. "Surely you don't need any further proof that it was Holsteen at the controls of the plane?"

"I just have to go," he said, apparently prepared to give no other explanation than that. "It's important, believe me."

"I believe you," she said, giving him that much, yet suddenly fearful almost to the point of physical illness. The risk she had taken was enormous—not only the physical risk, but the risk of her heart and her values. It occurred to her that her relationship with Sloane might have been based on lies from its very inception. If Sloane hadn't come to find and identify Gary Holsteen's remains, what had he come for?

"And you can't tell me why it's so important?" she pressed, hoping he would reconsider and give her an explanation that would make everything crystal clear.

She thought for a moment he was going to tell her; the look on his face indicated a sifting and sorting of thoughts, a weighty decision. "I can't tell you now," he said, and she was unbelievably disappointed. "Maybe someday." The way he said "someday" didn't give any indication whether it would be tomorrow or next year, and the way things now stood, the two of them had precious few "somedays" left.

"I see," she said, not seeing anything. If he loved her—if he truly loved her, had not just said he loved her—then she felt there was no reason he couldn't confide in her now. She couldn't imagine what was out there, anyway, that was suddenly so important to him—and possibly so awful—that he was afraid to reveal it even to her. It was more frightening to wonder if that something was what he had really been looking for all along.

"By all means go back," she told him stiffly. If he did go without telling her why, there would go with him a vital part of their relationship. Something would die out there and in dying would cause a breach between them bigger than all the miles between Washington and Brazil. Already Diana could sense a widening gap, and while she couldn't deny she still loved him, she felt she had every right to be hurt by the growing suspicion that he had used her, tricked her into lending her support to a cause that wasn't noble at all.

By the time he returned later that afternoon, she was still suspicious. In fact, in the thought-filled interlude between his leaving and returning, during which even her continued fear of being watched by the jaguar had faded in importance, she had become more adamant in her belief. No real love had ever been based on a foundation of lies and deceit. Her heart paining her, she told herself it was better things had turned out this way. Now she could make a clean break in the face of his deceptions

What upset her all the more on his return was the way he appeared to be going about his business as if nothing whatsoever had changed between them, even going so far as to greet her with a disturbingly enthusiastic kiss when he emerged from his mysterious afternoon's jaunt in the underbush. She responded more eagerly than she would have liked. But the seed of distrust had been sown, and his nonchalance, even his vigorous kiss, would not change her mind.

Whether he had located whatever it was that had pulled him back out into the plane wreckage, she didn't know; he certainly didn't give any intentional hints of it to Diana. She, however, couldn't help having her own suspicions regarding his failure or success, since he announced that they *would* be leaving the next day. He seemed to move with a kind of controlled buoyancy as he went about gathering and sorting through their gear in preparation for the next day's exodus from the battle zone. He laid out dried fruit and nuts for their supper that night and for breakfast the next morning, saying that there seemed no point in lighting a fire that might attract unwanted attention before they could safely make their escape. He made Dan as comfortable as possible, covering him with the extra alpaca blankets and giving him another pill when he asked for it.

Diana grew more and more nervous as the night progressed and Sloane made no move whatsoever to unzip their sleeping bags, which were still locked in mute witness to the joys of the night before. That night now seemed as if it had happened a million years ago.

After they'd eaten, Sloane suggested they turn in early, because they would have to be sure to take full advantage of the light the next day. Watching him begin to remove his gun, his boots and then his shirt, Diana was horror-struck by the realization that he apparently had no intentions of making adjustments to their sleeping arrangements of the previous night.

He looked at her and smiled, his teeth gleaming white in contrast to a tan that extended all the way down to where his trousers were being unbuttoned by his large, strong hands. When he dropped his remaining clothing, the mere sight of him made her go pleasurably warm inside. But there was more to love than physical attraction. There was more to it than the certain knowledge that he wanted her. There was more to it than the gut feeling inside of her that told her she still wanted him, too.

Sloane checked the sleeping bags for any unwanted visitors, then slipped inside. He propped himself into a sitting position, the covers falling to reveal his muscled tanned chest and flat stomach. Diana hadn't even started to undress. She felt uneasy with his eyes questioning her reticence. "Coming?" he asked finally. "If you're worried about Dan, don't be. Those pills will have him out until morning."

She wasn't worried about Dan. What did worry her was that last night she had thought she would never tire of climbing into bed with this man. Now, a mere twenty-four hours later, sleeping with him again was impossible.

Nevertheless she removed her gun and her boots, slipped off her bush jacket and began slowly to unbutton her blouse. Sloane was watching. "Turn your head, please," she whispered, asking that of a man who had already seen, touched, explored—and pleased—every inch of her body.

"But I want to see you," he said. "Seeing you gives me pleasure. Besides, you didn't see me complaining when you watched me strip down, did you?''

Diana blushed. He knew, then, how her eyes had fastened on his nakedness. "Please," she said. Though he looked as if he were going to object again, he shut his eyes instead. Diana finished unbuttoning her blouse, but before slipping it off she knew she couldn't keep on pretending everything was the way it had once been—as much as she might have liked to.

"I'm sorry, Sloane, I just can't," she said, her voice catching in her throat.

He opened his eyes. "I don't understand," he said, seeming confused, although Diana couldn't see how he could be.

"I'm sorry," she repeated. "It's simply impossible for us any longer."

The hurt and the disappointment were plain on his face. Diana was angry that he wouldn't see how he had compromised their relationship. "But why?" he asked. "Last night—"

"Last night was different!" she said in loud interruption, as if his very mention of the previous night was sacrilege. She couldn't believe he was going to make her stand there and spell it out for him. "Last night I loved you. Last night I thought you loved me."

"And that's changed?"

"It changed when you lied to me," she said, furious that she was finding it so difficult *not* to go over to those joined sleeping bags.

"Lied?" he echoed, the consummate actor.

He actually looked mystified. "I never lied to you, Diana. *Never!*"

"You told me you had come out here to find and identify an airplane and the remains of the man in it."

"You think that was a lie?" he asked.

"Yes," she said, "I do. I think whatever you really came out here looking for was still missing after you had found and identified Gary Holsteen's remains."

She knew he was getting up to come to her, and she was ashamed and disgusted that his nakedness could almost make her forget that he had betrayed her trust...betrayed her caring...betrayed her love. "Don't come any closer," she warned, trying to still the trembling in her voice, trying to keep from going to him and losing herself in his muscular arms, pressing herself against his hard and velvety warmth. "I don't want you ever to touch me again!"

He stopped, looking painfully vulnerable without any clothes on, looking confused, looking as if he didn't really understand, as if he didn't know what to do now. He had to be made to see that Diana was no fool, easily taken in by his make-believe love.

"Diana, I..." he began, as if attempting to make those explanations Diana wanted, but having second thoughts. He walked over to his pile of clothing, found his pants, stepped into them, pulled them up and fastened them. He then knelt beside the joined sleeping bags and unzipped them, separating them into their individual units. He pulled one bag off to one side, leaving it there, then turned to Diana. "I have never lied to you," he said. "Never. The story about my family and Holsteen is true, every word of it."

"If it was, then you didn't come *just* for the sake of family honor, did you?" she accused, wishing he would tell her something—anything—that would make her regain her faith in him.

"No," he admitted after a lengthy pause, "I didn't." Diana waited, thinking he would say more, *hoping* he would say more, but he didn't.

"And you're not going to make any further explanation than that?" she asked. She found it impossible to believe he couldn't see how she was holding out to the very last in the hope that he would yet set everything right between them. "You don't think I deserve more?"

"I've already said I have hopes of telling you—"

"I know!" she interrupted him. "You have hopes of telling me *someday*." Damn it, she was starting to cry!

"Saying any more now would make things worse," he said, as if he actually believed that was the consolation she needed to compensate for her tremendous feeling of loss. "Believe me."

Diana wondered how she would react if he would not say another word, just come over to her, lift her in his strong arms, carry her over to his sleeping bag, smother her with kisses and. . . .

"You can go to bed now," he said, not moving one step closer. He turned away, looking back only after Diana was burrowed deeply in her separate sleeping bag. "I love you, Diana Green," he said. "Surely you must at least know that's no lie."

But Diana didn't know anything of the sort at the moment. She only knew, as she rolled onto her side, turning her back to him, that her heart was breaking.

CHAPTER TWELVE

TWO DAYS LATER Diana could hardly believe there were so many miles of jungle without one clearing large enough to set down something as seemingly small as a helicopter. It had been so long since she had even seen the sky and the sun, she was wondering whether they were still up there beyond the intricate weave of tree limbs and creepers—animal and vegetable—that composed the impenetrable roof of greenery above her. The sounds of gunfire that had followed them intermittently the whole first day had now disappeared completely. But although she would never have admitted it to Dan or Sloane, it had not been the gunfire that had frightened her most. What kept the chills periodically racing up and down her spine, even now as she sat in relative safety, was her uncontrollable fear of being watched and followed. That there was no visual trace of the predator did not still Diana's intuitive uneasiness. Once more she checked the surrounding underbrush for signs of *its* presence, finding nothing—as usual—to feed her apprehension except, perhaps, the gathering gloom of yet another Peruvian nightfall.

She glanced at Dan, who sat propped up against the trunk of a nearby tree; his concentration on nothing in particular spoke of his efforts to combat severe pain. "Dan, are you feeling okay?" she asked, although she felt hopelessly unable to suggest how she could make him feel better. He had been entirely uncomplaining, his exceptional fortitude making Diana keep her own complaints in check whenever she was sorely tempted to voice them.

"You're insinuating, I suppose, that I look like hell?" he said, the trace of a smile playing across his lips. Diana was amazed that he could manage even the appearance of good humor, especially since the stained bandage on his shoulder told her his wound was once again open. "Undoubtedly, however, I shall soon be looking much better," he said, "since I detect your boyfriend returning at this very moment to inform us he has just booked us into luxury accommodations for the evening."

As usual, Diana didn't hear anything until mere seconds before Sloane emerged from the surrounding jungle. She tried to be consoled by the fact that if Dan, with his keen sense of hearing, hadn't detected the prowling of the jaguar, it seemed highly unlikely the cat was around.

Compared to those of the previous evening, the lodgings did turn out to be luxurious—although, since they arrived after dark, Diana was more than a little intimidated when Sloane focused the beam of his flashlight on a small shadowy entrance. The opening really looked too narrow, but she moved a yielding border of undergrowth and stepped through.

"Here, hold the flashlight, will you?" he asked her. "And keep it aimed about there." The scanning beam turned up a pile of dry wood, and Sloane knelt quickly beside it. "I took the liberty of getting this ready," he said. "I figured there would be little chance to look for firewood by the time I got you both back here. Unfortunately, I wasn't able to get enough to last through the night, but we should at least be able to coax a warm meal out of it. And there should be no danger—it's doubtful that a fire surrounded by rock wall on all four sides could be spotted."

He applied the flame of his lighter to the balls of dry moss beneath the tented kindling. Dan watched from the darkness, leaning against one of the stone walls for support.

"What exactly is this place?" Diana asked, the darkness preventing her from seeing her surroundings clearly.

Sloane didn't answer immediately, first concentrating on making sure the moss caught flames, rearranging it for better ventilation. Finally satisfied, he answered, "An Incan building foundation. From what I could make out in the little daylight I had available, it looks as if there are more, maybe even the ruins of quite an extensive community."

His face, turned toward Diana, was illuminated by flames now dancing higher. Oh, he was handsome! He reached for the flashlight, taking it from her. She tingled as a result of even that brief touch. She moved in closer to the fire, not necessarily for its warmth but for the escape it offered—if just momentarily—from the darkness. "I'll get us something to eat," he said.

"I'm feeling quite energetic," Diana admitted, although she was glad when Sloane didn't renege on his offer to get them supper. "What about water?" She had her heart set on once again eating something besides dried fruit and nuts.

"I'll use what's in the canteens," Sloane said, "and there's a stream not far away where we can refill in the morning."

Diana made herself as comfortable as possible under the still very primitive conditions. Wondering what she looked like, she ran her fingers through her hair, surprised when she didn't immediately come up with something small, alive and moving.

Sloane went about fixing their meal with a minimum of motion, and before long the water was boiling, bubbles forming within the plastic sack of..."I think it's one of the chicken casseroles," he ventured. "The label was torn off."-He dropped tea bags into containers, added water, then handed Diana and Dan each a cup.

They all lapsed into a reflective silence that continued throughout the meal. "You both look beat," Sloane said finally. "Why don't you hit the sack and let me clean up here?"

"I'll help," Diana volunteered, hoping her actual lack of enthusiasm didn't come through.

"Thanks, but no thanks, Diana," he said, extending his hand for her plate. "Do yourself a favor and get some shut-eye. We don't know for sure that it won't be a few more days, just as tiring as this one, before we finally find that clearing we're looking for."

She crawled over to her sleeping bag and unzipped it, preparing to slip inside. She suddenly felt she didn't have enough energy to undress.

"I think maybe you should at least take off your boots, Diana," Sloane suggested. "Here, I'll help you."

Diana didn't bother pretending she wanted to do it herself. "I really am a chain around your neck, aren't I?" she said when one boot was off and Sloane was in the process of helping her remove the other.

"It's all been my pleasure, lady," he said, placing both of her boots off to one side.

"Thanks for saying so, anyway," Diana told him, feeling reality escaping before she was even completely inside her bag. She was only vaguely aware that Sloane zipped it around her. She thought she was dreaming when she felt his lips tenderly brush her forehead. He was really such a remarkable man. What horrible, horrible secret could he be hiding from her?

DIANA CAME AWAKE to the sound of birds, opening her eyes to gaze at the complete interior of the enclosure for the first time. Like what remained of the buildings at Machu Picchu, this one's straw roof was long gone. Above her, though, there was a natural canopy composed of jungle limbs, vines and leaves. The fire had gone out, now little more than a rough circle of pale gray ash. Sloane's sleeping bag was laid open across from her, he and Dan nowhere in sight.

Scrambling out of her bag, Diana reached for her boots. But she wasn't in such a hurry that she didn't take the time to turn each boot over and give it a violent shake. Quite amazingly, this morning's ritual turned up nothing. "Nine times out of ten, it won't," Sloane had told her. "It's the tenth time, however, that makes you thankful you've been so diligent the other nine." Her boots on, she came to her feet and headed for the doorway.

The original entrance in the rock was high enough that even Sloane could have walked through it without stooping. It was cramped only because there was a thick undergrowth crowding from the outside. Not only that, but the exit had been made even more narrow by several branches that someone—Sloane, perhaps—had worked diagonally to keep anything dangerously large from getting inside. Whether it would have offered a successful barrier to some of the jungle's small dangerous animals was debatable.

Diana cautiously peeked ahead before walking through, confident that Dan and Sloane wouldn't have gone very far without her. "Sloane?" she called, her voice scaring a monkey in a nearby tree, whose shriek scared her in turn.

"Over here, Diana!" Sloane called, although he was nowhere visible. "Turn left and follow the path." At a time earlier in her trip, Diana wouldn't have recognized Sloane's definition of a pathway. It was noticeable now only as a faint trail of squashed plant growth, but she found him nevertheless.

"Come on," he said, immediately taking her hand. She knew she should have pulled away, but she simply couldn't bring herself to do so. "I want to show you something Dan discovered while the two of us were looking around the place this morning." He sounded excited. "I can guarantee you'll find it interesting."

"Speaking of Dan, where is he?"

"Around," Sloane replied cryptically, then turned to give her a mischievous smile. "Actually he diplomatically volunteered to give us a few minutes of privacy."

Diana was going to say that the last thing she wanted or needed was time alone with the man who had hurt her so deeply, but Sloane was already drawing her attention toward a segment of jungle up ahead. She followed the angle of his outstretched arm, seeing greenery, lots and lots of greenery, all growing in magnificent profusion, all entwining its way upward...around a stone structure nestled within a pod of spiraling plant life. For some odd reason it all looked familiar, as if Diana had seen it before, possibly pictured in some book.

"My God!" she exclaimed in a burst of recognition. "George Culhaney said it was here!"

"Yes, he did, didn't he?"

"He's been here," Diana said. "He's stood right here. He said it was round, with no apparent windows or doors—"

"Well, he was certainly right on that score, at least as far as I can see," Sloane said.

"George said his party was attacked by Indians," Diana added in worried remembrance.

"Hostile Indians around here forty years ago are not necessarily still here," Sloane pointed out. "At least, I've seen no sign of them this morning, have you?"

"I only wish I had paid more attention to George," Diana said, trying to rack her brain for specifics. "To be quite frank, I always assumed he was exaggerating. Although he did insist there were several newspaper and magazine articles written up on the incident. He even asked me to come by his place in Los Angeles to look at them."

"Well, the dirty old man!" Sloane clucked his tongue and shook his head in mock disapproval. "I've heard of asking a young lady up to see one's etchings, but—"

"Very funny," was Diana's response, although she said it jokingly.

"Well, the old man certainly saw this," Sloane said. "I've never come across anything quite like it."

"You have any ideas what it is?" Diana asked, deciding she was going to have to take some pictures for George. She remembered how he had mentioned he hadn't been able to bring back even one photograph. Wouldn't he be pleasantly surprised to have Diana show up on his doorstep with bona fide proof that his Incan Keep was indeed out there in the Peruvian wilds!

"It was probably used as some kind of watchtower," Sloane said. "Most likely as part of the city's defense system. As I already mentioned, it does look as if there was once quite a little settlement here. I suspect this is something our friends Carlyle and Sipas would be willing to fight yet another battle over."

"Really? You mean, this is an important find?"

"Offhand I'd say yes, that is a safe assumption," he answered. "Aside from The Keep and the building we stayed in last night, I've found what looks like three temples, a possible palace complex, and what might well have been a public granary. None of which looks as if it has been tampered with by professionals or amateurs. Which means Dan is going to come out of this a very rich man, holding out this archaeological plum to Carlyle.''

Sloane immediately read what was flashing across Diana's mind. ''Dan has to live with his conscience,'' he said, ''and he's so far in with Carlyle now that there's no getting out.''

''But what about you? Couldn't you gain by this?'' Diana asked.

''How?'' Sloane questioned. ''In order to find anything small enough to take out of here—and to turn over to the authorities, I might add—we'd have to dig for days. We'd never get away with it. The same if we tried to send anyone in. This is Carlyle's territory any way you look at it.''

So even this find would be no help to Sloane. He seemed disinterested in it as far as personal gain was concerned, so Diana was surprised when he said, ''What if by some rare stroke of luck I did happen to get my financial situation straightened out before I thought I would? What if I hopped a plane one day soon for Seattle? Would you go out and have dinner with me? Maybe a drink? Maybe talk over old times? Maybe say you'd marry me?''

''What's the point of this conversation?'' Diana asked, furious that he was unfeeling enough to play this kind of game with her. ''The way you've explained it, in great detail, I might add, you'll be working until you're a hundred to pay off all your debts. And as I've explained to you, I couldn't possibly have any kind of relationship with a man who keeps things—important things—from me. I certainly could never marry you!''

"What that really means is that you aren't prepared to forgive me for not telling you what I was doing out in the jungle on our last afternoon at the wreckage, doesn't it?''

"Will you please just leave it be?" Diana pleaded. She had no desire to go over it all again, coming out in the end with the same heartache.

"Well, there is no one who wishes he could tell you more than I do,'' Sloane said.

"But you still can't tell me, right? Right!'' She gave him a mocking smile.

"There would be little point in telling you—now,'' he said. Diana found that statement no more clear than she ever had.

"But there possibly would be a point in telling me *someday*,'' she said. "Yes, I know!'' She was trying very hard not to sound sarcastic. "Well, if you'll excuse me, I'd like to go get my camera and snap some pictures before another *someday* has Carlyle and his henchmen arriving here with hacksaws to take this city away piece by piece, stone by stone.''

She turned and fled back to the small ruined building that had sheltered them through the night. She couldn't bear standing there beside them any longer while he kept on pretending that he still loved her, that there might yet be a chance for them to be together permanently. He was lying: he had to be! If things could be so

easily explained *someday*, they could be just
as easily explained today.

She ferreted through her gear for her camera,
knowing the moment he filled the doorway behind her. She came to her feet and faced him.
"Please...please...please," she said, feeling helplessly exhausted as if the energy
had suddenly been drained from her, leaving
her a defenseless shell. She would never forgive him for what he had done to her; for
what he was now doing to her. She blamed
him for a future in which she knew she would
be comparing every man she met with this
one.

He reached out, drawing his lean fingers
along her smooth cheek. She raised her hand,
covering his large one as the tip of his thumb
began a faint tracing of her soft trembling lips.
"Sloane..." was all she could manage before
he silenced her with a kiss.

When she didn't try to pull away, he put his
arms around her. He held her, moving her backward until she was pressed against the stone wall
of the building. His lips kept anchored to her
mouth the whole time, now twisting slightly to
one side, then the other, their pressure lovingly
forcing her mouth open in response. "I love
you," he whispered at the breaking of the kiss.
"My God, Diana, if you only knew how much I
do love you!"

He pulled back slightly, gliding his large
hands into her open jacket, moving to peel it off

her shoulders and letting it fall in a heap between her boots and the wall behind her.

"Sloane..." she began again.

"Shh," he whispered, his finger pressed against her lips to silence them. He began to unbutton her blouse, his hands sliding beneath the fabric to trace her skin with erotic shivers. He kissed her neck, her shoulders, her breasts. A groan came from deep in his throat as his hands gently cupped and caressed....

Slowly he dropped to his knees, his fingers working at the waistband of her slacks.

"No, no," she moaned softly, her sounds of protest a low purring that came from deep inside of her. She couldn't stop him because she didn't want him to stop.

He stood, but his hands stayed on her hips, holding. His face was not an inch from her own. Every muscle in his body seemed tensed, his eagerness, his readiness evident as he pressed against her pliant softness.

"No..." she pleaded, yet her hands, as if through a will of their own, lifted into his thick dark hair, her fingers tangling in the silky strands. His hands slid up her body, each palming one of her breasts. His open mouth descended, taking hers in a consuming kiss that despite its passion was only a prelude. His tongue against her own was probing, preparing her for a ceremony as old as time itself. His skilled hands molded the contours of her body, sending uncontrollable impulses coursing through her. As Incan virgins must have once been prepared

for other ceremonies held long ago—perhaps in
this very place—Sloane was preparing her for
the rite of love.

Leaving her weak and in panting breathlessness, he finally knew her body was once again
his, no longer able to resist. Yes, he knew, he
knew, and. . . .

"Oh, Diana, I love you," he moaned. And
the fire of their passion, so quickly ignited, now
began to turn toward its consummation, as both
of them so desperately wanted despite the barriers everything outside of their love had erected
between them.

She wrapped his neck with her arms, all reluctance gone in the wonder of the moment. She
leaned her face against his shoulder. "Yes," she
whispered in willing consent. "Yes. . .oh yes. . .
oh. . . ."

She sighed the ecstasy of ages past, present
and future. Around them rose the walls of hard
stone, their tightly fitted seams no less securely
joined at that sublime moment than were Diana
and Sloane's straining bodies.

"I love you!" she screamed, her voice echoed
by the distant cry of a jaguar poised somewhere
within the denseness of verdant undergrowth
beyond the protection of Incan stones. "I love
you!"

LOVE, THOUGH, WASN'T ENOUGH—not even for
them. Diana saw that, without illusion, as soon
as the heat of their flaring passion had tempered. In her love, and in the hopelessness of

that love, she had once again given herself, but now again, she was able to see things clearly. Regrets filled her as later that morning they packed up to head for the river Dan had reported spotting through a small break in the trees.

Even Dan must have sensed the desperation in Sloane and Diana, the utter hopelessness of their ever being able to stay together. Turning to her as they were leaving George Culhaney's lost city behind them, he said quietly, "Some people never even have the moment, Diana. You're really one of the lucky ones, even if it might not appear that way now."

There were simply too many things working against them, and not just Sloane's poverty, which had suddenly become almost insignificant in the face of the real problem of lack of trust and mutual confidence. So Diana had decided it was best to take their painfully few moments of love and store them up like worn and faded photographs. Perhaps on melancholy nights she would remember and be glad for what she had had for a little while. Perhaps.

The river wasn't all that far. In fact, Sloane suggested, after finding an extensive network of overgrown Incan irrigation channels, that it had probably been the city's chief source of water. It was not wide now, but gave every evidence of being larger and swifter at other times of the year. Its shoreline displayed an impressive deposit of large trees, uprooted upstream by powerful hydraulic forces and now dropped haphazardly at low-water intervals. Diana was fascinated to see Medusa-headed root systems, denuded of all soil and looking like mirror images of the limbs and branches sprouted at the top of massive tree trunks.

"A little too swift for a helicopter to set down safely, wouldn't you say?" Dan remarked, his face muscles drawn taut with the pain of the wound once again soaking his bandage. For the first time Diana realized what the two men had had in mind. "I wouldn't want to risk a chopper of mine getting its pontoons hung up on any of those submerged snags, either," he continued.

"What about that as a potential launchpad?" Sloane pointed upriver to where a conglomeration of uprooted trees and other jungle debris had formed an interlocking maze. The logjam, located at a bend in the river, jutted from shore out to a point approximately midstream.

"Might work," Dan replied after a quick moment of further scrutiny.

Diana thought of Dan's previous comment that the helicopter might have to come down and pick them up from the treetops. She looked from Sloane to Dan and then back to the logjam. "You must be kidding!" she said, knowing they weren't.

"One more act of daring-do lies between us and escape," Sloane said. Diana felt a rush of nostalgic emotion in realizing this was surely the final adventure they would share. "Don't underestimate your survival capabilities. After all, what's being airlifted by a helicopter from a pile of logs after all you've been through?''

''It certainly won't be able to land,'' Diana said, her observation totally unnecessary.

''Which makes boarding a little more difficult but certainly not impossible,'' Sloane responded, calling to Diana's mind a vision of herself suspended from a trapeze above an audience of awed circusgoers. She used to be spellbound by such performances. She had certainly never imagined.... There were so many things she had never imagined. She would have asked if it wouldn't be better just to keep on looking for a clearing, except she knew the present option wouldn't be under such serious consideration unless the alternatives had already been carefully weighed and discarded as impossible.

The wound in Dan's shoulder was their prime concern at the moment. Although he continued to put up a good front, he was growing weaker, having lost a fair amount of blood. Besides, every second spent out in such unsanitary surroundings only increased the likelihood of infection. That being the case, it was selfish of Diana even to wish they might stay on a little longer just so she would have a few more precious moments with the man she loved but could not— would not—marry.

''How can Dan possibly go up a ladder in the condition he's in?'' she asked, wondering if that small point had somehow escaped both of them.

"When I initially made arrangements for the copter, I told them to be sure to bring a sling," Sloane said, "just in case we were forced into using an inconvenient pickup locale. Although I must admit I was hardly contemplating a place quite as inconvenient as this one."

"A sling?" Diana wanted clarification, even if she did have a rough idea of what he was talking about.

"You fasten it under your arms, and a winch pulls you up," Sloane explained, pretty much confirming Diana's suspicions. Although that might be a good deal easier than going up a ladder, it still wasn't something to look forward to.

"Isn't even that going to hurt Dan's arm?" she asked, with a glance at Dan, who wasn't looking at all well.

"We'll improvise," Dan said, trying to give her a smile that, because of his pain, made him look like a caricature of himself.

They moved farther upriver, finally coming to the first large log that connected the bank to the jam. Diana was not reassured by the rotting wood, wet surfaces, moss-slippery patches of green, dangerous limb snags and air holes riddling the whole construction.

"I rather think it's now or never," Sloane said, removing the pack he was carrying on his back and kneeling to retrieve the signal box from it. He laid the black box on the fallen tree trunk nearest him and flipped a switch that seemed to do very little except activate a small red light on the console.

"Rescue comes to those who wait," Dan remarked hopefully. He went off to one side, still trying to hide his increasing physical discomfort. It was clear that he did not want to mar the final moments of two such unlucky lovers.

Diana and Sloane sat together on the bank, somehow finding silence less painful than trying to put their feelings into words. It didn't seem possible that it was all about to end, that she and Sloane would go their separate ways after all that had happened between them, after all the memories they now shared. It hardly seemed possible that....

She saw the faint movement in the underbrush nearby and stiffened in apprehension. She still had the strong feeling that there was an evil presence in this jungle, an evil presence with an awareness that the three of them were on the verge of escaping....

It wasn't the jaguar, though, that appeared from concealment as Sloane motioned Diana to silence by putting his finger to his lips. It was a burro-sized animal with a bulky form and moderately long legs. It was a uniform dark brown, its skin forming a thick rounded crest on the nape of a neck that grew a short mane of stiff hair. It had short ears, small eyes and an elongated muzzle.

"Tapir," Sloane whispered, nodding in the direction of the animal that was now entering the water. "Looks rather piglike," he went as as he noticed Diana's bewildered expression, "but actually it's related to the horse and the hippopotamus."

Diana breathed more easily as she and Sloane carefully watched the strange but harmless beast. The tapir immediately showed itself to be a good swimmer, because its drift in the current was minimal as it headed for the opposite shore. Suddenly, though, the water around its head seemed to boil. "What's happening?" Diana asked loudly, unable to formulate a reasonable explanation for what she was seeing. The tapir seemed to stop swimming; it was being swept downriver, still at the center of a frothing circle of water.

"Piranha!" Dan said, on his feet and pointing excitedly.

Sloane wrapped a protective arm tightly around Diana, trying to turn her face into the shelter of his chest before she could see the tapir's head disappear a final time beneath the surface. Even as they heard the helicopter approaching, she shuddered at that sudden, vicious assault on the otherwise calm beauty of the scene, unable to free her mind of what she had seen.

"Rescue has arrived!" announced Sloane, giving her a quick reassuring squeeze and helping her to her feet.

The helicopter appeared above the trees and hovered over the water. Sloane waved and

pointed toward the logjam, making a few complicated hand motions that Diana would never
have been able to interpret had she been the
pilot. Sloane, though, apparently had more
faith in his pantomimes than she did. "This is
it!" he said. "You'd better take off your jacket
so there's no chance of it getting tangled." She
did as she was instructed, not sorry to be leaving
it, since it was soiled beyond redemption and of
no possible use except as a souvenir. "Ready?"
he asked. Dan was already beginning to work
his way slowly out onto the pile.

"Oh, my film!" Diana exclaimed suddenly,
realizing she had been on the verge of leaving it.

"Get it," Sloane said.

The copter had moved to a position over the
end of the logjam from which it could come
even lower without hitting any trees. The sling
was already being fed from a side door.

Diana quickly rummaged through her things,
locating the small plastic containers holding her
exposed film. "Where'll I put them?" she
asked, realizing that without her jacket she
didn't have enough pocket space.

"Here, give them to me," Sloane suggested,
kneeling with her and quickly filling the pockets
of his pants and jacket.

"What happens if *your* coat gets tangled?"
she asked, not so much worried about her film
as she was about Sloane's safety.

"I've had more practice at this sort of thing
than you have," he assured her with a wide

smile. They stood. The copter was in place, the sling dropped. "Every adventure has to have its suspenseful rescue," Sloane said, reaching for Diana's hand and giving it a squeeze. "Shall we get on with this one?" He made it all sound like such fun and games, as if this were one good ending to a nice tale, but Diana, even with all she had been through, had certainly never contemplated quite such a finale.

Sloane started climbing up the jam after Dan. Diana followed, feeling a sudden reluctance but aware that she had no choice. She had come too far, in every sense of the word, to turn back now. Rescue hovered overhead and she had to make for it. Sloane crawled, Diana crawled. Sloane told her to watch for a patch of dried leaves that concealed no more support than a hole. Diana watched for it and stepped around it, feeling very much as if she were back on that jungle bridge once again.

Déjà vu.

All the while the helicopter hovered above and in front of them, wind from its blades making ripples on the piranha-filled water.

They finally caught up to Dan, who looked thoroughly drained by the ordeal. His face was white even under his heavy tan. His eyes were glassy, with large dilated pupils. The pain-tautened lines of his face, etched deeply beneath the stubble of his beard, made him look like a very, very old man. The bandage wrapping his wounded shoulder was so saturated that red was splattering the tree trunk at his feet. "It won't be long now," she encouraged him.

"I hope not," he said weakly, somehow still managing that trace of a smile as if he were the one doing his best to keep Diana's spirits up.

Then, before Diana even knew what was happening, Dan shut his eyes and fell sideways. She and Sloane automatically reached out for him, Diana being the one who actually took hold before his weight ripped him free of her fingers. "Sloane, my God, save him!" she yelled, not ready to believe Dan had come so far to perish on the verge of rescue.

He hit the water instead of breaking bones against any of the logs. The water apparently revived him, because he managed to hold onto a dead limb with the hand of his good arm and was kept from being swept downriver, although he obviously didn't possess the strength to pull himself to safety. Sloane, who had immediately begun clambering back down the jam past Diana, was already scampering along the intricate pathway that would give him access to Dan in the water. With luck he would get there in time, before Dan's strength gave out and he was forced to....

God help them, she prayed, the horror dawning on her with a force that exploded fear like rockets at a picnic. "Don't go into that water!" she screamed. "Dear God, Sloane, get him out but don't go into the water!" She could see

Dan's life trickling away, his bullet wound leaking billowing invitations to disaster.

The tapir had been swept downriver, the center of a frothing circle of water!

Diana, too, began making her way back down the logjam in an effort to get to Dan, although she knew she could never be the one to save him, even if she reached him in time. She wouldn't have the strength necessary to pull him from the water. But Sloane. . . . Diana knew the strength in his arms, even though she mainly felt it muted to gentleness whenever he held her. She had however always recognized the sheer potential of that power locked within his ropy muscles, hard flesh and durable sinew. She only hoped he could get there soon enough to save Dan's life. Diana tried desperately to remember how much time had elapsed between when the tapir had entered the water and the water around it had commenced boiling. Not long, not long at all, and the animal hadn't been wounded. . . .

She couldn't see, realizing for the first time that she was crying, tears blinding her. Somehow—not noticing when, not yet feeling the pain—she had ripped the sleeve of her blouse, a vivid red scratch visible now on her arm.

The helicopter had changed position, its pilot having thought it better to bring the sling in at a different angle. Sloane, though, was now sufficiently close to judge that Dan's good arm would never be strong enough to keep hold of the sling for the pull from the water, and there was probably no time to secure the device around the wounded man's upper body.

Sloane squatted at the spot where Dan was miraculously still holding. He reached down, grabbing hold of Dan's wrist with one hand while prying the man's fingers loose from the wood with the other. Then, with both of his massive hands wrapped around Dan's wrist, he leaned forward so that Dan actually disappeared completely below the surface of the water, then heaved up and back. The maneuver managed to beach the upper half of Dan's body over the log.

In a second fluid movement Sloane released Dan's wrist, came forward over him and hooked his fingers into the waistband of the man's soaked pants. With another tug Dan's whole body was hauled onto the jam. The water was silent except for ripples and small pink whirlpools now drifting out of sight downriver.

Diana reached them on the water's edge, falling into Sloane's arms, shaking with horror at the breathless danger of the past few minutes. As usual, she felt sheltered by the protective strength of this man she loved, her sanity saved by him as surely as he had saved Dan from the piranha.

"Let's get out of here, shall we, Diana?" he said, his face buried in her hair, kissing it. "I've had quite enough adventure for one lifetime."

Her realization that civilization wasn't that far away gave her the strength to leave her safe haven, stepping back while Sloane took the lowered sling to fasten it around the unconscious but breathing Dan. "Let's hope he stays out long enough to be saved the pain of his ride up," Sloane said, stepping back to wave the helicopter winch into motion. Almost immediately the rope went taut, and Dan's limp body was lifted. Sloane brought Diana back next to him with one arm, holding her tightly while they watched.

"You next," he said, leaning to kiss the side of her cheek reassuringly. "It won't be long now."

Suddenly a ladder dropped from the helicopter door, and a man appeared, waving frantically. Diana looked toward where he was pointing, seeing, almost upon them, confidently following the trail of Dan's splattered blood, the giant jaguar that had made them its target. Sloane saw it, too, taking his gun from his holster. "Looks like you miss out on the elevator and have to take the stairs," he told her, keeping one eye on the approaching beast while his free hand reached twice for the swinging ladder, bringing it over to them on the third try.

"Sloane, I—"

"For God's sake, Diana, don't argue with me now!"

"—love you," she finished, reaching for the ladder, hooking her right foot on the bottom rung and attempting the long climb to safety. When she heard two shots she stopped, her heart caught in her throat. The look down was scary, nauseating her as the ladder weaved back and forth over water that was filled with deadly little fish just waiting for a meal to replace the one they had missed when Sloane pulled Dan from the water. The shots had apparently been fired in an effort to scare the jaguar or stop its progression, achieving neither objective. The huge cat continued on its way, stopping on its own initiative only when it had reached striking distance.

Diana knew she should have been climbing, but she couldn't move. She was helplessly rooted to the spot, dangling in midair while below her the man she loved was confronting the beast that for her had always personified the jungle and all its hidden dangers. It was beautiful and evil, its black spots the color of midnight against a contrasting backdrop of sunshine gold; its body compact, powerfully muscled, tensed more and more as it stored up the energy that would soon be released in a lunge for her lover. If the cat were successful, all Diana's preceding horrors would be minor in comparison to this, all her precious memories suddenly shattered in this final terrifying assault.

The cat leaped and Diana screamed warning, waiting for defensive gunshots that never came. Instead she felt a jerk on the ladder that almost shook her loose and tumbled her into the water. Sloane, having jumped when the cat had jumped, was now on the ladder with her, both of them swinging even farther out over the river. The jaguar, having missed, whirled in frustration to attack again, confused to find its intended victim gone.

Diana's elation, though, was short-lived, replaced immediately by new terror as the helicopter tipped precariously. Sloane, on the lower edge of the ladder, struck the river, the resulting drag making the copter drop even farther. He was suddenly up to his waist in water, trying desperately to climb up while each new rung became submerged as fast as he could put his foot on it. He seemed confronted by a hopeless dilemma.

Diana felt numb, hardly even aware that she herself was a long way from being safe in her precarious perch on a shaking flexible ladder that exaggerated each and every movement made by the helicopter trying to stabilize above it. She was whipped this way and that as the chopper tipped, righted itself, then tipped again in overcompensation. It began to move out along the river, Sloane's legs skimming the surface of the water as if he were bait being used to troll for shark.

The chopper finally rose, bringing its human burden safely above the water. Back on the logjam, the jaguar watched for a moment, then sat nonchalantly back on its haunches and licked an injured paw. To Diana looking down from this distance, the animal appeared less threatening, like a tame and affectionate house cat cleaning up after a meal. Beyond it the jungle was a blanket of emerald green, its beauty masking the life-and-death struggles still going on beneath its deceptively peaceful surface.

She surrendered to the steadying hands that reached down to pull her to safety, and was soon joined by Sloane, whom she wanted merely to hold her...hold her...hold her...and assure her that their nightmare had finally come to an end.

CHAPTER THIRTEEN

"As soon as the chopper lands, keep low until you get out of the blade downdraft," Sloane instructed, pointing toward where Diana should head on exiting.

She nodded her head that she understood, more concerned at the moment with whether or not an updraft would swoop from the canyon to raise havoc with their approach. Below her she saw people watching: the helicopter was putting down while the *turistas* were in swarm!

A few tourists were drawing in for a closer look. Sloane leaned out and waved them away. The copter dropped closer to the ground, stirring up a virtual whirlwind of dust and dirt.

One woman in a blue dress lost her hat and headed out after it. Several other people, seeking to avoid a similar occurrence, clamped their hands down tightly on the tops of their heads.

The helicopter touched solid ground. Sloane tapped Diana on the shoulder, and she stepped out. She took a mouthful of dust and had sudden visions of being blown off the edge of the escarpment. What a grand finale that would have made!

She bent low, fearing the slicing twirl of the copter blades, even while knowing they were well above her. Scuttling for the sidelines, she finally reached a spot that wasn't anything like the wind tunnel she had been hurrying through.

"Quite a breeze," she commented with a laugh, turning to where she assumed Sloane was behind her. He wasn't there. He was in the helicopter and it was lifting. For a brief instant Diana thought that something was wrong, that the chopper was merely going to circle for another approach. It didn't circle, though. It took up a course that paralleled the canyon and headed away.

Diana watched until it was a distant spot in the sky. She was numb. No matter what she might have thought about the dreaded moment when she and Sloane would have to part, she had never expected anything like this. The least he could have done was say goodbye.

On the other hand, Diana told herself without conviction, maybe it was better this way, without prolonged farewells. Automatically she put one foot in front of the other and headed for the hotel.

She was still the principal object of attention. The tourists were undoubtedly envious of her arrival compared to their grueling trip by train. But those around her kept their distance. Maybe Diana didn't look as if she were up to talking to anyone. She certainly didn't feel like trying to make polite conversation with complete strangers.

It seemed a century ago that she had waved
Carol off down the Hiram Bingham Road, but
it really hadn't been all that long ago. Just a few
days, really. Unbelievable what one could
squeeze into a few short days of living! Diana
knew those days would take years to forget.

She walked up on the veranda, feeling more
eyes focused on her. She must look a sight, she
thought, but let them stare! She sat vacantly
down at one of the tables, running her hand
through her short blond hair, thinking maybe
she would keep it short as a reminder of her
adventure, knowing she would never find a hair-
dresser to duplicate the cut.

Someone was standing by her table. She
glanced up, somehow expecting—somehow
hoping—it would be Sloane, but it wasn't. It
was the waiter. *"Buenos días,"* Diana said
wearily.

"¿Chicha de jora, señorita?" he asked, seeming to sense she needed a drink.

"Sí," Diana answered, a rush of memory
bringing back to her the day the waiter had first
recommended the liquor. Maybe she had been
dreaming everything in between. Maybe she
hadn't been out in the jungle with Sloane at
all....

She watched the waiter disappear into the service area, to return shortly with a tray and her
drink. When he reached the table, he deposited
her glass on a small napkin, putting her hotel
key next to the glass.

"You'll want to freshen up, yes?"

"Yes," Diana agreed.

"We will be sorry to see you leave us," he said. "All those who stay to really see the ruins are special."

Diana was amazed at the discretion that prevented his asking her the obvious questions. Perhaps it did not seem strange to him that she had virtually disappeared from the hotel. "Thank you," she said, and the waiter quietly left.

Diana sipped her drink and toyed with her key. Most of the tour groups were heading into the ruins, and she watched them, not really seeing. She wondered just how long it was going to take her to begin functioning normally.

Her drink finished, she went to her room, showered and crawled into bed, dozing on and off until the tourists were long gone.

She changed into her white wool dress and went back outside to the veranda. Some of the hotel guests had already gathered there, but Diana knew none of them, nor did she particularly care to. She ordered *pachamanca*, because she had first had it there with Sloane on the eve of their departure. She was disappointed when it came made with stuffed chicken instead of lamb, but she was not surprised. Nothing was the same anymore.

After dinner she stopped off at the desk to have her travel arrangements adjusted. It took only a phone call. Back in her room, she mechanically laid out her clothes for the follow-

ing day, packing everything else, then returned
to bed.

The next morning she was a little less in a daze
as she showered and dressed, spending a good
deal of time standing in front of the mirror,
wondering if that was really Diana Green she
saw reflected in it. The difference she saw there
must be due to her dark tan and shorter hair,
she reasoned. The tan rather surprised her, since
she hadn't realized she had got that much sun.
She remembered frequent days in the jungle
when she had hardly seen the sunshine through
the trees.

She went out for breakfast, finding the sun
long up, dirty dishes on several tables telling
that other guests were already out exploring.

She looked down into the canyon at the river
with its rushing water. Above her the sky was
completely deserted of clouds, and off to one
side the Hiram Bingham Road was a dull scar
on the mountainside. All around the landscape
was green, beautifully lush like velvet.

The waiter arrived and took Diana's order for
breakfast. As she ate, she couldn't help comparing each mouthful to her usual morning fare of
raisins and nuts. Surprisingly enough, the latter
stood up well in comparison.

Later Diana chose a corner table to witness
her final *turistas* swarm. She had a final *chicha
de jora*, although she had about decided she preferred *chicha morada*.

Afterward she got her bag and walked over to

the line for the *camionetas* that would soon be moving off down the mountain. The man behind her in line had a splitting headache, or so he said.

Diana sat by one of the windows in the VW bus, unphased by the way the vehicle weaved dangerously close to the edge of the precipice. It hardly seemed likely the bus would go over, since none of them ever did; so why should she worry unnecessarily about this one?

She slept most of the train ride back to Cuzco, a couple of times getting off at the stops to stretch, once even buying a small bunch of bananas from an old woman. She munched on the bananas, thinking of Sloane, then dozed some more.

At Cuzco she found a cab and directed it to the hotel, where she went to her room and soaked in a hot tub. She slept exceedingly well, considering she had spent most of the afternoon catnapping on the train.

Later she made her way to the dining room, finally beginning to adjust to the fact that Sloane had swept into her life briefly and then swept out again. If this dull ache inside her could be called "adjusting."

She took a cab to the airport a couple of hours before flight time, just in case there were problems, but there were no problems, although for a moment Diana thought there were going to be. She had just checked her bags and was heading for a seat in the lounge when the clerk at the

airline check-in desk called her back. "Miss
Green, this was left for you this morning," the
clerk said, handing Diana a large manila envelope.

She took the envelope with her to one of the
chairs and opened it. Inside was a photograph
album, giving off the smell of recently developed film.

Maybe Diana really had forgotten that she
had left all of her film stuffed in Sloane's
pockets. Or maybe she had known all along, yet
had not been ready, what with everything else,
to come to grips with the fact.

She spent all of her time until plane departure
turning the pages of the album. The black and
whites were all eight-by-ten glossies with accompanying negatives. The slides were all neatly
inserted in plastic sheets, each sheet holding
slots for twenty.

On the plane she leafed through the album
again, happy that the seat beside her remained
unoccupied so she wouldn't have to make small
talk or explanations as to how she had ended up
posing for photos that had her decked out in a
safari outfit with gun, leaning against a fallen
bridge in the Andes. Her hair had been long
then, probably already full of the first of a long
line of bugs.

She hadn't realized Sloane had snapped quite
so many shots of her: Diana at the watering
hole, Diana washing her hair, Diana making a
face over supper, Diana making a face over a

berry Sloane had picked and told her was edible in a pinch, Diana making a face over.... She couldn't believe she had apparently spent so much of her trip with her features screwed up into ridiculous puckers. Well, it was better than having them screwed up with tears. She had a feeling the time for tears wasn't entirely past.

The pilot announced that they were beginning the descent into Lima. She shut the album on her lap, glad she had it. She would have preferred Sloane to have given it to her personally, but this was the next best thing.

Seeing the pictures had already set her mind to sorting which of them she would submit with her travel article on Machu Picchu. Also, seeing the pictures of that Incan city she and Sloane had stumbled upon in the wild, she had suddenly recognized all sorts of potential for story development. What she had there was probably better stuff than all of the copy she could ever have milked out of Carlyle or Dan about smuggling Incan artifacts. Everyone—editors and readers alike—enjoyed a good human-interest story. What could be more of one than the tale of George Culhaney, a man who had made the discovery of his lifetime only to lose it; a man whose descriptions of a lost city had been mocked and disbelieved; a man who hadn't given up hope of rediscovering his city until old age had forced him to; a man who still made yearly pilgrimages to Machu Picchu in order to stand on the jungle's edge and bemoan his lost moment in history. That man was going to be vindicated by Diana Green, reporter. So in the end life did go on, even her life. She was already beginning to pull herself up by the heels, wasn't she?

She would never forget Sloane, never stop loving him, but the panacea of work would allow her, she hoped, to live with the pain of his leaving. She had, after all, the wonderful memory of the times when they had been close, so close. Not years, but still. . . .

Boarding her plane in Lima, bound for the States, Diana decided she would call George when her plane touched down in L.A. She had his address and his telephone number. She had her pictures. There was certainly no time like the present to become fully immersed in a time-consuming work project. She also remembered she had to be sure to call Carol and report. It was hard to imagine that the two weeks Carol had been going to allow before contacting the authorities weren't even up yet.

CHAPTER FOURTEEN

SHE WAS SURPRISED when the car George Culhaney sent to pick her up at her Holiday Inn
turned out to be a Rolls-Royce. She wasn't quite
sure just why she was surprised, since with even
a modicum of thought she could have reasoned
that it must have taken a good deal of money to
finance his expeditions in search of lost cities in
the Peruvian wilds, especially in the 1930s, let
alone allow him to keep returning year after
year, for forty-plus years, to an isolated mountaintop in the Andes. Yet her surprise remained
even as the polite chauffeur ushered her into a
back seat where she was immediately enveloped
within the expensively opulent fragrance of
handcrafted leather. In fact, despite all the
evidence she had had to the contrary, she had
always pictured George Culhaney as being se-
questered in some cloistering low-cost garret,
surrounded on all sides by his old books and his
painful memories.

She was still mulling over the ridiculousness
of her obviously distorted perception of the man
when the car pulled off the suburban roadway
and paused briefly before the massive barricade

offered by the wrought-iron gate. The gate was
thrust between two sections of a solid rock wall
that extended in either direction as far as the eye
could see. The gate disconnected along its center
seam, its two halves swinging open in a wide arc
to reveal a driveway composed of crushed white
quartz. Diana couldn't be sure how the gate
mechanism had been triggered, but she assumed
it had been done by utilizing some electronic
device inside the car, since as far as she could
determine, the chauffeur had had no outside
communication with anyone after leaving the
hotel.

Whatever remaining notions she had of
George being holed up in some lonely garret,
they were completely obliterated when, after a
twenty-minute drive through forestlike landscape, she glimpsed the house through the trees.
"I was a very spoiled, very rich, very young
man," George had told her on their train ride to
Machu Picchu from Cuzco, and the phrase
"very rich" had somehow rolled then off her
consciousness as easily as water rolls off the
back of a duck. However, he had obviously not
been kidding. Diana wasn't familiar with the
cost of real estate in the Los Angeles area, but
she still knew an expensive chunk of property
when she saw it, and she was seeing it now.

The final approach was through a gauntlet of
towering palm trees, each topped with a waving
cap of spiky fronds. To each side of the bordered roadway stretched a wide expanse of

emerald green lawn that terminated, in each instance, in an orchard of some kind of fruit or nut trees. The house itself appeared large even from a distance, mirrored to twice its natural size by a small lake filled with water lilies that made the scene almost theatrically lovely. Diana wasn't sure of the architectural style, especially since the house showed indication of having undergone several additions that, rather than detracting from its special beauty, gave it a charm all its own. Had she been hard pressed to come up with an overall description, she would probably have labeled it English Tudor, counting six brick chimneys before the car finally pulled up in front and came to a stop. As the chauffeur got out to come around and open her door, Diana was aware that the photographs in the album on the seat beside her had managed to secrete their cheap stench to the air around her, that smell having completely overpowered the rich aroma of the leather.

She was suddenly a little cowed by her surroundings. Her initial fantasy of showing up on George's doorstep as the woman who was going to set the old man's life right before he died now seemed a bit ludicrous. She suspected that the emphasis she had put on George's frustrations in the field of archaeology must have been purely the result of an atmosphere now literally miles removed from this present epitome of genteel and civilized living. With some uneasiness she found herself questioning whether George Culhaney could really need the comfort of what she had come to tell him; at least not as much as Diana had been imagining he needed it. It would seem, by all outward appearances, that George had around him more comfort than any one man could possibly need in a lifetime.

"Miss Green?" a man asked, coming down the steps to greet her. He wasn't George Culhaney. By his black livery Diana could only assume he was some kind of servant. Most of the people Diana knew found servants far too great an extravagance in the present day and age. "Mr. Culhaney has instructed me to show you inside."

The moment Diana entered the house she felt on firmer ground. Stepping through the front door was like stepping across time and space into an entirely different world from the one that existed outside in the too bright California sunshine. She was as comfortable inside the building as she had been awkward outside it. In fact, it was now the liveried servant who seemed out of place, Diana fitting right in amid the decor that included two massive slabs of gray stone, carved with Incan motifs, that flanked the large area beyond the doorway.

The visible interior of the house seemed a virtual museum of antiquities: massive carved heads, an Incan sacrificial altar, case after case of smaller objects ranging from clay pipes to exquisite gold figurines.... One case displayed so much precious metal, primarily in the form of jewelry, Diana estimated there could have been more than enough to pay off even Sloane's monumental debts.

She felt the tug at her heart that thoughts of Sloane automatically triggered inside her. She couldn't help wondering where he was now, what he was doing and if he ever thought of her as she was thinking of him. She told herself not to get bogged down in needless nostalgia, especially since there was no way she could have changed the way things had turned out. As much as she loved Sloane, as much as she would probably always love him, she simply had to accept the inevitable reality and get on with her life. She was here to do a job, get a story, get her life back on the right track. Still, it was hard not to think of Sloane when a step through a doorway had plunged her into a setting that did everything it could to recall her memories of that place in which she had found love and then lost it.

Her growing melancholia wasn't helped any by her entrance into the room in which George Culhaney was waiting for her. Because the room, even more so than the ones she had passed through to get to it, was evocative of that Peru that she had left only a few hours by plane behind her. On one whole section of wall, behind a large couch, was a fresco of Machu Picchu. Diana was momentarily so caught up in the artist's accurate conception of the Peruvian landscape that she unwittingly ignored George, who had risen to greet her. Oh, how the picture, a mere one-dimensional rendition of the reality, took Diana's mind soaring like condors riding those late-afternoon updrafts at the Incan citadel! It was almost as if she were there again, gazing upon that city as it was misted periodically by the majestic sweep of low-flying clouds, Sloane beside her, both of them drinking in the spectacle and sharing it as they had shared each other's love. But it wasn't Sloane who was standing beside her. It wasn't his tightly muscled body, his deep dimples, his sensuously full lips, cleft chin, square jaw, dark brooding eyes....

"What a pleasant treat it is for me to see you again, Diana," George said, taking her hand. "You can't imagine how delighted I was when you called to say you were in Los Angeles." How desperately Diana wanted it to be Sloane and not George standing there, his hands squeezing hers. "Come on over here, my dear, and sit down," he went on, leading the way to the couch.

The room was filled with the colors of Peru: gray rug; green wallpaper; emerald moiré on the chairs, floral chintz on the couch; large potted plants with wide, brilliant green foliage; orchids tumbling in colorful profusion over the edges of yellow porcelain bowls. French doors opened onto a solarium that was choked with a tangle of even more exotic greenery. Amid that clutter of vines was a large jaguar, sculpted from warm sun-colored marble. A colorful parrot sat on its perch, eyeing Diana quizzically through the open doors.

"Tired from your trip, are you?" George

asked, misinterpreting Diana's somewhat dazed expression. He was dressed in a light blue three-piece suit complete with tie. Diana couldn't recall ever having seen him dressed any less formally.

"To be absolutely frank, I'm a bit over-whelmed by my surroundings," Diana admitted. "I don't know why, but I was expecting something a little less...." She paused, searching for the right adjective.

"Oh, I see," George said, grinning in obvious insight. He sat back against the cushions of the couch. "Why would this George Culhaney take a modest Circle-SA tour when he could charter a plane and then a helicopter in to Machu Pic-chu?"

"Something like that," Diana conceded, laughing at George's obvious good humor. No matter what the setting, he remained an entirely charming and enchanting old gentleman. Here was one person with whom Diana could count on being safe. Here was one man who wouldn't be threatening her well-being as Sloane had threat-ened it, as Sloane's memory was still threatening it.

"Well, it's simply a case of George Culhaney not wanting to broadcast overly loud his yearly pilgrimage to wallow in bitter memories," he said. "So much attention was focused on my trips there in the past that I don't go out of my way in my old age to invite any unwanted publi-city. And God only knows what could take the reading fancy of the masses in this day and age, right? Circle-SA, and other innocuous tours like it, offer me the desired anonymity of getting in and out of Machu Picchu with a minimum amount of fuss and fanfare. Besides, I've never really been a snob, and one can meet the most charming people on those little tours. Miss Diana Green certainly being a prime case in point.''

''You do have the knack for saying just the right thing at the right time,'' Diana responded, hoping George's pleasant bantering could make her forget Sloane, knowing it was highly unlikely that it would. George, after all, had been one of the characters there in the wings when Diana had met Sloane. He had been there at the breakfast table the morning after Diana had received her first kiss from Sloane. He had been on the train joining in the conversation as Sloane pointed out the sights. He had been sitting with her on the hotel veranda when Diana had thought Sloane had left her for good at the depot in the canyon. She wondered how different she would be feeling now if Sloane had left her life after that parting kiss on the train. But, then, if he had left her there she wouldn't be here now, since she would never have stumbled upon George Culhaney's lost city out in the jungle.

''So, how does it feel being back on more familiar terrain?'' George asked, and Diana was grateful that the pleasant modulation of his voice called her back from that remembered precious moment when Sloane had risen from his chair, moved across the veranda toward her, took both of her hands in his and told her how marvelous it was that she had come to share the glory of a Machu Picchu sunset with him.

"Actually, it does feel good to be back," Diana said, not sure that was really the truth. She wished this room didn't remind her so much of Peru, because Peru reminded her so much of Sloane, and she wanted to forget Sloane. No, that wasn't quite true. She didn't want to forget him. She merely wanted to smooth off the sharp edges of a memory that when brought to mind now was far too cutting.

"It is admittedly a thoroughly fascinating country—Peru," George said, getting a look in his eyes that was vaguely reminiscent of the extreme vacantness Diana had seen registered there on several different occasions in the past. However, George's memories were apparently less apt to completely consume him here than nearer the source of his unrealized dreams, because his gaze quickly refocused on Diana. He smiled. "As a matter of fact, most of the artifacts in the house come from that area. Not, unfortunately, turned up by my own hands."

"You do seem to have an extensive collection," Diana commented.

"Actually, the best of my pieces are in the vault downstairs. You'll have to let me show them to you if you have the time. Are you off to Seattle this afternoon?"

"I plan to spend a few days more in L.A.," she said, wondering if now was the time for her to show him the photographs couched within the album she held on her lap.

"Excellent!" George said, seeming genuinely delighted by that prospect. "It's always a pleasure to show my best pieces to someone who has a knowledge of the area. An artifact, after all, isn't just the piece of clay, stone or metal it's made up of, is it? It's a compilation of many things, not the least of which is the sense of history that went into its making in the first place. I have friends—avid collectors, mind you—who gather up objects purely for their commercial value, with no care in the world for the history behind them. I've always found such activity less a matter of collecting than of gathering up shiny objects like a pack rat."

The servant who had appeared to show Diana into the house now entered the room with an ice bucket and tulip glasses on a silver tray. In the ice bucket was an open bottle of champagne.

"You will join me in a bit of liquid refreshment, won't you?" George said, turning to Diana after informing the servant that he would pour the wine himself. "Granted, it's not the *chicha morada* or the *chicha de jora* you're no doubt accustomed to by now, but I'll guarantee it's French, pleasantly refreshing, and a very good year." He handed Diana a glass and then lifted his own in a toast. "To Peru, then," he said.

"To Peru—the good memories," Diana responded, wondering if her memory of Sloane would ever be brought to the point of being only good and not painful.

"Yes," George went on, as if Diana's addition appealed to him more than the original. "The *good* memories." He took a sip, seemingly savoring the sparkle of the liquid on his tongue before swallowing. "Now, tell me about your present accommodations. Will you find it comfortable spending several days in...the Holiday Inn, is it?"

"Yes," Diana said, wondering why she was a little embarrassed by her choice of hotels. She was about to explain that, since her stopover in Los Angeles had been spontaneous, she hadn't had time to make better reservations, then realized that she would have probably ended up in a Holiday Inn, or its equivalent, no matter what the circumstances. She was hardly able to afford the prices of the Beverly Hills or any of the other more luxurious accommodations.

"You have family and friends to visit here in the city?" George asked, sipping more champagne.

"No," Diana said. Then, after a short pause, thinking perhaps that there was no time like the present to launch into her explanations for being there, since when she had called George from her hotel she hadn't gone into any real detail, she added, "Actually, my main purpose in being in Los Angeles is *just* to see you."

"I'm flattered," George said, sitting his tulip glass on the teak coffee table positioned directly in front of the couch. "Really, I am."

Diana, though, didn't want George to get the impression that this was purely a social call. She was there on business, after all. She was there in an attempt to get her head on straight, to get back into the groove of things, to prepare herself for returning to Seattle and making her bid for the world of journalism that went beyond cream-puff stories found on the women's page.

"I came to see you about your lost city," she explained. "You mentioned you had newspaper clippings and the like."

"Coming to check up on the old lunatic's story, are you?" George asked. However, his tone of voice, and his accompanying wide smile, indicated he really wasn't insinuating that was the case.

"I want you to let me do a news story," Diana said, deciding to leap in. "I want an exclusive."

"An exclusive?" George echoed. He laughed, unable to help himself. "My dear, there's no exclusive awaiting you here. Too many people have been this way before you, pointing out the dotty would-be archaeologist whose amateur dabblings left several of his dear friends dead in the jungle. And, not meaning to seem uncooperative at this point, I'm afraid I'm not too sure I want it all brought up in print once again. Old age doesn't steel a man to scornful laughter any more than youth does."

"Please don't answer me yes or no until you have a chance to see these," Diana said, passing the album to George, who looked more than a little curious as he took it. He turned back the front cover. "It's the photos nearer the back of the book that I want you to see," she added, realizing her host was now looking at the picture of her standing by the machete-downed jungle bridge.

Diana and Sloane had admitted their love for each other at that bridge. He had collapsed his hard body on top of her. She had felt his weight, the want of his virile manhood. She had known even then that he wasn't prepared to make any commitments, yet she had plowed right ahead, thinking to hoard memories for after he was gone. Well, he was gone, and she had her memories. The only problem was, those memories were more painful than consolation. She couldn't help wondering if she wouldn't have been far better off without them.

"It looks to me as if you managed to get just a bit off the beaten path, Diana," George said, glancing up to lock her gaze with his own. "You didn't mention any projected trips into deep jungle when last we talked."

"Here," Diana said, reaching out to hook her finger into a spot nearer the end of the album. She should have brought only those pictures of the lost city, since she had no desire now to go over all the other photographs of her taken by Sloane. They represented memories she wasn't yet prepared to share with any inquisitive third person. She flipped the pages, thankful when she turned up one of the photographs of

George's Incan Keep. She heard the old man's immediate audible gasp. "I want to tell the world that you weren't as crazy as some people thought you were," she told him.

"Where did you get these?" George asked shakily, having flipped several other pages, all of which portrayed one building or another, each partially digested by jungle undergrowth and clinging vines. "Where?"

She told him only a modified version of how it had come about, mainly because the truth was too entwined with her feelings for Sloane and Sloane's supposed feelings for her. When she had finished telling the tale she had George convinced the whole thing had been pure luck, Diana having simply decided to see a bit of the jungle, and a guide having volunteered his services. She didn't mention Sipas, or Dan Jacos, or Dennis Carlyle, or even Sloane. She didn't mention the downed aircraft, either. All of that was quite beyond the point anyway. And Diana wasn't ready, even with George, to be queried about why she had gone into the jungle. Explaining the real why would necessitate opening up the heartache of her love for Sloane and his supposed love for her in return, on and on ad infinitum. She simply wasn't up to it.

In the end Diana's watered-down version seemed to satisfy George, probably because he was acutely aware of enough major archaeological finds that had come about purely as the result of just such accidents. Besides, what the old man found of paramount importance wasn't the how or the why but the mere fact that it had been done. Here was his proof in black and white, and in color: his Incan Keep, the same structure that had caused skeptics, jealous of his youth, wealth and discovery, to label him deranged because no such structure had ever turned up before. Well, he would have the last laugh now!

George's initial reaction was that they should immediately fly back to Peru so that he could see his discovery for the first time since the catastrophe of so many years before. He seemed frustrated and a little piqued when Diana admitted she was no more able to come up with the pinpointing coordinates for the ruins than George had been when he had returned to civilization after being there. Nor did he seem overly impressed by Diana's warnings that the area, when she had left it, had been the center of some kind of jungle warfare between robbers of archaeological sites.

"Such battles have been going on for as long as I can remember," he told her in no uncertain terms. "I didn't let them scare me in the past and I refuse to let them scare me now." She told him a helicopter had picked her up not too far from the ruins, and suggested he could check with the pilots in the area, since there was hardly likely to be all that many of them. George seemed to think it would be an even better idea to contact the man who had acted as Diana's guide. He, the old man figured, would probably have thought more about the practical aspects of relocating the ruins than Diana had done.

Diana frustrated George further by saying she didn't have the vaguest idea of where her guide had gone after their little expedition. "He mentioned Brazil," she told him, still determined not to go into specifics.

If she wondered briefly how things might turn out if George did come to finance a return expedition including himself, Diana and Sloane, she countered that thought with suspicions that she and Sloane had already had plenty of time to settle their problems, if there had been any solutions available to them. Getting back together with Sloane now, for possibly just another brief moment in time, would mean only more pain for the both of them, plus the anguish of yet another parting, and Diana wasn't masochistic enough to want any of that. So if George wanted to go back, he would have to do so alone. Diana had enough memories of Peru, and of Sloane, to last her a lifetime.

"I'll get people on it," George said, obviously determined not to let the lost city slip through his fingers a second time. Diana didn't have the heart to tell him that if Dan Jacos had recovered from his bullet wound and sold his information about the city's presence to Dennis Carlyle, there was a good chance George—if he ever did get to the jungle locale—would arrive on the scene only to find the whole complex had been hacked into movable pieces and carted away piecemeal. Thinking of Dan meant thinking of Sloane, since the two had disappeared together in the same rescue helicopter. Diana hoped there would come a time in the not too distant future when there wouldn't be something in every conversation, or in every passing thought, that ended up reminding her either of Sloane or of the times she had spent with him.

GEORGE INSISTED Diana move out of the Holiday Inn and into his house. There was plenty of room, he said, and if they were going to collaborate on this story, there was no sense in Diana's commuting each day. Besides, he would enjoy the company and would relish having an attractive woman around the place. If Diana resisted at first, it was only because the house was full of artifacts that reminded her too much of Peru...too much of Sloane. But she eventually accepted George's invitation, not only because she could see the validity of his arguments, not only because she could be seduced by surroundings that were definitely more luxurious—and more private—than her room at the Holiday Inn, but because she couldn't bury her head in the sand every time she chanced upon something that reminded her of Sloane. It was far better for her to face these little obstacles now and be saved the bother of facing them later. Sloane was completely out of her life, and she couldn't continue to allow thoughts of him to influence her actions.

She called her newspaper, telling her editor that she would mail him the Machu Picchu travel piece. With surprising ease she got an okay for a feature story on the rediscovery of George Culhaney's lost city. That taken care of, she called her mother, telling her she would be spending some time in Los Angeles with a sorority sister. It was a little white lie, but Diana had no wish to endure any long-distance arguments in her present emotional state, especially since there was probably going to be a really big blowup once she got home, now that Diana had lost Sloane and had no intentions of ever surrendering the career she figured to be her panacea. She would be an investigative reporter despite her mother's fears for her safety. She called Carol Wiley, telling her that she had arrived back safely and thus there would be no need to send in the marines after her. But when Carol pressed for specifics Diana cut her short, saying she would call her back later and flesh out the details. There was no way Diana could yet bring herself to talk about her love for Sloane, not even over the telephone.

She came to enjoy the time she spent with George, sorting through his files. There were actually brief moments during her work when Diana thought she was once again getting control of her life. Then again, there were moments when she simply gazed off into space and momentarily allowed herself to relive days in the jungle with Sloane that could never really be recaptured, even in her daydreams. She continued to tell herself that work was all she needed, and she was pleased to find that George had kept and filed every article, every newspaper clipping, every picture he could get his hands on about the tragedy he had undergone in the Peruvian wilds. Diana couldn't help feeling a tremendous empathy for this old man, seeing as how his friends' dying had made his ordeal in the jungle more tragic than hers had been. Sloane was at least alive; that was one major consolation.

They spent most of their time in George's comfortable library, the old man working at his large desk, Diana working at the smaller desk that he had specially moved into the room for her convenience. "Diana, would you please come over here for a moment?" he interrupted her thoughts as she sat with the newspaper clippings spread out in front of her. The servant had just brought in a large manila envelope that had been delivered by private courier, and Diana had taken the opportunity of his arrival to stare out one of the expansive windows that usually gave access to a strikingly beautiful panorama of lawn and gardens ending at a stone balustrade that capped a high cliff top overlooking the Pacific Ocean. Today, though, the view was distorted by fog—or was it smog, Diana wondered—that couldn't help but remind her of the gossamer veils of mist that were forever flitting through the ruins of Machu Picchu. The natural progression of those thoughts had

brought her back once again to thoughts of
Sloane. As always, thoughts of Sloane brought
on a great feeling of sadness that all of her im-
mersion in work was never completely successful in combating.

She got up from her desk and crossed the short
distance of carpet to George. He had the manila
envelope open, its contents, three eight-by-ten
color glossies, laid out on his blotter. On seeing
the pictures of what were obviously Incan gold
artifacts, Diana felt herself hoping against hope
that here was something more from Sloane. However, she soon realized that she had to be grasping
at straws: the envelope in which these pictures
had been enclosed was addressed to George, not
to her. Besides which, it was highly unlikely that
Sloane could know of Diana's decision to stop
off in Los Angeles on her way home and take up
residence in the home of George Culhaney.

"What do you think?" George asked, referring to the photos.

"Exquisite pieces," Diana readily admitted.
She was particularly taken with the picture of a
jaguar mask of beaten gold. There was something about the way the pliable metal had been
hammered into the stylized representation of the
jungle cat's beautiful yet evil features that had
Diana immediately attracted while simultaneously repulsed. The latter sensation, she realized, was probably because a cat very much like
the one depicted by that gold mask had come so
close to killing the man she loved.

"They're being offered for sale," George said, fingering each photograph in front of him, rearranging them once again into a neat line. He centered the one of the jaguar mask in between the one of gold figures sailing in a gold boat and the other of some Incan deity that Diana couldn't readily identify. "A man I deal with in the city seems to think that I might be interested in these particular pieces for my collection." He looked up at Diana and smiled. "I think he might be right."

Diana wondered how it would feel to actually have the money necessary to even contemplate purchasing three such obviously priceless pieces of ancient artwork. She had been taken down to the vault beneath the house to see those treasures too valuable to be displayed on the upper floors. Diana actually believed she had never seen so many gold artifacts, except the time she had stood awestruck in the Bogota Gold Museum gazing at literal piles of them stacked on all sides of her. George's collection was extensive, gathered during a lifetime of interest in archaeology in general, and in Incan artifacts in particular. Surely a man with the wealth George had at his disposal might be persuaded to make a loan to the man who had done so much toward proving his lost city was a reality.

In almost the same thought pattern, however, Diana realized that a loan from George wouldn't really solve anything as far as she and Sloane were concerned. It would mean only that

Sloane would end up owing one creditor instead of several. With his acute sense of family pride and honor, Sloane would still feel obligated to spend his life paying George back, which would keep Diana removed from that happily-ever-after ending she wanted. Oh, it was hopeless, and she would be well simply to face that hard fact. She couldn't continue to think there was some miracle in the offing, some marvelous flash of insight that was going to make everything right in her world, when in truth it was highly possible that her world would never truly be right again—not without Sloane playing a bigger part in it than mere memory.

"Would you like to come with me to see these and what else is being offered?" George asked, bringing Diana back from her reverie. "I think the two of us would find the objects of exceptional interest, since they come from an area not all that far from Machu Picchu."

"I'd love to go," Diana responded. She was determined to confront, at every available opportunity, the ghosts that haunted her past. She would go with George to see these artifacts "from an area not all that far from Machu Picchu," and if she thought of Sloane as she looked at each piece, then in time those thoughts would be less painful for her than the ones she had called to mind yesterday or the day before. Someday, she assured herself, there *had* to come a time when she didn't feel like breaking into tears each moment she remembered Sloane and how their love had come to nothing, when love should have conquered all.

The procedure for viewing the artifacts being put on sale hardly turned out to be what Diana had anticipated upon accepting George's invitation. She had envisioned dressing to the hilt and arriving on the scene in the Rolls, while crowds milled, flashbulbs popped, champagne flowed and moneyed men and women finally wrote five- or six-digit numbers on monogrammed checks. Instead, George told her to wear something as inconspicuous as possible, and the two took a circuitous route that included three changes of taxis before they were finally deposited in front of a nondescript warehouse on the waterfront.

"It's never good policy to broadcast you're going off to a sale of items so valuable," George said, as if in apology for the slacks and turtleneck sweater he had substituted for the traditional three-piece suit that was his usual attire.

Standing on that seemingly deserted street, Diana caught a sudden chill. For some inexplicable reason she found herself feeling much the same sense of danger as she had experienced in the jungle. Which was more scary here, probably because George Culhaney seemed hardly equipped to fight off whatever unknown opponents might come leaping out from the wings. In the wilderness Sloane had been there to protect her. On the other hand, George seemed quite confident, and with an ease and authority that told Diana he had probably been this way on more than one occasion in the past, he led the way into the warehouse, out a side door and into the adjoining building, where Diana was confronted by her first sign of life other than themselves.

"Mr. Culhaney and friend," George told the great brute of a man who filled the width of the hallway. "I believe we're expected."

Cold gray eyes, set deeply behind bushy black eyebrows, scanned a list on a clipboard. The man, a pistol in a shoulder holster that was readily visible beneath the flaps of his unbuttoned suit coat, had to be over six foot five, possessing the kind of muscled body that looked uncomfortable in any kind of constricting clothes. Diana found his tremendous bulk anything but attractive—unlike Sloane's hard and sculptured physique, which had been aesthetically pleasing in or out of clothing. "Of course, Mr. Culhaney," the man said finally, putting a check mark in the appropriate place on the paper. He stepped back to let the two squeeze by, smelling unpleasantly of perspiration as Diana passed him.

George led the way through a maze of hallways, during which time they were stopped by two more men, each seemingly more muscled and bullish than the previous one. They ended up in a room that immediately reminded Diana of her conception of a museum storage area. Stacked around the perimeter were large stone blocks carved with representations of Incan deities. On tables arranged within the center of the room were myriad objects, some gold, some stone, some clay, all looking as if they had been hurriedly tossed on the scarred wood surfaces like trinkets on display at a garage sale. The conversation of the few people present, what little of it there was, was noticeably muted.

One of several people who had glanced up upon the door's opening, a distinguished older man who looked as out of place in his flannel shirt and jeans as George did in informal attire, detached himself from a conversation with two other men and headed for George's and Diana's direction. "Ah, there you are," he said, taking George's hand and shaking it.

"Miss Green, Mr. Thatcher," George said, making introductions. "Paul is a dealer who has been invaluable in my adding many important pieces to my collection, Diana."

"I can't think of a man I would rather have own them, quite aside from myself, that is, than you," Paul Thatcher said. He reminded Diana of someone who would have been right at home in a Brioni suit and strolling some fashionable gallery on Rodeo Drive. "The pieces you're interested in seeing, George," he said, "are being held for you in the back room. Would you like to see them now, or take a look at what's being offered out here on the main floor?"

"Is there anything out here worth seeing?" George's experienced eye had already surveyed and rejected most of the objects within immediate viewing.

"Some very nice pieces," Paul said with all the tonal qualities of someone who knew what he was talking about. "However, nothing that I think would hold a candle to those standards set by the rest of your collection."

"Any items the competition got to before we did?" George asked, all business.

"Not this time, George," Paul assured him with a wide grin indicative of a successful coup. "I've got an in with these people, and I've had one for a very long time. There was an interesting gold staff tip that I let go to Philips, and a gold headpiece—nothing elaborate, mind you—that I let Randolph have for old times' sake. However, the three pieces I've held out for you, as I'm sure you'll soon agree, have to be the pick of the lot."

The back room was more formal, but only a little. The desk looked as if it had seen far better times, as did the man who was sitting behind it when Paul opened the door. Unlike the other men Diana had encountered on the way in, this one looked as if he were dangerously hungry, his shirt and pants hanging in deep folds on his skinny body, his face scarred with a moon landscape of pockmarks.

"It's just a couple of regulars," Paul said in greeting. "Keep watch outside, will you, Carl, while I show Mr. Culhaney what we have saved for him." Carl got up on cue and left the room, closing the door behind him.

Paul spread a square of black velvet over the desk top, then squatted down to come up with an ordinary cardboard box. What he lifted from the box, however, was anything but ordinary. Diana gasped her appreciation of the foot-high Incan idol, even though she had already seen the photograph that should have prepared her for what to expect.

"Yes, it is a lovely piece, isn't it?" Paul agreed. That the idol was heavy was evident by the way he had to use both of his hands to move it across the desk to where George could get to it for closer inspection. He followed by producing the gold figures rowing their gold boat, and then finally came up with the jaguar mask. When all three items were lined up across the black velvet, Diana still thought the mask was the most exquisite piece. She watched, afraid even to touch, as if she were some little kid with sticky fingers wandering the halls of a museum under the watchful eye of not one but several guards.

George, though, made a thorough examination of each piece, his fingers gliding over smooth surfaces, searching for chips, scars, cracks or any indication whatsoever that the pieces had been repaired or modified by other than their original craftsmen. At last he seemed satisfied, stepping back to allow himself the luxury of a purely uncritical gaze.

"You were right when you said these were exceptional pieces, Paul," George said, knowing he could never have fooled Paul Thatcher by pretending they were otherwise. "It must have been quite a cache."

"A major one," Paul admitted. "And—not to get your hopes too high—I'm expecting a few more pieces in mint condition from the same locale."

"Then, you don't know how very glad I am that distribution is in your hands," George said. Diana knew without asking, without being told, that George had decided to purchase all three pieces. "I would have hated having Miller or Perkins leave me picking up leftovers."

"I've done well enough by Carlyle in the past that he knows how to treat me now that this particular find has come in. Besides...."

Diana missed entirely the rest of what Paul Thatcher had to say, her world having instantly telescoped. She was momentarily in the dark about who she was or even where she was. Her mind was too occupied with flashing back to that moment in the Hotel Savoy in Cuzco when she had first heard the name Carlyle muttered by Sloane's lips. She realized suddenly that George and Paul were no longer looking at the artifacts but at her. She had said something without knowing just what.

"Yes—Dennis Carlyle," Paul was saying, giving her a clue and showing surprise that this woman should know anything about the man currently supplying the bulk of his existing inventory. He would have suspected that Carlyle's name had been dropped in passing by George somewhere in Diana's hearing, except he could tell his friend was just as surprised at the young woman's murmuring Carlyle's full name as he had been.

"He's your supplier?" Diana asked, feeling her heart pounding inside of her. "He gave you these?" Her right arm swept the room, encompassing the gold objects in it, and her voice was so high-pitched that Paul glanced to George for some explanation. The old man obviously didn't have one.

"George, I have to talk to you—alone!" Diana said. None of this made sense. If Dennis Carlyle had supplied the artifacts in this room and in the other, then these objects were in the country illegally; and Diana couldn't imagine George being involved in anything illegal. But if the items were legal, then Sloane had lied to her about Carlyle, and she refused to believe he had lied. "George, please!" she insisted. She had to find out the truth no matter what the cost. If Sloane had lied about Carlyle, Diana would at least be able to complete her final break from him far more easily than she was otherwise managing, by finding out about it now. If he had been telling the truth, then she had to warn George about what he was possibly getting himself into.

"I'll leave you two for the moment," Paul said magnanimously. "I think I know you well enough by now, George, to trust you with the merchandise." He nodded coolly to Diana and left the room, closing the door behind him.

"Now, then, Diana, what is all of this about?" George asked patiently.

"Dennis Carlyle is a common grave robber," Diana said. "He's a thief in his own country. If he is in fact Mr. Thatcher's supplier, then those items on the desk, the ones in the other room, are most likely in this country illegally."

"I've dealt with Paul Thatcher for a good many years," George said, his voice low and calming. "He has a fine reputation as an art dealer in this city. I'm sure you can easily verify that if you will take the time to check it out. Accusing him of being willingly involved in clandestine activities, especially in stolen artifacts, is a very serious matter, my dear. It would be to no one's advantage for you to make such statements public before discovering you were really wrong or, more likely, hadn't been aware of certain extenuating factors."

"Dennis Carlyle is a despicable man who makes a career of robbing his own country's archaeological heritage and selling it in the marketplace," Diana persisted.

"Okay," George said with the patience of someone dealing with a child who is failing to grasp a very important point. "Even assuming for the moment that Dennis Carlyle is all that you say he is, that's not to find it naturally following that Paul Thatcher is a criminal, too—at least as far as doing anything illegal in this country goes." That statement baffled Diana and her face must have shown as much.

"While there may indeed be export laws in some countries, like Peru, to prevent the movement of certain goods out of their boundaries, more often than not there are no such laws in other countries to prevent those very same items from being legally imported," he went on. "Do you see what I'm trying to get at here, Diana? Even if Dennis Carlyle's methods of getting his artifacts eventually to Paul might violate certain laws of Peru, it doesn't mean they violate the laws of other countries."

"You mean, Thatcher might legally be able to import them into the United States once Carlyle has got them out of Peru into some other country?"

"Exactly!" George said. "And consider how much more difficult it is to prove accusations against someone like Carlyle who, according to your story deals mainly in goods pilfered from newly opened graves, goods that are nowhere on record as being in existence in Peru after any national-treasures laws might have been put into effect. The man, if he is as unscrupulous as you say, might well argue that the items in question were removed from Peru years ago, before there were laws to protect against their export. For that matter, who's to say that artifacts such as these weren't really part of the Spanish booty when the conquistadores sacked the Incan Empire and hauled thousands of such pieces back to Spain? You see the problem, Diana? I can only assure you that if I purchase one or all three of these gold objects on the desk, I will be given by Paul Thatcher all the paperwork I need to prove they are in this country legally. Which in the long run, and barring lengthy litigation, is all I really need; possession, as they say, being nine-tenths of the law.''

"It doesn't bother you, though, that these gold objects just might have been removed last week or last month from an archaeological site in Peru, smuggled out to another country to be imported here legally?''

"Bother me?'' George asked, as if he were genuinely considering that possibility now and had considered it in the past. "I think it would bother me if I bought these items, and others like them, knowing full well that by not buying them I could stop Dennis Carlyle from sacking archaeological sites.''

"But it *will* stop him, and people like him, don't you see?''

"Sit down, please,'' George said, motioning toward the chair that had been occupied by the skinny pockmarked man when they had first entered the office. Diana didn't feel like sitting, not really knowing what she wanted to do. She was upset that this likable gentleman, whose life she had assumed was devoted to the discovery and preservation of antiquities, was now metamorphosed into one of those men who supported Dennis Carlyle's little kingdom in the jungle; who make it so lucrative for Carlyle and Sipas to plunder Incan graves and whole Incan cities for a profit; who had paid for the bullet that had wounded Dan Jacos. And George didn't even look like a criminal!

"It's not as you think it is, Diana, not even if what you're saying about Carlyle is true," George continued. "It's not as if I can stop what he's doing by not buying the objects being offered here for sale. What I can do, however, by buying, is to assure that pieces of exquisite art, like this jaguar mask, are preserved for posterity."

"It doesn't bother you that you might very well be responsible for people being looted of their heritage?" Diana asked, wishing things could always be dealt with in simple black and white, without the confusing shades of gray conjured by rationalization. To hear one side, Carlyle was a thief, selling his country's heritage. To hear Dan Jacos tell the tale, Carlyle was a saint, putting food on the table of people who couldn't eat gold. To George, Carlyle was a man allowing remnants of a dead civilization to be saved by getting them to the highest bidder.

"I'm saving their heritage," George insisted. "Without me and men like me, what do you think would happen to it? Where do you suppose the Elgin Marbles, in the British Museum today, would be if Elgin hadn't had the foresight to pick up the crumbling pieces of the Parthenon friezes from the deteriorating heaps of rubble on the Acropolis and spirit them away from Greece? They'd be dust today, Diana—

nothing more. They would be lost to the world, not just to the Greeks. If someone isn't here to buy up these artifacts, tuck them under protective wings for safety, do you think people like Carlyle will stop what they're doing? No, my dear, they won't stop at all. What they'll start doing instead is dropping every gold item they find into one big common crucible, melting it all down and destroying the generations of history that went into the making of each small piece. They'll convert everything into one lump of yellow metal that can be easily disposed of without any questions being asked. That's what they'll do without people like me, Diana. Do you know how many tons of artifacts were melted down just like that by the Spaniards who conquered Peru and sacked it of Incan treasures? Countless tons! Do you want people like Carlyle to begin repeating that destruction by melting down what little there is left?''

"Do you know that Dennis Carlyle probably already knows about your lost city?" Diana pointed out. "Do you think you're even going to be able to see it before he has torn it apart looking for booty to sell buyers who won't give a damn that he pulled down your Incan Keep to get at it?" She felt ashamed of herself the minute she saw the look on George's face as a result of her words. It was as if she had offered candy to a baby and then pulled it away at the very last minute, the simple truth of the matter being that people were very much like emeralds, few perfect no matter what their outer surfaces might show. She didn't consider herself immune from that comparison, either. Her major flaw had been in not having fought hard enough, long enough, to convince Sloane that she could accept him and love him no matter what his financial situation.

There was a knock at the door. The door opened a crack, and Paul stuck his head into the office. "Well, George, have you made any decisions about these pieces?" he asked, apparently having diplomatically decided to ignore the inexplicable outburst of some acquaintance of a very good customer.

"Yes," George said. "I'll take all three. Just as you always knew I would."

Diana had little trouble seeing how it must have come about that George began rationalizing his present dealings. After all, she herself had become an expert in rationalization through her continual efforts to explain away just why it was that she and Sloane had failed to make their love work....

SHE STAYED ON LONG ENOUGH at the house to complete her article on the rediscovery of George Culhaney's lost city, although she knew that her visit to that warehouse with George had changed the relationship between them. No matter what the legal machinations involved in making objects stolen from Incan graves the lawful property of George Culhaney, Diana knew enough about Dennis Carlyle not to condone the practice. While she found herself unable to pinpoint any immediate victim of the crime, she felt certain nevertheless that it was wrong.

Diana was sure of one thing, though, when she boarded her flight for Seattle. That was that she was finally adjusting to life without Sloane. In fact, she had adjusted to the degree where she could actually admit to herself her real reason for stopping off in Los Angeles to see George. Her visit had had more to do with his being a part of that other world Diana had shared with Sloane than with her desire to write a newspaper article about the rediscovery of his lost city. Diana, Sloane lost to her, had simply been reluctant to release her memories. She was now prepared to say goodbye to George, goodbye to Sloane, goodbye to those memories that were so painful.

On second thought, maybe she was being a bit optimistic about freeing herself of the pain. She still got an uncomfortable constriction in her throat, as if she were suppressing a sob, whenever she recalled certain memories, like of the time at the bridge when she and Sloane. . . .

She shook her head to clear it, refusing to admit she had been on the verge of a relapse into the exact emotional state from which she had but seconds before been trying to assure herself she was cured. She pulled down the shade and fastened her seat belt, then settled back into a

fairly comfortable position and shut her eyes before the plane had even begun its ascent. She began thinking of just how she was going to break
the news to her mother that there would be no
more innocuous travel pieces coming from the
typewriter of Diana Green. When she had called
her mother to tell her where and when to pick
her up at Seattle-Tacoma Airport, she had
thought to break the news then that she was
determined to embark upon that career of investigative reporting. She had ended up, though,
once again deciding to hold off that potentially
volatile pronouncement until she was rested
enough for the battle that would follow.

She was vaguely aware, some time later, that
she had been dozing when the seat beside her
had become occupied. She still didn't open her
eyes, not feeling much like making small talk
with a complete stranger.

She dreamed of majestic landscapes that consisted of massive upthrustings of granite, of
deep gorges, of roaring rivers, of green jungles.
It was all pleasant and familiar, as if she were
renewing an old acquaintance. When those pictures began to fade, she tried vainly to recapture
them.

"If you're not careful, Diana, you're going to
end up sleeping both of our lives away," someone said. Diana's eyes came open at the sound
of that dangerously familiar voice that, like no
other, could stab her to the heart. She turned to
see him, Sloane, sitting there beside her. She

didn't know what to say or what to do. Her first impulse was simply to reach out and hold him, let him hold her while she smothered his handsome face with kisses.

"How long have you been there?" she asked instead.

"Since the plane took off from L.A.," he told her. He was even more handsome than she had remembered. "And some flying companion you've turned out to be, too," he joked. "Snoring for hours on end!"

"I thought I had seen the last of you," Diana said, finally managing to get words out. She was so choked with emotion, she could hardly speak at all.

"Did you, now?" Sloane said, smiling. "What kind of a fiancé did you take me for, anyway?"

"How did you find me?" she asked, choosing to ignore completely his reference to being her fiancé. She was deeply hurt that he could tease her so maliciously. At the same time she was wishing she had reached out for him, had let her arms wrap his muscled body, had kissed his lips...

"When I kept calling your apartment in Seattle without getting an answer, I remembered the name of the newspaper you write for. So I called your editor, explaining that I was the manager of the Hotel Savoy in Cuzco and that there had been a mix-up on your hotel bill; was there any way I could reach you? He obliged by telling me when you were expected back from L.A. I checked for your flight reservation, and here I am. What were you doing in L.A., by the way? Seeing George Culhaney and breaking the good news about his Incan Keep?''

"I'll tell you what I was doing in L.A. after you tell me just what you're doing here now.''

"You mean, it isn't obvious?''

"Frankly, no, it isn't.''

"Why? Because you're upset that I seemed to just up and kick you out of the helicopter while I disappeared into the wild blue yonder?''

Diana stifled a temptation to admit that, yes, that was why she was so upset—among other things. "I figured you had assumed the best breaks were the swift and uncluttered ones,'' is what she did say.

"Yes, at the time, I must admit, I was thinking something along those lines. I was also thinking about how I was going to get Dan to a competent doctor who would be discreet enough not to ask too many questions about his bullet wound.''

"How is Dan?'' Diana asked spontaneously, genuinely anxious to find out. She liked to think that she and Dan had actually become friends by the time their little adventure ended.

"He was doing just great the last time I saw him. He's probably up by now, back to ransacking Incan graves for Carlyle.'' Diana had sudden visions of Dan off in the jungle, busy tearing down George Culhaney's Incan Keep in an effort to see if it was filled with treasure. How ironic that would have been. "But back to my main reason for deserting you on our return to Machu Picchu," Sloane continued. "My haste was almost entirely spawned by my sincere hope for just the kind of reunion the two of us are now enjoying, and I simply wanted to get the ball rolling as quickly as possible."

"I'm confused."

"It seems I'm able to tell you what I was looking for in the wreckage that—"

"Tell me now, you mean? *Right now*?" Diana was incredulous.

"I did say I was hoping to explain it to you someday, didn't I?"

"I never dreamed someday would be quite so soon."

"Neither did I, but it seems the two of us have finally lucked out, Diana. Do you believe in happy endings? I hope so, for I think there just might be one in the offing."

Diana was almost afraid to believe such a thing was possible, she wanted it so badly.

"Nothing I did tell you, by the way, was a lie," Sloane said. "My brother did leave the plane in Leticia, Gary Holsteen did take over, Jack and Gary were the very best of friends, there were accusations of hijacking. My father did sell off everything to make good the claims, and artifacts from the cargo did show up in Lima, leading me to Dan Jacos, who led us to the plane."

Diana told herself not to set her hopes too high. This could all still come tumbling down around her.

"The plane, though, was carrying more than just a few crates of Manaus Indian artifacts when it went down. It was also carrying an estimated two million dollars' worth of uncut emeralds."

"It was carrying *what*?" Diana was uncertain she had heard correctly.

"Remember my telling you about David Journer?"

"The man who took care of you after your brother and father died?"

"Did you ever wonder what cargo he was shipping on my father's plane that could have had my father ending up giving him the coffee plantation in repayment for losses?"

"The emeralds?"

"David was a longtime prospector. He had been at it for years, looking for the one big strike that would put him on easy street. He figured he had it made when he came up with a pocket of green stones. The problem, of course, was getting them out and doing so as quickly and as secretly as possible. If men will kill for Incan artifacts, you can imagine what they'll do to get their hands on something less bulky and more valuable.

"It was always a tip-off, of course," he continued, "if a prospector suddenly packed up and headed downriver. The usual route was down the Amazon to Belém. However, David got in touch with my father and the two made arrangements to ship the gems out via Leticia and Lima."

"Surely your brother wouldn't have turned the plane over to Holsteen with so much at stake!"

"My father never bothered telling Jack. Jack had been known to have a pretty loose tongue when he'd had a few drinks, and he was often drinking heavily. He wasn't to know anything about the extra cargo until Lima, where arrangements had been made for a representative of I. Bern to pick up the merchandise and give an appraisal and purchasing bid. However, the plane never made it."

"And you found the stones? You actually found them after all this time?"

"It wasn't so difficult once I'd found the plane and then the wreckage of the cockpit. The gems were secured in a secret compartment that had been specifically designed to hide them. It had, luckily, survived the crash pretty much intact, though you can imagine how twenty years' worth of rust had affected it! My problem ended up being just getting the compartment open. For that I needed the extra afternoon."

"But why didn't you tell me all of this before now?" Diana asked. "Why the mystery? You can't imagine the wild things I was thinking." Oh, how fast and loud her heart was beating!

"Had me pegged there for a while as another Carlyle or Sipas, did you?"

"I couldn't imagine what your reasons were—it seemed they had to be pretty horrible if I couldn't be trusted to cope with them and understand. That's what hurt me the most, I think."

"That's sweet," Sloane said, leaning over to brush her cheek gently with his lips. "I certainly had no intentions of ever hurting you. Far from it. In fact, it was actually my not wanting to hurt you that made me keep quiet about the gems."

"You'll excuse me if the logic of that momentarily escapes me."

"If I'd told you I had found the emeralds, you might have got false hopes about my paying off all my debts."

"False hopes?" Diana echoed, her heart sinking. She knew it had all been too good to be true! "You mean, even with the emeralds you can't pay off your outstanding debts. Oh, surely, you've got enough to pay off at least some of them, enough so that you can now see yourself clear enough to...." She hesitated. Maybe he really didn't want to marry her.

"Marry you?" Sloane finished for her, his face going all sunny with one of his big smiles that caved in both dimples and made him look so handsomely boyish.

"Your not having money never did have anything at all to do with the way I felt about you,"

Diana said. "And it certainly doesn't mean anything to me now. Having you with me is all that matters to me. Other people get along fine without a fortune to—"

"Oh, but as it turns out, the revenue I received from the sale of the gems has left me very solvent. After all, the emeralds were estimated at a value of more than two million dollars when the plane went down. You can imagine how much they've appreciated on today's market."

"I'm not following you, then," Diana said in frustration. And she did so want to understand!

"I couldn't say anything to you about the emeralds in the beginning of our relationship because, quite frankly, I didn't know I could trust you when I first met you. By the time I did come to trust you, I also found I loved you, so it became my fear that kept me from telling you, even when I had located the cache."

"Your fear? Your fear of what?"

"Fear that I didn't really have emeralds at all, but pieces of green glass, or worthless beryl, or bottle-green tourmaline worth only a fraction of what David had always quoted. Not that David would knowingly have lied. But sometimes prospectors get carried away with expectations and overestimate the value of a find. The two million was David's figure. That couldn't have been officially verified until the I. Bern people got the gems for appraisal. But the gems never got that far. As for my father—well, what did he know about the value of gemstones? David had said two million, and that was good enough for him."

Sloane paused, the excited glitter still in his eyes in spite of his somber tone, then went on reflectively, "All credit to David, I must say— he ended up taking only the plantation in compensation, when at the time it was worth nowhere near two million dollars. Nor is it now. He also left me everything in his will when he died, so I came by my legal claim to the emeralds two ways: not only by being David's sole heir, but because my father had made recompense to everyone, David included, who had cargo lost on that downed aircraft."

"I still wish you had told me all of this before," Diana said softly.

"And if the gems had turned out to be worthless?" Sloane asked. "Can you imagine how I would have felt, knowing I had held out false hope for us where there had never been any hope? I had to be sure, Diana. I couldn't be sure until I had dumped my find on the black velvet of an I. Bern appraiser's desk and had him take his jeweler's loupe to each stone."

"And they *were* real?"

"Quite real." He produced a small box from his suit-coat pocket. Diana suddenly realized that, for the first time since those brief moments in the Tambo de Oro and during dinner at the Hotel Savoy in Cuzco, she was seeing Sloane in a suit. He looked handsome enough, but she thought she preferred him in less formal attire.

Maybe she had just got used to seeing him dressed for far more rugged travel than that offered by a commercial airline. Maybe she had just got used to him—period.

"Go on, open it," he encouraged her.

Diana flipped open the small lid. "Sloane, it's gorgeous!" she exclaimed, looking at the large green stone that appeared so cool against black velvet. "It's absolutely beautiful!"

"Green like the jungles of Peru," Sloane said. "Green like Diana Green. I thought that made an emerald especially apropos for the occasion. Don't you agree?"

"It's so big," Diana murmured, overwhelmed.

"I would have preferred one of the stones from the packet I picked up in the wreckage," Sloane said. "But as I was in somewhat of a rush, trying to clear up my business and still make this plane connection, I had to settle for a cut stone from the I. Bern safe. I hope it meets with your approval. Does it?"

"My approval?"

"Certainly. You're going to be the one who has to wear it."

"Me?"

"It's a ring, Diana," Sloane said. "Or haven't you noticed that yet? Actually, it's your engagement ring."

"My what?"

"That is, if you accept my proposal of marriage. If you turn me down I want you to have the ring anyway. A kind of payment for services rendered, since I couldn't have done any of it without you, now could I?'' Diana was speechless. "I figure it will make a nice heirloom to pass on to the kids,'' he added, grinning sheepishly.

"The kids?''

"Sure,'' Sloane said. "Kids usually do happen when two people get married, don't they? You did say yes to my marriage proposal, didn't you, Diana? Or was I just hoping so hard that I only thought you did?''

"Oh, Sloane, of course I'll marry you!'' Diana breathed as he took the box from her, removing the ring from its dark velvet cushion to slip it on her finger. The gem's faceted sea-green surface caught and held the light, burning with a cool and verdant inner flame that was so hypnotic it was only Sloane's touch that could pull her gaze from it. He drew her close against him, his hand gently cupping her chin, tilting her face upward to more easily meet the pliant firmness of his lips being lowered to hers. Their kiss telescoped their world until it included just the two of them, leaving them oblivious to the bemused stares and smiles of fellow passengers who hadn't yet forgotten what it was once like to be young and hopelessly in love.

Here's how to get your volume NOW!

MAIL IN	$	GET
2 SPECIAL PROOF-OF-PURCHASE SEALS*	PLUS $1 U.S.	ONE BOOK
5 SPECIAL PROOF-OF-PURCHASE SEALS*	PLUS 50¢ U.S.	ONE BOOK
8 SPECIAL PROOF-OF-PURCHASE SEALS*	FREE	ONE BOOK

*Special proof-of-purchase seal from inside back cover of all specially marked Harlequin "Let Your Imagination Fly Sweepstakes" volumes. No other proof-of-purchase accepted.

ORDERING DETAILS:

Print your name, address, city, state or province, zip or postal code on the coupon below or a plain 3" x 5" piece of paper and together with the special proof-of-purchase seals and check or money order (no stamps or cash please) as indicated. Mail to:

HARLEQUIN ROMANCE TREASURY BOOK OFFER P.O. BOX 1399 MEDFORD, N.Y. 11763, U.S.A.

Make check or money order payable to: Harlequin Romance Treasury Offer. Allow 3 to 4 weeks for delivery.

Special offer expires: June 30, 1981.

PLEASE PRINT

Name

Address

Apt. No.

City

State/Prov.

Zip/Postal Code

Let Your Imagination Fly Sweepstakes

Rules and Regulations:

NO PURCHASE NECESSARY

1. Enter the Let Your Imagination Fly Sweepstakes 1, 2 or 3 as often as you wish. Mail each entry form separately bearing sufficient postage. Specify the sweepstake you wish to enter on the outside of the envelope. Mail a completed entry form or, your name, address, and telephone number printed on a plain 3"x 5" piece of paper to:
HARLEQUIN LET YOUR IMAGINATION FLY SWEEPSTAKES,
P.O. BOX 1280, MEDFORD, N.Y. 11763 U.S.A.

2. Each completed entry form must be accompanied by 1 Let Your Imagination Fly proof-of-purchase seal from the back inside cover of specially marked Let Your Imagination Fly Harlequin books (or the words "Let Your Imagination Fly" printed on a plain 3" x 5" piece of paper. Specify by number the Sweepstakes you are entering on the outside of the envelope.

3. The prize structure for each sweepstake is as follows:

Sweepstake 1 - North America

Grand Prize winner's choice: a one-week trip for two to either Bermuda; Montreal, Canada; or San Francisco. 3 Grand Prizes will be awarded (min. approx. retail value $1,375. U.S., based on Chicago departure) and 4,000 First Prizes: scarves by nik nik, worth $14. U.S. each. All prizes will be awarded:

Sweepstake 2 - Caribbean

Grand Prize winner's choice: a one-week trip for two to either Nassau, Bahamas; San Juan, Puerto Rico; or St. Thomas, Virgin Islands. 3 Grand Prizes will be awarded. (Min. approx. retail value $1,650. U.S., based on Chicago departure) and 4,000 First Prizes: simulated diamond pendants by Kenneth Jay Lane, worth $15. U.S. each. All prizes will be awarded.

Sweepstake 3 - Europe

Grand Prize winner's choice: a one-week trip for two to either London, England; Frankfurt, Germany; Paris, France; or Rome, Italy. 3 Grand Prizes will be awarded. (Min. approx. retail value $2,800. U.S., based on Chicago departure) and 4,000 First Prizes: 1/2 oz. bottles of perfume, BLAZER by Anne Klein. (Retail value over $30. U.S.). All prizes will be awarded.

Grand trip prizes will include coach round-trip airfare for two persons from the nearest commercial airport serviced by Delta Air Lines to the city as designated in the prize, double occupancy accommodation at a first-class or medium hotel, depending on vacation, and $500. U.S. spending money. Departure taxes, visas, passports, ground transportation to and from airports will be the responsibility of the winners.

4. To be eligible, Sweepstakes entries must be received as follows:
Sweepstake 1 Entries received by February 28, 1981
Sweepstake 2 Entries received by April 30, 1981
Sweepstake 3 Entries received by June 30, 1981
Make sure you enter each Sweepstake separately since entries will not be carried forward from one Sweepstake to the next.

The odds of winning will be determined by the number of entries received in each of the three sweepstakes. Canadian residents, in order to win any prize, will be required to first correctly answer a time-limited skill-testing question, to be posed by telephone, at a mutually convenient time.

5. Random selections to determine Sweepstake 1, 2 or 3 winners will be conducted by Lee Krost Associates, an independent judging organization whose decisions are final. Only one prize per family, per sweepstake. Prizes are non-transferable and non-refundable and no subsitutions will be allowed. Winners will be responsible for any applicable federal, state and local taxes. Trips must be taken during normal tour periods before June 30, 1982. Reservations will be on a space-available basis. Airline tickets are non-transferable, non-refundable and non-redeemable for cash.

6. The Let Your Imagination Fly Sweepstakes is open to all residents of the United States of America and Canada, (excluding the Province of Quebec) except employees and their immediate families of Harlequin Enterprises Ltd., its advertising agencies, Marketing & Promotion Group Canada Ltd. and Lee Krost Associates, Inc., the independent judging company. Winners may be required to furnish proof of eligibility. Void wherever prohibited or restricted by law. All federal, state, provincial and local laws apply.

7. For a list of trip winners, send a stamped, self-addressed envelope to:
Harlequin Trip Winners List, P.O. Box 1401, MEDFORD, N.Y. 11763 U.S.A.
Winners lists will be available after the last sweepstake has been conducted and winners determined.
NO PURCHASE NECESSARY.

Let Your Imagination Fly Sweepstakes
OFFICIAL ENTRY FORM

Please enter me in Sweepstake No. _____

Please print:
Name

Address

Apt. No.   City

State /   Zip/Postal
Prov.   Code

Telephone No.   area code
(   )

MAIL TO:
HARLEQUIN LET YOUR
IMAGINATION FLY SWEEPSTAKE No. _____
P.O. BOX 1280,
MEDFORD, N.Y. 11763 U.S.A.
(Please specify by number, the Sweepstake you are entering.)